The Trumpets

By

Braxton DeGarmo

Christen Haus Publishing

COPYRIGHT

DEDICATION

This book is dedicated to those who hold fast to their biblical worldview while reaching out to those around them with the Good News of Christ.

Revelation 8:1-2

1 When the Lamb opened the seventh seal, there was silence in heaven for about half an hour. 2 Then I saw the seven angels who stand before God, and seven trumpets were given to them.

ONE

Shawn Westhope didn't like what he saw but at the same time wasn't quite sure what he was seeing. The Sierras around Mammoth Lakes had received record snowfall, a true blessing considering the severe drought conditions facing the State of California prior to this winter. But was this too much water, too quickly?

Repeated atmospheric rivers had dumped over 28 inches of rain on the state since October 1st, the beginning of the state's water year. That amounted to over 78 trillion gallons and 148% of their average *annual* rainfall. The majority of the state's reservoirs now held levels that were at or above historic averages. However, with this record rainfall, major flooding had become a problem. Tens of thousands of homes and nearly 90,000 people had been evacuated in recent weeks, and fast-water rescues had taken place in several places in the state. Levy breaks in northern and central California had destroyed crops or threatened farmlands responsible for nearly three-quarters of the country's produce.

Plus, the combination of record rains and wildfire-damaged terrain also caused massive mudslides. Dozens of homes had been damaged or destroyed by mudflows, and hundreds were under evacuation orders as the hillsides they perched upon had fallen away below them.

Snowfall in the mountains had reached levels few in those mountains had ever seen. Over 58 feet of snow had fallen around Mammoth over the winter. As of today, the ski resort reported a base of nearly 30 feet, and blizzard conditions made skiing there treacherous for all but the foolhardiest skiers. For this time of year, the snowpack sat at over 250% normal. Over two feet of additional wet snow had fallen just a few days earlier, and yet another bomb cyclone had been forecast to arrive over the state this very day, starting in the northern end of the state and moving south. The last one hit San Francisco with 80 mph winds and took out power for over a quarter of a million homes and businesses.

Shawn stood atop the earthen Long Valley Dam at Crowley Lake along the Owens River, just 15 miles south of Mammoth Lakes. The lake's unique tall columns in the chalk cliffs along the eastern shore remained out of view behind Lifeguard Point and under water with the lake full. At this level, the lake was 12 miles long, five miles wide at its widest point, and held over 183,000 acre-feet of water. The snowcapped Sierra Nevada range provided a beautiful winter backdrop for the lake that belied the potential danger covering those mountains.

Shawn was an engineer and inspector with the state's Division of Safety of Dams. The division was responsible for the integrity of over 1,200 dams within the state, both privately and government-owned. His Region 6 responsibilities included part of the South Lahontan Hydrologic Region in which the Crowley Lake watershed sat, but the dam was fully within his area that included Mono County.

He worked closely with the inspectors in the Division of

Flood Safety. One of their men, Mick Mulholland—only a distant relationship to *the* Mulhollands of Los Angeles—had called him.

"What do you make of it?" asked Mick.

Shawn shrugged. "Not sure from first look. Has it changed since you first saw it?"

The man shook his head. "Don't think so. As I told you, a photographer friend of mine was out here taking pictures of the lake and mountains. He stumbled upon it and sent me that photo I sent you. Unfortunately, the photo held nothing to reference the size. I saw it firsthand yesterday, and it's no different today."

"Okay, but we've also been precipitation-free for two days."

The dam was 126 feet high with an overflow spillway along its northern end. It had been built in 1941 for flood control, regulation that was essential for the Owens River that supplied Los Angeles with 48% of its drinking water through the Los Angeles Aqueducts. Numerous hydroelectric facilities also sat downstream—the Upper and Middle Gorge plants being first in line.

Shawn thought about the age of the dam. It hadn't shown any signs of trouble, but then, the season's rainfall and snowfall had been extraordinary. He walked along the steep hillside formed by the dam, taking care not to slip in the slushy and muddier areas. To lose his footing would result in a long, bruising tumble to the bottom. After traversing about halfway across the dam, he dropped about 20 feet down and returned to his colleague waiting by the scar. He spotted nothing of concern along the way.

"Mick, I don't see any other areas, but I didn't go all the way across either. Looking back from the middle out there, this scar was obvious. So, I figure if there's anything else like it over there, I should have seen it."

The scar he mentioned, and the reason he'd been called, was a roughly oval area about eight feet wide and 15 feet long. It sat about ten feet below the top of the dam and 50 feet from the northern end. The defect measured from six to eight inches deep, enough to remove the surface vegetation helping to prevent hillside erosion.

"I don't see any obvious seepage issues and the spillway's working as expected, so I wouldn't expect any overtopping. I'll get hold of LADWP and get them to reinforce this area with rock. Hopefully, they can do that before the next atmospheric river hits."

The Los Angeles Department of Water and Power owned the dam. The city also owned the power plants along the way, as well as the aqueducts.

Mick nodded. "I'll talk to my contacts there, too. Maybe double-teaming them will get a faster response. That next deluge could hit here in two days."

"Sounds good. In the meantime, I'll put this on our list of concerns and check back at the first of the week. I'll also ask the guys in Bishop to check it daily for changes. Definitely needs another look if we get more rain."

The pair walked back to their trucks, discussing anything besides rain, dams, or floods. Those topics were always on their minds, as well as the lead stories for every news channel in the state. They relished any conversation that could take their minds off work.

"Whatja think about San Diego State? Who would have guessed they'd make it to the Final Four?"

Shawn was more of a baseball fan, but he could get caught up in March Madness like anyone else. And like everyone else, major upsets along the way had destroyed his bracket early on. He doubted anyone's bracket had made it to this point.

"Great playing. They should take Florida Atlantic."

"Maybe. I'm not placing any bets on any team this year. Not the way this tournament's been going."

Shawn laughed. "I hear you."

They shook hands and agreed to keep in close touch. Shawn was about to pull out behind Mick but stopped. As he watched the other man pull away, cross the dam, and head onto Owens Gorge Rd, a thought came to him. He turned off the truck and walked to the back. From there, he gathered up half a dozen stakes, a three-pound sledge hammer, and a can of landscaper's spray paint in fluorescent orange.

Back at the scar, he carefully pounded the stakes along the edge at strategic points. He drove each as deeply into the ground as he could. Then he painted the exposed edges from the soil level on up. He also sprayed the ground where he could—where there was no snow—extending lines from the scar outward as well as along the perimeter.

Sure, it seemed old school, but he now had markers he could use to measure changes in the defect. From the stakes, he could determine any changes in depth, while the painted ground could help him monitor changes in size.

He felt confident that this was just some superficial slippage from all of the water that had been dumped on the area . . . and that the dam was safe. He didn't want to think of the consequences should he be wrong.

TWO

Aric Afton's semester so far had become a prime example of nothing being constant except change. The previous fall, his award for courage had produced a change in the atmosphere on campus in which the LGBTQ+ crowd seemed to tolerate him. Some even condescended to talk with him. And then there was the "excitement" of being monitored by the FBI in its search for his brother, Adam. Yes, it had been a memorable semester.

But now, both were gone—the FBI and the tolerance of the LGBTQ+ crowd.

The January term—or J-term, as they called it—had sped by. Only a fraction of students attended class that month, and many relished classes that took them overseas to study music, art and architecture, or languages, although those options paled in comparison to the offerings provided in the years before the pandemic.

Now, two months into the spring semester, he found the level of animosity toward the Christians on campus by the LGBTQ+ and BLM groups to exceed those of his first semester when he became known as "the guy" who stood up for free speech. He had been spit on, screamed at, taunted, ridiculed for his beliefs, and physically threatened on more than one occasion. His size was the only thing keeping those bodily threats from materializing.

And what had changed? Nothing he had done had led to the persecution. He continued to show respect for all of his fellow students. He continued to go out of his way to make friends. No, he hadn't done anything to cause the animosity he felt aimed at him . . . unless accepting Christ and believing in the Bible's teachings were enough to be the reason.

One of those lessons was that the world would hate him, and all believers, because of the world's hatred for Christ. Jessica sometimes reminded him of that and said that it could be considered something of a badge of honor, proof that he was on the right track. Sometimes, though, it just felt like that badge's pin kept sticking him in the chest with every breath.

No, the real trigger was someone else. Sam Goode had returned to campus . . . as Sam and not as Ashley Love. He had become an activist for the other side—speaking out about the depression and physical issues he had encountered trying to live as a transwoman. The LGBTQ+ crowd hated him for it while the local press largely ignored him.

By extension, that hate extended toward Aric, the guy who had saved Sam's life after Sam, as Ashley, had jumped into the icy waters off the lighthouse pier to commit suicide two previous Januarys ago. As long as Sam remained absent from campus, that crowd seemed to remember Aric as saving the life of one of their own. With Sam back at school, Aric was now guilty of saving the life of someone who opposed their agenda, a traitor to their cause. Aric had been so much as accused of saving Sam's life just so Sam could come back to haunt them, the LGBTQ+ crowd. By default, Aric had become an extension of Sam's activism even though they shared no classes, rarely saw each other on campus, and never spoke together about the trans movement. In fact, Aric found himself shying away from speaking about the transgender mania simply because of Sam's activism.

So, just like the weather, every day brought new changes. However, the specific change on his mind at the moment was quite different. He rushed from his morning class, his only class for the day, and headed toward the admin building where his friend and mentor, Prof. Lynch Cully, had his office. On his way, he saw his girlfriend, Jessica Larson, leaving the library. He made a quick detour.

"Hey, Jess!" he called out after her as she turned the other way. He rushed up to her. "Hey." He smiled and gave her a quick kiss on the cheek. As she returned the smile, her dimples once again caught and amazed him. It was as if he could fall into those dimples. He loved her smile.

"Hi. Didn't see you. What's up?"

"I'm heading over to Lynch's office to meet him for lunch. Wanna come with us?"

"Maybe. You're done for the day, but I have to be back for my one o'clock class. Plus, where are you going? Not another one of those dives he likes to explore, I hope."

Aric shrugged. "We were thinking about the Union Park Tavern."

She nodded. "Okay. I like UPT, and they're fast."

Ten minutes later, having joined Lynch and ridden with him into town, they waited for a table at the tavern on the west side of Union Park, a small, one-block-square green space with a playground that had seen better days. For some, the UPT might fit Jess' definition of a dive, but they had one of the best fish fries in town, including lake perch and walleye choices, and great sandwiches. Once seated, they scrutinized the menu and made small talk until ordering.

"So, Aric, what's the occasion? You said you wanted my opinion on something," said Lynch.

Jess chimed in. "He wouldn't tell me either. Said he'd tell us both together." She poked Aric's arm.

Aric pondered just how to address the thing on his mind. "You know how the Bible says that in the latter days old men will dream dreams and young men will have visions?" The other two nodded. "Well, I think I had a vision this morning as I was waking up. It was weird. Not really a dream, but like a dream, except I was actually sitting on the edge of my bed when it happened."

"Maybe we should have asked my dad to join us at this meeting." Jess' father, Thomas Larson, was the pastor of the church that Aric and Jess attended.

"Aric can always consult with him, too. I can't say that I've had much firsthand experience with visions or dreams, but I know that God speaks to each of us through His Spirit. I've had an occasional prophetic word for someone, but no dreams or visions. So, tell us what you saw." Lynch took a sip of his iced tea, which had just been delivered to the table.

Aric took a drink of his Coke before speaking. "Well, it was like I was suspended in space looking down on the United States. The country was all dark except for areas of light scattered within its borders. And despite being dark, I could tell where the bigger cities were supposed to be. Some areas of light were small and faint, some were much larger and brighter, but it wasn't anything like photos from space showing all of the cities lit up at night."

"In what way?"

"Well, the east and west coasts were barely lit up and the biggest cities had hardly any light. There was a brighter band of lights scattered along the Mississippi River, but again the big cities, like New Orleans, St. Louis, and Chicago, were not brightly lit. And instead of bright white lights, like on photos from space, there were areas of red light and orange, but mostly yellow."

"What about the middle of the country, away from the Mississippi?" asked Jess.

"Well, there were scattered small dots of faint light, but the bigger cities, again, didn't light up. No Denver or Phoenix. And, as I think about it, Kansas City and Atlanta were weird."

"How?" Lynch had a look of fascination.

"Well, the cities themselves weren't very bright, but each had a brilliant red light coming from the area. In Atlanta, it seemed to be northeast of the city, but in Kansas City, it was south of the city itself."

Lynch pulled out his phone and began to search for something on it.

Jess asked, "What about this area?"

Aric nodded. "Yeah, most of southeast Wisconsin seemed to light up yellow, leaving Chicago and Milwaukee dark."

A moment later, Lynch held up his phone for Aric to see. The screen displayed a map of Kansas City. Lynch pointed to a spot south of the city. "Is this where you saw the light?"

Aric nodded. "Pretty much. I mean the scale is a lot different. I was seeing the entire country, not details of each city. But that's roughly where the light seemed to come from."

A few seconds later, Lynch held up his phone again, but with Atlanta displayed. "And is this where the light seemed to be outside of Atlanta?"

Aric nodded. "Sure does. I mean, that seems to be where I sensed it to be. Why?"

Lynch sighed. "I may be barking up the wrong tree, but those dots of red are where the International Houses of Prayer are located in KC and Atlanta. Maybe the lights are areas of prayer with greater prayer or 24/7 prayer centers lighting up more intensely."

Aric bobbled his head in agreement with that possibility.

"What about an electric grid failure? Could these light areas be places with some kind of backup power systems?" asked Jess. "With all that fuss over the Chinese spy balloon a month or so ago, some people were talking about the potential for a nationwide EMP attack. With the attack on that pharmaceutical company last fall, that really struck home."

Lynch waggled his head as if saying that, too, was a possibility. "An EMP attack seems unlikely. That would take out all backup systems as well as the main grid. But you could be on target about a grid failure. When all that fuss about the balloon rose up, I did some reading. There are about 30 essential power substations across the country. If a handful or so of them fail, it could trigger a domino effect of outages and lead to a systemic failure of the nationwide power grid. The transformers in those substations cost millions and would take 3 to 5 years to replace. Plus, they're all made overseas."

Another thought came to Aric. "And what about solar activity? I was reading about how a strong enough solar magnetic storm could take out earth's power grids. Something called the Carrington Effect."

Lynch nodded. "There *has* been a lot of solar activity lately. You know, all of these are possibilities. Aric, I suggest you make this a focus of prayer and see if the Lord gives you the right insight into it. And when He does, keep us posted."

Aric agreed. He would indeed search out an answer through prayer. And yet, as he ate, he felt that Lynch's first impression might be on target. He tried and tried to recall where the brightest areas were located on the "map." Maybe he could correlate those with other prayer centers.

THREE

Adam Afton felt both a sense of freedom and of being lost. While feeling lost without the backup and information provided by his program, UltraNet, he also experienced a freedom he hadn't felt in over a decade. Much like leaving behind a major time suck, like Facebook, he had hours available to do more than sit in front of a screen.

Still, his first month after leaving UltraNet behind in its virtual limbo had seemed like withdrawal from alcohol. He recalled that ordeal firsthand.

Now, five months later and reunited with his family in St. Louis, he found new purpose in life. Besides making up for lost time with Rachel and their kids, he also had seen his parents and sisters more over that period than he had over the previous three years combined. He no longer hid in the shadows. He became reacquainted with old buddies. Birthdays and holidays brought new joy. Having fun was no longer a stranger to him. It was as if Jesus now showed him everything he had been missing.

He also spent time studying the Bible. There, too, it was as if his eyes had been opened to things he'd never seen before. Why hadn't he noticed those things while growing up? Aric had. So had his sisters.

He wondered about that until one day, he realized that maybe God had allowed him to go through the turmoil he'd experienced in order to teach him something. One thing was sure, had he not gone through that phase of his life, he would never have been in a position to develop UltraNet or to stop AlterNet in both of its incarnations. While that hadn't stopped the global beast from advancing its agenda, he had slowed them down.

Without that time of tribulation, he also would not have developed the skills he now had, talents he needed to launch his next endeavor—cybersecurity, with a focus on Christian organizations that were seeing a significant uptick in censorship and virtual attacks. All he needed was a catchy name. Afton Security sounded too dull. AA Cybersecurity was too old school. Others that came to mind just seemed, well, weird.

He took his knowledge of UltraNet and created an "abbreviated" version that had safeguards to prevent its use on the dark web or performing other illegal intrusions, should it ever fall into the wrong hands. He developed a collection of tools that could prevent such things as denial of service attacks, website hijacking, and ransomware demands. And with this, he made the software powerful in combing and collecting data from public databases, particularly those operated by the government.

One arena, in particular, had found these latter strengths useful.

"Alítheia Media Group, how may I direct your call?"

"James O'Neal, please. It's Adam Afton," replied Adam.

"One moment."

O'Neal had been the founder of one of the most honest independent journalist companies in the country. They had undercover reporters everywhere and had exposed corruption in major corporations, government agencies, district attorney offices, and more. Sadly, although the corruption was openly exposed, few of the bad actors ever faced prosecution. Still, the act of exposing the slime to the sunlight had its effect.

While facing potential prosecution himself, O'Neal had reorganized the company to include a board of directors with control of the company, so that should he face jail time, the company could continue. Within months, despite his exoneration, they had ousted him from his CEO position, fired him, and then wanted his return when the donors dried up. From that, O'Neal reinvented himself and formed AMG, with *alítheia* being Greek for "truth."

"Adam, wow, that info you sent me is dynamite."

"I knew you'd like it."

When it came to uncovering corruption, Adam knew that he and James were like-minded brothers-in-arms.

"This truly looks like a money laundering machine to fund Democrats. We're going to organize a handful of investigators to make phone calls and go door-to-door to interview a few dozen of these people. Looks like they've been smurfed for sure."

"You think? Maybe Rand Engle, age 82, really did make 12,115 donations totaling $214,225."

James laughed. "Sure, and Mary Wright, age 78, almost matched him."

Adam had been scouring the Federal Elections Commission website and database when he came across the public records of a Democrat fundraising platform, GoBlue. He decided to test his new program by culling those records, sorting and combining them by names and addresses, ranking the donors, and compiling the list of those who gave to the platform in 2022. GoBlue had registered tens of thousands of small to medium donations through a few dozen elderly people. The number of donations far exceeded what would be expected of a normal person. In Mr. Engle's case, he would have had to make a $17 donation every 43 minutes, 24/7, to match the records. This was clearly fraud as well as a scheme for money laundering and funneling hundreds of millions of dollars into Democrat political coffers illegally.

"We're set up to go. We've put together lists of people in New York and Arizona that we want to call and interview. We'll ask them on camera if they actually made the donations attributed to them. I think we're going to open some eyes with this one."

"Good. I hoped you'd make use of it. I'm working on two other PACs right now, one Democrat and one Republican."

"Fantastic. We want to be equal opportunity folks and pull back the curtains on both sides of the aisle." The man laughed.

Adam smiled at both the thought of shedding light on this dishonest political action committee as well as the idea that he was able to continue his work of exposing corruption without having to resort to hacking. Everything he had provided O'Neal came from public records.

After disconnecting his call, Adam checked his watch. As he recalled, Aric only had a morning class on Thursdays. He hadn't talked with his brother for over a week, so he decided to give him a call.

"Hey, Big Bro, can I call you back in 15? I'm with Lynch and Jess, and we just finished lunch. Heading back to campus now."

"Sure. Call me when you can."

Interesting, he thought. Lunch with Jess was a common

occurrence. Lunch with Lynch on a Thursday, not so much. He wondered what was up.

True to his word, Aric called back just before the 15-minute mark.

"Hey."

"Funny that you called me. I was telling Jess earlier that I missed having you close by. What's going on?"

"Well, hadn't talked with you for a while, and I miss you, too." He laughed. "So, lunch with Lynch, eh? Something going on?"

Aric told him about the vision. He then described the possible interpretations offered by his lunch companions. "I'm going to try to come up with a map of prayer centers and see if it jives with what I envisioned."

"If you want, I can do that for you in no time flat." Adam felt confident that his new program was up to the task in its current state. He also felt a slight twinge of regret for mothballing UltraNet. That program could have Aric's map completed within an hour or so.

"What? I thought you gave up UltraNet?"

"I have. I'm putting together a new program kinda like it but only able to search publicly available data. It's got a way to go, but it's already produced some interesting results." He described what he'd discovered about the GoBlue PAC. "And you can tell Lynch the search was totally above board."

"Wow. That's amazing.   I know he'll find that interesting. He's still in touch with President Graham."

Lynch Cully had been the ex-president's chief of security during the man's election campaign. After Graham's abduction in Oregon, Cully had been the one to find him imprisoned in a cabin in an Oregon wilderness area. The ex-president now faced incredible hostility and several politically-motivated investigations aimed at keeping him from seeking re-election. There were even rumors that he'd be indicted on falsifying records in New York.

Adam had little doubt that Graham would call on Lynch's expertise from time to time. He would have to give thought as to how he might help.

"So look, as much as I like catching up with you, I called to get your input on something, too." Adam paused. "I told you I was going to start a new business in cybersecurity. I'm struggling to come up with a name, and you've always been more creative than me."

"I'm flattered. What have you considered already?"

They bantered back and forth with names and ideas for a few minutes. Aric agreed with him about most of the options he'd come up with.

"Hey, I have an idea," said Aric. "I was reading from 2 Samuel, chapter 20, today. How about Pelethites Cybersecurity? That's pronounced pel-ay-thee'. "He spelled it for Adam.

"Huh?"

"Yeah. The Pelethites were King David's bodyguards, some of the mightiest of his mighty men and warriors. If you're looking to protect fellow believers, it's perfect."

Adam thought about that for a moment and then smiled. Aric was right. It wasn't just unique; it was perfect for his mission. He knew he could count on his younger brother.

FOUR

Werner Koch watched as his executive assistant, Edvin Bergstedt, exited his office. Months had passed since the PfenRich Pharmaceuticals and AlterNet2 debacles, and Edvin still seemed to walk on eggshells around him. The young man went out of his way to please Werner, despite having been assured on multiple occasions that he was not being held responsible in any way for either event. No one could have predicted the electromagnetic pulse attack against the drug maker, and Edvin had been in no position to stop the viral attack on their AlterNet reincarnation. He didn't have the IT skills to stop it even if he had been in such a position.

And while the demise of PfenRich, the world's largest pharmaceutical manufacturer, had taken a toll on the World Order Council's long-range plans—and a major hit on Werner's personal wealth, other companies had stepped up to fill the breach. Several of PfenRich's top virologists and mRNA experts had moved to BioLogis, a new company funded by the Council, Gates Foundation, and the Wellcome Trust. A significant loan from the World Monetary Fund had enabled the "startup" to purchase the remaining PfenRich assets, and even though they acquired those manufacturing plants and labs for pennies on the dollar, the purchase still amounted to billions of dollars.

Now, as spring attempted to make its return to the northern hemisphere, the dust of that acquisition had settled, and BioLogis had taken up where PfenRich had ended. New mRNA vaccines were once again in the pipeline and the delay had been but one quarter's blip on the timeline.

Werner pressed his intercom. "Edvin, could you come back? I forgot something."

Thirty seconds later, his assistant was standing before him. "Yes, sir."

"Where are we in follow-up to the Cataclysmal Plague 2025 exercise?"

Edvin bent over Werner's desk and rummaged through the pile of papers he had placed there minutes ago. He pulled a folder from near the bottom of the pile.

"Here's the brief. I can give you the highlights if you wish."

Werner nodded. "Yes, please."

"Well, sir, I think you're already aware of what's been publicly promoted through their website. They state the need to focus on ways of making the people trust their governments and health officials, the need for a global network of public health leaders to direct each nation's response to a future contagion, and the need for speedy vaccine—"

"Yes, yes. I know all of that, plus giving the WHO the ability to manage all resources. What was decided behind the scenes?"

Edvin nodded. "The enterovirus under development is on track. Also, the mutations of the avian flu have progressed to where the strain can be passed between mammals. We had to move both from the Ukrainian biolabs because the Russians were getting too close and about to expose them. Wuhan is being scrutinized too closely, so a new virology lab in China is proving to be up to the task. The virus is ready, but quantities are limited. So, widespread dissemination is not possible at this time. Also, the WHO has finalized the amendments to their International Health Regulations and will coordinate with member nations. Publicly, they're saying they've abandoned the idea of vaccine passports, but the IHR changes will embody the concept. However, while the next virus will be ready soon, the committee requests a six-month delay from the originally planned release because public trust in government and health officials is at an all-time low. They hope to improve that level of trust before initiating the plan."

Werner nodded his approval. That was what he had hoped to hear, although the six-month delay was longer than he anticipated. Still, he understood the rationale, and the postponement would assure the final development of the virus that would produce their severe epidemic enterovirus respiratory syndrome—SEERS-23. Plus, it sounded like they might have a choice between that and the avian flu, H5N1.

The wait would also have another benefit. The implementation of the new IHR changes would no doubt face stiff opposition from certain elements within the U.S. They would argue the need for senate ratification, which would be impossible to get despite gaining control in the midterm elections. The Sidon administration would see that the new rules were enforced. Precedence was on their side. Only six percent of international agreements, whether they were called treaties or not, had ever been ratified by the U.S.

Senate.

"Oh. One more thing, Edvin. Where do things stand with the various investigations of Graham?"

While not directly involved in those proceedings, Werner had a clear interest. They needed to keep the ex-president out of the next race. Keeping Sidon in office was critical to their work. For that, they had a close ally in the U.S. whose billions of dollars continued to fund district attorneys who would do their bidding.

"I've heard that the grand jury in New York is close to indicting him. However, there is much more pushback to this than expected. Numerous legal scholars are publicly commenting against this and even some on the left are calling it political, criticizing it as the stuff of banana republics, and saying it will backfire."

"Perhaps, but it is a perfect distraction while we implement the new IHR changes."

Werner had no idea how far they would get in dealing with the ex-president. In their perfect world, perhaps they could trigger an armed rebellion that would allow the institution of martial law. *Hmmm*, he thought. *How far would we have to go to make that a reality?*

FIVE

Peter Manning sat at the console in the LADWP control offices just northwest of the small city of Bishop, California. As an electrical engineer, his primary job was one of supervising the turbines of the hydroelectric plants along the Owens River, as well as those along Bishop Creek to the west of town and a handful of others further along the transmission lines into the city. Secondarily, he oversaw the maintenance crew that serviced these plants and kept them in good working order. For small facilities, they did an extraordinarily good job of providing green power. Of that, he was proud of the work they did.

All told the dozen plants produced about 122 megawatts of electricity at peak. True, that paled in comparison to, say, the Hoover Dam with its 2,080 MW of output or the Grand Coulee Dam with 6,800 MW of electrical generation. Yet, they provided enough electricity to power 179,000 homes in the L.A. metro area. That might be a drop in the Pacific considering the fact that L.A. consumed roughly 180 gigawatts of electricity daily, but the 320,000-plus people in those 179,000 homes appreciated it.

Rolling blackouts, partly because of the drought's effect on hydroelectric power generation, had become all too commonplace. Now, with the record rainfall and snow, those blackouts were a thing of the past, hopefully. If anything, controlling, or more precisely, limiting the water flow through their turbines had become a top priority to keep them at an ideal generation level. Too little flow had resulted in low power, but too much threatened the integrity of the turbines. It was a simple wear-and-tear equation.

In truth, Pete and his team had become somewhat complacent because of the low water conditions of the previous three years. He was the first to admit that. For the past couple of months, they had their hands busy maintaining the turbines to get optimal power out of them without allowing too much stress on their moving parts. With all of the water overflowing into the spillway at Crowley Lake, they had to watch their equipment carefully. Still, he was satisfied they had found the "sweet spot" where they could handle the turbines while maximizing the electricity being created.

Pete took another sip of coffee as he gave his screens another perusal. He nodded at the data which showed maximum power coming from all of the turbines. He heard footsteps behind him and turned to see who it was.

"Hey, Pete. Did you hear Shawn Westhope was called to Long Valley? Is there a problem?"

Wally Prescott, a senior aqueduct and reservoir keeper, was Pete's counterpart on the water side of LADWP. He had his hands full with the increased water levels, too. Already, earlier in the month, a 120-foot section of the aqueduct near Olancha had been undermined and destroyed by runoff. The herculean task of repairing that breach took 100 men and a full week of work. But they had completed the task and restored the water flow to the four million rate-paying customers in L.A. who used that water.

However, the threat to the aqueduct remained. The

high water levels challenging them both saw over 1,000 cubic feet per minute of water going over the spillway at Pleasant Valley Dam just downstream from the control center. Already that water overflowed into the dry, rocky arroyos and ditches along the valley and covered lower roads. And Owens Lake—once a thriving area where steamboats plied the water until the aqueduct system took its water and turned the area into a dry, alkaline salt flat— was filling again, causing major problems of a new kind by disturbing that alkaline salt.

Plus, the headgates of the Los Angeles Aqueduct system sat roughly 20 miles downstream. Monitoring their water levels to prevent too much water from flowing into the aqueduct, which threatened sections of aging concrete, had become a 24/7 task. More importantly, maintaining the dam that allowed that water's diversion was critical. To lose the dam would mean a massive rebuilding project of the headgates and would cut off water to the city for much longer than a week.

"I heard that he went there with Mick Mulholland. Some kind of soil slippage along the face of the dam. He contacted the folks downtown about getting a load of rock up there to reinforce the defect."

"And?"

Pete shrugged. "Don't know. Haven't heard anything further. That was just a couple of hours ago."

"Oh. Well, I hope there's nothing to that."

"You and me both. If you hear anything else, let me know, and I'll do the same."

Wally gave him a thumbs-up and walked out the door. Rather than turn back to his monitors, Pete bowed his head and said a quick prayer.

Pete's true passion was teaching, specifically the Bible. He had considered himself a Christian all his life but had never truly given his life to Christ or accepted Him as his Lord. He hadn't been to church in years.

A prophetic word of knowledge about what could have been a tragic accident changed that. Ten years earlier, a complete stranger had come up to him to tell him that God wanted him to avoid a certain electrical substation he was scheduled to work on. The man gave him details on what was about to happen, and something about the message hit him as true. Unusual and definitely outside his comfort zone, but true. Pete didn't sleep all that night and called in the next day to say he'd be late. Fifteen minutes after he was originally scheduled to be there, a major explosion and fire rocked the substation. Every detail of the prophetic word came true, and had Pete ignored the message, he would have died. Three other men had. Pete resumed church attendance and became born again that very week.

Now, he was a pastor of a small, but growing, congregation in Bishop, with his job at LADWP being his version of tent making, a reference to the Apostle Paul. With the way things were going in the country, he decided to spend time teaching on the end times, what is theologically called 'eschatology.' During that study, he found his own beliefs changed. No longer did he believe in a rapture of the church. Nor did he still read the Book of Revelation literally or accept that there would be some global tyrant called the Antichrist. He now saw the Old Testament roots of John's apocalyptic book and believed he and his family were part of that generation who would see Christ's return.

As he watched the monitors, his mind was elsewhere. A member of his church had asked a probative question: how do we know when a nation had passed the point of no-return for God's wrath? From their conversation, it was clear that the woman wondered if the U.S.—indeed, the world—had passed that point. If so, then perhaps the period in time that the Bible called the time of Jacob's Trouble had come.

Taken from Jeremiah 30:7, those who believed in a rapture equated this time with seven years of tribulation. There were no seven-year periods actually described in the Bible. For Pete, it would be a time of severe persecution and distress for Jews and Christians alike, but also a period of unknown length preceding Christ's return. He understood that it could be as short as three-and-a-half years, based upon the Book of Revelation, but he had no reference as to when such a period might start.

So, had the world passed the point of no-return? He had sought that answer in both the Bible and in prayer. Repeatedly, he was led to the first chapter of the Book of Romans, verses 24 through 32:

> *Therefore God gave them up in the lusts of their hearts to impurity, to the dishonoring of their bodies among themselves, because they exchanged the truth about God for a lie and worshiped and served the creature rather than the Creator, who is blessed forever! Amen. For this reason God gave them up to dishonorable passions. For their women exchanged natural relations for those that are contrary to nature; and the men likewise gave up natural relations with women and were consumed with passion for one another, men committing shameless acts with men and receiving in themselves the*

due penalty for their error. And since they did not see fit to acknowledge God, God gave them up to a debased mind to do what ought not to be done. They were filled with all manner of unrighteousness, evil, covetousness, malice. They are full of envy, murder, strife, deceit, maliciousness. They are gossips, slanderers, haters of God, insolent, haughty, boastful, inventors of evil, disobedient to parents, foolish, faithless, heartless, ruthless. Though they know God's righteous decree that those who practice such things deserve to die, they not only do them but give approval to those who practice them.

Those words certainly described the world around him. If indeed the country had entered that period, what were believers to do? Prayer was a given, and his church had become more devoted to that practice than at any time since they joined together as a congregation.

Yet, Pete was feeling the need for them all to become more evangelistic, for the time of Jacob's Trouble could possibly be aligned with the three and a half years described in Revelation as the time of the two witnesses. And the more he studied, the more Pete recognized that the two witnesses weren't necessarily two specific individuals, but the church as a whole. By God's direction, no one was to be condemned on the testimony of just one person. Two or more witnesses were needed. If the world was to be condemned, the church would provide the required witnesses.

Pete began to feel a burden for family, friends, co-workers, and neighbors. They needed to not just hear the gospel but to gain some understanding of it as well. Time was short. Eternal decisions needed to be made before it was too late.

SIX

Aric joined his fellow believers on campus for their weekly Sunday afternoon assembly in a meeting room of the library. As a recognized club within the college, they had free access to the room, but that standing had come at a cost. A year earlier, they had lost that official recognition when complaints were filed about their strict code of following a Biblical lifestyle to be eligible for an officer's position. Similarly, their requirement of signing a statement of faith and of being a member in good standing in a local church in order to join was offensive to those who complained.

Of course, they took a stand against those complaints saying that not following those standards effectively eliminated the charter of the group. After all, what was the point of having a biblically-based, Christian club if you didn't have to be a follower of Christ or believe in the Bible's teachings?

Still, their arguments fell on deaf ears . . . at first. The college said their club violated the campus diversity, equity, and inclusivity guidelines and anti-discrimination code. The club argued for their first amendment rights . . . and won after a lawsuit was filed on their behalf. The college knew it stood no chance of winning that case in court and reversed its ban on the club.

Yes, they had won, but the cost had been one of extra

scrutiny of everything they did. They were the most closely watched group on campus. Hypothetically, the BLM folks could burn down a building and remain an approved club. If the Christians misspent a dollar of club funds, that could shut them down.

Aric sat with Jess and her brother, Chris. That day, he might have preferred sitting with someone else.

Jess raised her hand when Alan, the club president, asked if anyone had a praise report or something good that happened to them that week. Aric wasn't aware of anything special happening to her, so he was curious as to why she raised her hand.

"I wouldn't call it a praise report, but Aric had a vision Thursday morning." She turned and poked him in the arm. "Go on, Aric. Tell them about your vision."

Aric wanted to shrink back. Yeah, there were a few people in the room whose opinions and feedback he would appreciate, but not the whole group. He didn't like being singled out.

"I, uh . . . Yeah, okay. I had this vision as I was waking up Thursday morning." He proceeded to tell them about the "dream" and the possible interpretations that he, Jess, and Lynch had come up with. "Look, I don't expect everyone here to have an interpretation, but I would ask that that you pray about it, specifically that God give me understanding about it."

Jess smiled. "He's leaning toward the—"

Aric nudged her to stop. "Don't bias them. Let them pray about it."

She sat back looking a bit sheepish. "Okay."

Alan resumed the meeting. "Anyone else?"

One of the other gals raised her hand. "Since we're

asking for prayers, I have a nine-year-old cousin who asked me a question, and it's been bothering me. He asked if it was going to become a law to let people kill Christians." The usual background murmuring of their meetings went quiet.

"He's only nine?"

She nodded. "Yeah. I don't know where that came from, and I told him no."

Several voices expressed their agreement.

"I'd have said the same thing. Man, I sure wouldn't want my little brother stressing over something like that."

"But what do you think? Could that really happen?"

"No, not in this country."

"But the Bible says it could."

"Maybe, but it's more likely that authorities will just look the other way, not pass such a law."

A lively discussion followed until Alan asked all to quiet down. "Guys, we have plans for the day. Remember? Anyone else?"

When all who responded were finished, he continued. "Okay. Well, our friends with The Spark have informed me that they're all set up at Eichelman Park in Kenosha and ready for us to join them. So, team up and head over there."

The Spark was a local band headed up by the worship leader at their church, along with his wife and others from the church.   They frequently joined forces with the club to bring open-air praise and worship sessions to various parks in the city. The live music would attract people to the group, and the club members formed small teams to talk with those people and spread the gospel. While these gatherings seemed impromptu, they were all planned, and permits were obtained.

Eichelman Park was in downtown Kenosha near the

Southport Marina, where it overlooked Lake Michigan. With a beautiful garden surrounded on three sides by long pergolas, a crescent-shaped beach protected by a breakwater, and a small playground, the green space looked resplendent with its mature maples and oaks beginning to bud out. Soon, those large trees would provide shade for dozens of picnickers on any given summer day.

Today, although the air temperatures had reached the forecasted upper 60s, the wind off the lake remained a bit on the chilly side. Despite that, Kenoshans were typically hardy souls and the promise of a sunny day in the 60s in early April still brought them to the park.

As the music started, Aric looked around the park. As expected, the music began to draw a crowd. Members from a variety of churches in the area joined together to sing. He joined in but was soon distracted by the arrival of a police car. They parked along the main road adjacent to the park and the officers remained in their car. That seemed suspicious to Aric. They had never required a police presence before. Plus, most patrol cars carried one officer. It was obvious there were two officers in this one. A few minutes later, a second patrol car arrived. It, too, held two policemen.

Aric sought to focus on the praise music and closed his eyes to do so. At some point during the second song, he heard a commotion off to his left. He opened his eyes and looked to see what it was.

A group of about 20 people, all hooded and wearing masks, approached their gathering. Several were screaming profanities. Others openly denounced Christ and His followers. As they neared, a few began to reach into the satchels and bags they carried, and soon eggs were flying into the midst of the worshipers and others gathered there.

Leaders among the various churches represented there began to encourage their people not to retaliate. From up front, Chris, the worship leader, did the same. The protesters heard this and further taunted the assembly. Those gathered there continued to encourage each other to turn the other cheek.

Aric saw an egg barreling toward Jess' head. He reached out and caught it before it could hit her. The egg cracked and slimed his hand. He tossed the goo to the ground and tried to shake his hand clean. He didn't want to soil his clothing with it, so he bent down and wiped his hand on the grass. As he did so, he noticed the police officers standing by their cars. They made no effort to stop the protesters.

Aric understood what the various leaders were trying to do—de-escalate the situation. However, a small voice inside Aric's head said, "Show them My love." Aric thought about that for a split second. They, the college club, were there for evangelistic reasons after all. He stepped toward the protest group and noticed that his move caught the attention of the police.

"Friends, welcome! We're glad you came to learn more about Jesus!" he yelled. "C'mon over and let us tell you more." He spread his arms in a welcoming gesture.

Some of his friends looked at him like he was crazy, but the protesters stopped in their tracks. They, too, looked at him. Some cocked their heads as if questioning him. Some backed away as he took another step toward them. With the masks and hoods, you couldn't tell what emotion registered on their faces, but Aric guessed that they had never encountered his response before.

"Jesus loves you, too, whether you know it or not. He

died for you, just as He did for all of us, but you have to accept Him as Lord and Savior to enter the kingdom of heaven!"

A couple of the egg throwers reached into their bags and retrieved eggs, but in launching them toward Aric, all of the eggs broke in midair and went no further than ten feet. A second attempted volley produced the same result. Their third attempt saw the eggs break in their own hands as they lifted them out of their bags. They screamed in frustration as they dipped their hands into the bags and came up empty-handed. They tossed the bags to the ground and broken eggs spilled across the grass.

Aric's friends followed his lead in welcoming the protesters. Yet, no one took more than a step or two toward the people. Within minutes, the protesters all ran off. As they did so, one individual's hood flew off, and Aric recognized the pink-haired head. And the figure running next to him seemed familiar, too. He had seen that running style before . . . if you could call it a style.

Aric turned toward the police cars to see that they, too, prepared to leave. Except for one officer, who was talking with his partner. Aric had no idea what he said to his fellow officer, but that man left the cars and approached Aric.

"What's your name?"

"Aric, with an A."

"Son, I have to give you credit. When you first stepped toward those folks, we were prepared for the worst. You're a big guy after all, and we all thought you were about to retaliate. But you opened yourself up as a target, while also inviting them to talk with you. That took guts."

"Yes, sir." Aric wasn't quite sure how to respond.

The policeman gave Aric his card. "Look, I have to get

back to work, but . . . well, I don't know what just happened here, but I want to. Give me a call. I want to know more. I'll be expecting your call."

SEVEN

Shawn wondered what he would find upon his return to Long Valley Dam. Statewide, over an inch-and-a-half of rain had been added to the annual water year, but that was a statewide average. The Sierras now had over 200% more rain than average for the end of March.

The latest atmospheric river had delivered inches more of rain to the mountain range's lower elevations and a few feet more of snow to those higher up. Of significance, however, was that the elevation for snow had risen several hundred feet thanks to the warming weather in general. The critical importance of that was seen in the rising levels of snowmelt now contributing to the runoff entering the rivers and reservoirs across the state.

As a result, several reservoirs were now having to release water to accept the inflowing volume. Those releases contributed further to flooding downstream, where community after community didn't need more water. Ironic … after years of drought and water conservation.

The trip to the dam via US-395 was typically quick and easily navigated, but an inner voice told him not to cross the dam in his truck. He wasn't concerned about not making it across to the north side. He was concerned with adding the stress, even temporarily, of his three-ton Ford F-250 on top of what he already knew to be a soggy hill of rock and dirt.

In fact, he had asked the workers at the dam to barricade the road across the dam on both sides after his first trip there.

The trip around the north side of Crowley Lake, through Benton Crossing, and back down Benton Crossing Rd. to reach the access road to the dam added an hour to his trip. However, he was glad he made the trek. The degree of flooding from the Owens River in Benton Crossing was something he'd never witnessed before.

The Upper Owens was typically a meandering stream, ten to twelve feet in width, which snaked through dry meadows and rocky arroyos before entering the headwaters of Crowley Lake. Brown's Owens River Campground catered to fishermen and hikers just east of the bridge. Shawn was surprised to see much of the campground under water. As he stopped to peruse the scene, he noticed that the bottom lands to the west of the river were also submerged.

Although shallow in most spots, that would add another two square miles or more to the area of the lake, if he recalled those distances correctly. He tried to do the rough math in his head but gave up and used his phone's calculator. That was the rough equivalent to another 1,300 acres, which at a guesstimated average of five feet of depth would come to about 6,500 more acre-feet of water behind the dam. The next calculation revealed that this amounted to another 212 million gallons.

He didn't like that number . . . and more water was rushing in every minute.

He added a little lead to his foot. He needed to get to the dam.

En route, he called Mick Mulholland. "Hey Shawn, everything okay?"

That response alone threw Shawn off.   The man

always answered with "what's up?" To ask the question he asked revealed his concern, too.

"Have you been in the Benton Crossing area?"

"Not a chance. That's a remote area. We're dealing with major flooding affecting entire towns. Pardon the pun, but I'm swamped right now. No way I'm going to have time to head into the mountains."

"Understand. I'm sure you're flooded with urgent calls. Pun intended." He wasn't going to be out-punned. Come hades or high water. As he thought that and considered where the country was headed, he recognized that maybe both had arrived together.

"Yeah. Funny, and oh so true. So, again, everything okay?"

"Not sure. I'm heading back to Long Valley Dam, and my gut told me to head north around the lake. I just passed the bridge over the Owens and the campground. It's mostly under water. I estimated that means another couple of hundred million gallons in the lake. I don't recall what the dam's spillway is rated for. Gonna have to call into the office for that, but I'm worried I'm gonna find the dam being topped or close to it."

"No, no. I don't want to hear that. Do you want me to alert LADWP?"

"Not yet. I'll have a better assessment in 30 minutes. Call you back."

"Okay, buddy."

As he drove on, the rain resumed. That was not what they needed at the moment. At times, the rain poured so hard, he had to slow to a crawl. The flats ended, and he began the long, slow ascent into the foothills. The turnoff onto the gravel of Owens Gorge Rd was maybe four miles ahead and a couple of hundred feet higher in elevation. He expected to see snow but was shocked to see that the recent rains had cleared that. He had no idea how high the rain reached, but the higher in elevation it went, the worse the threat became.

After 45 minutes, he finally reached the turnout just north of the dam leading to the parking area near the spillway maintenance building. More bad news.

The spillway was a raging whirlpool as the water was sucked down into the tunnel leading to the bottom of the dam. He could only imagine what the water racing out at the bottom of the dam looked like. He would soon see it firsthand. The parking area closest to the spillway was under water, too.

He twisted around in his seat and grabbed his rain gear from the backseat. He donned the plastic pants and hooded jacket and emerged from his truck. The brim of his ball cap poked out from under the hood and barely protected his face from the rain. When facing the wind, it offered no protection at all. He raised his hand to act as a visor, but the visibility remained awful.

He fought the wind to get to the top of the dam and was knocked to his butt as he reached it. The gorge funneled the air and accelerated it to gale force speeds. He couldn't get back to his feet, so he crawled to a point where he could look down into the gorge. The water jetting from the spillway tunnel looked like it came from a pressure washer. He moved to a point where he hoped to see the scar on the hillside. As best he could tell, his stakes were gone, washed away. That meant the defect had deepened, or widened, or, more likely, both.

More importantly, it meant the LADWP hadn't reinforced the spot with rock. And that did not bode well.

The rain and wind would continue to erode that section of the dam.

He crawled back towards his truck until he was beyond the lip of the earthen structure and could fight his way back to standing. With the wind now at his back, it almost pushed him to the pickup. He climbed inside and fished out his cell phone from inside his soggy gear. No reception.

He exited the vehicle again and headed toward the maintenance building. As he recalled, they had a land line there. Upon reaching the door, he was confronted with an electronic lock and realized he should have looked up the combination recorded on his phone *before* going back into the rain and wind. Trying to protect his phone as he again opened his jacket to retrieve it, he fumbled it with wet hands but finally pulled up his notes app and recovered the combination. Once inside, he fought to close the door against the wind.

Man, it sure feels good to get out of the weather, he thought. The rain drummed against the roof of the building. He flipped on the lights and found the phone nearby on an old metal desk that looked like it had been there since the dam's construction. With his phone in hand, he retrieved the number for his contact at LADWP and dialed.

"Munson."

"Sonny, it's Shawn Westhope."

"Hey, Shawn. Look, I got your message about the rock. The road to our main source's quarry was washed out with a mudslide. We're trying to get the rock from another supplier, but it might take another day or two."

"Sonny, I'm in the Long Valley spillway building right now. You need to expedite that, and I mean it. The water's maybe a foot, foot and a half, from topping the dam. The spillway's—"

He felt it before sensing it any other way. A subtle but increasing vibration underfoot caught his attention. Before he could say another word, the vibration grew into a shaking. With that, a flash of recognition hit him. He hadn't personally experienced it before but an old-timer in his office had described it to him in very visceral terms. He had no time to finish the conversation.

He dropped the phone and dashed to the door. The wind flung it open as soon as he turned the knob to engage the spindle. He didn't care. He needed to get to his truck.

With adrenaline pumping through his body, he forced his way against the wind to get back to his truck. The ground felt as if an earthquake now shook it. Inside his truck, he started it up and moved it into reverse. He needed to back up and turn around. As he did, he saw the maintenance building begin to lean. The earth beneath it gave way and the yawning crevice now reached toward him.

Just as the old timer had told him. This was a problem of seepage on steroids leading to a serious piping failure. The rushing water of the engulfed spillway had eroded into the hillside around the tunnel. It followed the tunnel, removing earth and rock from around its concrete form until a new pathway, or pipe, for the water existed . . . and that had now resulted in a washout. The dam was about to fail, and he needed to get out.

As he tried to accelerate, his back wheels began to spin in the soil that now seemed to liquefy around his truck. As his truck began to fall into the growing fissure, he flung open his door and jumped.

EIGHT

Adam shuffled his notes, reviewed them one last time, and made the call.

"Calvary Chapel Bible College. How may I direct your call?"

Adam had heard through new contacts that the two-year bible college had become the target for those who jeered at their message and mission. The attacks had accelerated after the success of the movie *The Jesus Revolution*. Indeed, anything with the name Calvary Chapel seemed to draw the haters. Adam had reached out to the head of technical services at the school, which was located northeast of San Bernardino in the mountains west of Bear Mountain Ski Resort.

"Silas Grimshaw, please. This is Adam Afton."

"Thank you. One moment."

After a moment, the man came on the line. "Adam, I've been hoping you'd call soon. We had another DOS attack yesterday. Fortunately, whoever was behind it didn't realize we were on spring break and the attack didn't affect us much."

"Hi, Silas. I saw that taking place as I monitored your site. I can offer you a couple of things. First, I'm able to pinpoint where the attack came from should you want to file charges against them."

There was a slight pause on the other end.

"Do you think we'd get anywhere with that, with making a complaint and asking for criminal charges to be filed?"

Adam shook his head, despite knowing the other man couldn't see him. Habit. "Honestly, no, particularly in today's social and political climate. But it could tie back into my second offer."

"Oh?"

"I could create a piece of custom software, scripted code, which could detect when a DOS attack is starting and divert the attack to a fake page or dummy website. Or I could divert it back on the attackers. That's how my first suggestion can tie into the second."

"Whoa. You can do that? Why hasn't something like that been created before now?"

"To answer your questions, yes, and I don't know. It may be that this solution is resource intense. That is, it ties up the CPU on the server to an unusually high degree. If your website is on a shared server, that can become an issue. It could still shut down your website. To get around that, I would suggest that you place your site on my servers. I have these protections and more built into my servers. Makes no difference whether your site is built on WordPress, Elementor, or any other site creation software. And I'm competitive." He mentioned the three different hosting plans, with pricing, that he'd developed.

"So, if we switch to you for hosting, you guarantee no disruptions."

"Well, not a total guarantee. Some things, like a devastating solar storm or other natural disasters, could take out the servers, although I've done my best to harden them. Things like that are beyond anyone's control . . . and, they likely would take out more than my servers. Plus, interruptions caused by a disruption of the internet itself are beyond my control."

"So, how many companies do you currently host?"

Adam suspected that this question would arise. Going against everything taught in Marketing 101, he decided that honesty was the best policy.

"To be honest, I just started marketing this service and your college would be the first. Because of that, I'm willing to give you six months free to test my service. And I plan to give that offer to the first ten sites to sign up. Plus, I will do all the work of moving your site from its current server to my servers, and if you aren't happy with the service, I'll move it back."

He had never been much of a salesman, and much preferred working in the background, but he had been practicing his spiel. So far, he was pleased with how things were going.

"I don't know that my CEO is going to like being the first, free or not."

"I understand. I'm only working with fellow believers and focusing on Christian groups that have been facing attacks like the ones you've told me about. I can give you personal references if you like."

He had a list of people who had agreed to give him such a reference. Lynch Cully was among the top on the list, as was FBI S-A-C Chip Wiese, who had spearheaded the takedown of the child trafficking ring that Adam and Aric had exposed. President Graham had also agreed, but getting through to him was next to impossible, and he was facing his own attacks now.

"Okay, let me talk it over with—"

The line went dead. Adam tried to call back. Something was wrong. His call triggered a message telling him that all calls into that area code were being diverted to this message. Why?

He used the laptop in front of him to call up the school's website. After a few seconds, a 504 Gateway Timeout error appeared. He tried the UCLA website. Same result. Next, he tried the KTLA and FoxLA websites. Same thing. The internet in L.A. appeared to be gone. Had there been a huge earthquake? He tried The Epoch Times, NewsMax, Fox News, CNN, MSNBC, and Yahoo portals. None had information about what might be happening in Southern California.

NINE

Pete arrived at work on time, but his mind wasn't on the day ahead. As he listened to the report from his night manager, he felt troubled by the news of still-rising water levels in the gorge. Yet, he felt confident that they had everything under control. He worried more for Wally and his aqueduct maintenance teams.

"You know, the spring runoff from the mountains was an annual occurrence we handled without a problem in years past," said the night manager.

The guy was correct. Pete had been there for almost a decade, almost as long as he'd been a Christian. They did handle the spring runoff well.

It was when the man added, "Why should this year be any different?" that Pete felt a bit nervous, almost as if they'd just been jinxed. Of course, as a Christian, he didn't believe in jinxes. So, why was this spring different? Record rainfall and a snowpack that had everyone talking.

As Pete settled in with his coffee and ran his first review of the monitors, he saw nothing of concern. Everything appeared to be like it was when he left the previous afternoon. So, why did he feel so unsettled?

It was as if God's Spirit was telling him to prepare to run. In his half-sleep right before waking, he felt as if he was running from danger. The impression had jolted him awake.

The morning progressed as with any other day. His coffee had worked its magic in keeping him alert, but it was time to recycle it. He pressed an intercom button to the back office.

"Hey Q, can you relieve me for a break? I need to use the head and get another cup of coffee."

A moment later, Quentin walked into the room and assumed the task of monitoring the system. Pete stretched for a moment, then headed out to do his business. In the break room, he lifted the carafe from the coffee maker and began to pour a cup when the lights flickered.

Pete paused and the realization dawned on him that they were now on their backup generator. He almost dropped the carafe before running from the room and back to the control room.

"What happened?"

Q kept moving through various screens on the monitor.

"I-I'm not sure. Everything here seems okay."

Pete leaned over the desk and reached past Q to hit a button on the keyboard. Static appeared on the screen.

"Crap. The feed from Upper Gorge is gone."

He cycled through to another screen. The feed from Middle Gorge appeared on the monitor. What they saw froze them on the spot for a moment. A string of expletives came from Q's mouth. A giant wall of water could be seen racing down the gorge toward the power plant. Seconds later, the feed disappeared and static again filled the screen.

Pete rushed to a nearby wall and hit a panic button. In a flash, alert sirens echoed through the building and nearby grounds.

"Get out! Get out! The dam has failed. Get to high ground!

He ran from room to room screaming the same thing

before bolting outside. To anyone who could hear him, he yelled the same thing. He saw Q's truck accelerate out of the parking lot, followed by two others. That meant three other workers unaccounted for. He tried to recall if they were out on assignments elsewhere, but his mind couldn't focus.

There were also half a dozen private homes in Birchim Canyon just below the power plant. He ran to his truck, climbed in, and hurried down Rough Creek Road to its dead end. He laid on his horn the whole way and turned around, continuing to honk. On the return, he saw three homeowners outside their front doors.

With his windows down, he again screamed, "The dam has failed! Get out! Get out!" He kept honking the horn to get the attention of anyone else at home.

Two of the three ran inside, and he saw them, along with family members, rushing back out to their vehicles. The third man ran to one neighbor's house and then the next, sounding the alarm.

Pete now heard the noise of thunder rumbling from the canyon. He had to leave. Biblically, as a watchman, he had sounded the alarm, and now it was up to the individuals he had warned to act. They had two, maybe three, minutes to clear the gorge.

He floored the accelerator and flew up Gorge Rd. to get to higher ground. As he drove, he remembered that two of his men were doing maintenance on the turbine below them in the small earthen dam at the end of the Pleasant Valley Reservoir. As soon as he topped the crest of the gorge, he retrieved his phone and called one of the men. He felt relief as the man answered on the second ring.

"George, get out of there! Long Valley Dam has failed. There's a 50-foot wall of water coming your way. You have minutes to clear out."

George didn't answer, but he didn't hang up either. From the noise and the screaming in the background, he knew his message had been received loud and clear.

Next, he called his wife, followed by the elders of his church, to warn them all. Under normal conditions and upon leaving the gorge, the Owens River became a meandering stream that snaked back and forth through the plain on which their city sat. However, the river had already overflowed its banks. The water heading their way would quickly spread across the plain and while its devastating force would dissipate, that didn't mean the destruction would be minimal. Plus, much of the water would continue down the course of the river, threatening every structure downstream. This was going to be bad.

Pete bowed his head and prayed for protection over his workers, the town of Bishop, and anyone along the river. He looked up to see the wall of water tearing down the gorge. He had guessed it to be 50 feet high from the video he had seen, but now he recognized that the funneling effect of the gorge had produced a tsunami maybe 75 feet high.

Not that he ever expected this to happen, but he had been curious and had done the math should the dam ever fail. Based on data provided by LADWP and the state, over 60 trillion gallons of water sat behind the Long Valley Dam. And that was at average water levels. With the heavy rains and melting snowpack, hundreds of millions more gallons could be added to that tally.

He tried to place a call to the LADWP headquarters. No doubt they were already aware of the disaster that faced them. No signal. That meant power to the nearest cell tower was now gone. Despite various laws on the books regulating those towers and mandating battery backup for a minimum of two to four hours, the recurrent wildfires had done damage to many towers. As such, the batteries from towers in areas of low population, like Bishop, sometimes were robbed to replace those in more populated locations. That was going to add to the disaster, as many people would not have adequate warning to escape.

He contemplated the chain of events that were likely to occur. No, he thought, this isn't just going to be bad. This is going to be calamitous.

TEN

Heather Dickson checked her appearance in the hallway mirror before heading to the garage of their Bel Air home. She strove to look approachable and not ostentatious, like so many of her friends at the Bel-Air Country Club. Although, in reality, some of her friends on the tennis courts of MountainGate Country Club—where they held a tennis membership because she liked their courts better than the clay courts at the Bel-Air—seemed much more dire to impress than her golf and social friends at the Bel-Air. Some days it was difficult to decide at which place to spend her time.

But today was Monday. Few of her friends at either club used those facilities on Mondays, and this was her morning for community service—her choice, not court-ordered, she would always add when she mentioned it.

Their gated community of Windy Hill sat on the west side of the 405, on that side of the Sepulveda Pass where the Skirball Fire of 2017 destroyed six of their neighbors' homes. Fortunately, the firefighters contained the fire before it moved farther up the hillside to their house. Still, it had been a frightening experience.

But the situation had had a secondary result. The fire had been started by a homeless illegal trying to cook a meal. Well, she no longer used the term "illegal" and preferred her own description: undocumented sojourner. She loved the word, sojourner. An acquaintance had introduced it to her when she mentioned something about God telling the Jews to treat sojourners well because they had once been sojourners someplace in the Middle East. She couldn't quite remember where, and they'd never had a Bible in the house so she could try to look it up. Besides, she didn't think the Bible had an index where she could look up the word to find the right page.

The plight of that sojourner almost losing his life in the fire while just trying to cook a simple meal had made her think about the homeless. And what she learned led her to volunteer at the St. Joseph Center in Venice. As one of over a dozen facilities set up to help those people, the center provided numerous educational and mental health services to the homeless, as well as housing assistance, meals, and food.

At first, she had offered her help simply to serve meals in their Bread and Roses Café, which offered clients meals in a restaurant-style setting, as opposed to the soup lines and long tables so many associated with homeless feeding programs. When they learned she had cooking skills that her friends raved about, she assisted with their culinary classes where they trained people to cook and then helped place them in restaurants and institutional kitchens. Now, she helped manage their food pantry, while also using her contacts to find their culinary students jobs.

The work at the center had become more challenging. The homeless population had increased a staggering 32% over the previous year. No one quite knew why Venice attracted so many homeless, but they were there, and the center struggled with the demand for their services. The food pantry was particularly hard hit by the increase in the number of homeless and rising food costs. Regular donors had cut back for a variety of reasons and many food items were simply in scarce supply.

She climbed into the 2018 BMW 3-series for the trip to the facility. Her husband had purchased the car specifically for her trips to Venice after learning that it was the least stolen car in the country for some reason. While she preferred her Range Rover Autobiography SUV, she found the Beemer suitable as she slogged her way along the 405 to the 10. The 12-mile trip into Venice typically took just over an hour. Today, the rain added another 15 minutes to the commute.

She pulled into the monitored parking lot off Marine St and noticed it seemed emptier than usual. *Guess I'm not the only one who's late*, she thought. After entering the pantry, she shook off the water on her umbrella and secured her things in her locker.

"Hi, Jeannie. Sorry I'm late. The 405 was a soggy parking lot today, not just its usual stop'n go."

Her co-worker shrugged. "Just got here a few minutes before you. And the rain's keeping the clientele away, too."

Heather checked her in-box. In addition to the various donation receipts to be completed and inventory sheets, she found a note from Olivia Canon, the center's VP of Administration. *Come see me,* was all it said.

"Jeannie, Olivia left me a note to come see her. It's quiet here, so I'm going to track her down now, if you don't mind."

"Not at all. Go." Her coworker gave her a slight shooing away motion with her hand.

Heather went to Olivia's office to find it empty. David Brown, the CFO, was in his office next door. "Good morning,

Heather," he said from his desk. "Olivia said you might be stopping in. She went to the café and said she'd be back in 15 minutes. That was, oh, twenty minutes ago, so I guess she'll be back any minute now."

Heather nodded. "Thanks, David. Should I wait or head back to the pantry?"

He laughed. "Knowing how she gets sidetracked, I'd opt for the latter. I can tell her you stopped by."

"Okay. See you later."

As she exited the office area on the second floor and opened the door to the stairwell, she bumped into Olivia. The woman carried a stack of papers that seemed too much for her to handle.

"Hi. I was just at your office. Here, let me help you with that." She grabbed half of the woman's load and opened the door back into the hallway.

"Come on in," said Olivia as they arrived at her office door. After laying down her load, she stepped back to the door and closed it. "Have a seat."

That took Heather back a bit. Why the privacy? Was she in trouble? Had there been a complaint? Olivia's tasks included human resources, and Heather had heard tales of other closed-door meetings with Olivia. Of course, Heather was a volunteer, so it wasn't like she could be fired. They could tell her that her services were no longer needed. Heather realized she wouldn't like that.

"Heather, we've all heard good things about your work in the food pantry, but I want you to know that we're changing your position there to a part-time paid position."

Heather felt disappointment wash over her. At least there hadn't been any complaints about her. She had come to enjoy helping people at the pantry. She even provided simple menus and meal preparation ideas to the people coming in. True, those were nothing like the gourmet meals she served friends at home, but they were nutritious, without being difficult for someone with minimal cooking skills. She wondered what she might do now.

"Oh. So, I guess you're saying you won't need me there any longer. Is there—"

"No, no, not that. Not that at all. We'd like to offer you the position."

Heather had not expected that. Olivia knew about her background, where she lived, that her husband was a multimillionaire real estate developer, and that she had no need for a paying job.

"Oh, well, thank you, but I don't need a paycheck. I'm happy volunteering."

"And you've served us well, but we believe that people deserve to be compensated for their time. There is one catch, however."

"Oh?"

"We would need you to come in three days a week, not just Mondays."

Heather took a big breath in.

"Three days? I-I'd need to talk that over with my husband. It would definitely mean some changes at home."

But would it? She thought about it. The real changes would be two fewer days playing tennis and having lunch with friends at the club. Yes, she and her husband, Rory, often hosted clients, as well as friends, for dinner on Friday nights. She would have to work around that, if it was okay with him. He had told her time and time again that her dinners had helped clinch a deal. He might not like such a change. Olivia's voice brought her back from her thoughts.

"Heather, I'm going to be straight with you. When you first started here a few years ago, few of us thought you'd last long. You seemed like the typical one-percenter who wanted to feel good about herself by doing a good deed for the less fortunate. We've had them before. The well-to-do who signal their virtue by coming here to help, only to give up within a month or two. But you've stuck it out. You've worked wherever we asked without complaining. We think you deserve more than just a thank you or certificates at our volunteers banquets each year."

"Thank you. I have to admit, I did almost give it up after that first month. But now, my whole perspective on life has changed. I am honored with your offer, but I seriously need to discuss this with Rory. I have commitments to help him with his business, too, and they could be affected if I accept this job."

Job? Was she really being offered a *job*? She had never had to work at a job before. Now, it wouldn't be so easy to cancel a day if she needed to. She would be committing to something unlike anything in her life experience. Was she prepared to do so? Did she truly have it in her?

She had more questions, and as they discussed what would be expected of her, the power went off.

ELEVEN

Werner arose from his chair on the veranda overlooking the water and prepared to go inside to sit down for their evening meal at the Starnberg Lake house. He had been told that Elisha, their personal chef, had prepared a classic meal of maultaschen, sauerkraut soup, spargel, and bauernbrot. The hearty meal of meat dumplings, white asparagus, and farmers bread was just what he needed after their 30-kilometer bike ride along the *Nördliche Seestraße*, or Nordic Walking trail that followed the shoreline of the lake.

"*Herr* Koch, you have a call in your study," said Heinrich, their houseman and custodian of the premises in their absence. "It is *Herr* Bergstedt."

Werner looked at his wife and said, "Dear, please go ahead. I will be with you in a minute." He watched as she entered the home and then followed before diverting to his study. While he used his cell phone for the majority of his business, he turned it off during meals. However, they still had a land line as an emergency backup. For Edvin to call on it at meal time meant he had important information to share.

"Edvin, we are about to eat. What is it?"

"Yes, sir, I am so sorry to disturb your meal, but I did not think you would want to wait until morning to hear this."

Werner's assessment was correct.

"Go ahead."

"There has been a major disaster in Los Angeles. I am still getting updates but hope to have most of the details within the hour. I would like to give you a report on this at your home, if that is acceptable. I can come in an hour, to allow you time to finish your meal."

Werner's imagination began to whirl at the mention of a major disaster. An earthquake? A terrorist attack? A bombing that wasn't terrorist-linked? Likely not pestilence. Although their enterovirus was ready, they had not yet coordinated its release.

"Yes, by all means, Edvin. Come. Join us for some of Elisha's famed cherry torte, and we will talk."

"Yes, sir. Thank you. I will be there in an hour."

"Can you tell me what this is about?"

"A dam has failed. I will have the details for you when I arrive."

Werner ended the call and joined his wife in the dining room. As he prepared to enjoy his soup, he said, "Edvin will be here in an hour, dear. He will join us for dessert." From the knowing smile on her face, he understood that she knew all too well that there was more to his visit than cherry torte.

As they ate, Werner had a difficult time focusing on their conversation and on enjoying the meal. Climate change had resulted in over two dozen weather events the meteorologists called atmospheric rivers, and those had produced flooding. A dam's failing certainly fell into the realm of possibilities. Yet, what dam's failure could produce a major disaster, to use Edvin's terms? He hoped the young man wasn't exaggerating.

Adam had a listing of internet service providers in the

L.A. area. He tried three numbers, each in a different area code among L.A.'s dozen-plus codes. Each call went to the same message about the area code being unavailable. On his last call, to a provider in Irvine, someone finally answered.

"Cosmos Internet Solutions. If you're calling about your website, we know, it's off-line. Everything is off-line."

Adam's eyes widened. The man confirmed his concern that the internet was down in the L.A. area. "Great, someone's there. What's happened? I can't seem to get through to anyone."

"I don't know what happened, but the power is out all around us. Not sure why we're still getting calls, but once our backup generator goes down, we're done here, too. We're using what time we have to power down our servers safely."

Adam continued to play along as if he was a customer. "Oh, good, thanks. We put a lot of work into our site."

"Yes, sir. If there's nothing else, I have other calls coming in."

"Sure. Bye."

Adam had a partial answer. He wondered how long it would take for the major news portals to report on whatever happened in Southern California.

He debated calling the L.A. County sheriff's office but suspected they would be overwhelmed with calls. He looked up numbers for other contacts he had in the area and prepared to make another call, but his phone rang first. CallerID told him his little brother was on the line.

"Aric. What's up?"

"Hey. We're hearing all sorts of rumors about something big going down in Los Angeles. I figured if anyone I knew had some info, you would."

Adam chuckled at the thought that he'd become his brother's go-to news source. "Wish I could help. I was actually on a call with someone in San Bernardino when the call failed." He proceeded to tell Aric what he knew so far.

"Well, that jives with what Lynch told me. He was able to connect with an old friend in Homeland Security. Word is that the entire L.A. metro area is in a near-total blackout and that the power failure extended from LA to Vegas, parts of north San Diego, and everything between Bakersfield and LA."

Only weeks had passed since he mothballed UltraNet and already Adam began to think maybe he shouldn't have. The program could have tapped into reconnaissance aircraft and satellites, as well as secure government communication channels. But no, he would resist the temptation to restart it.

He again checked The Epoch Times and Newsmax websites. "Breaking News" headlines now appeared on both about a disaster in L.A. but clicking on the links revealed only that it was still a developing story.

"Just checked Epoch Times and Newsmax, and neither had any info yet. But it appears the rumors are spreading like a California wildfire across the country."

"Thanks. Our break's over, and I need to get back into class. Guess we'll all find out when the rest of the world does."

Adam nodded as he clicked off. Yet, he realized he didn't like being "like the rest of the world." He had become accustomed to knowing "things" like this ahead of everyone else.

Werner checked the time and smiled as the doorbell chimed. Precisely one hour. The man must have driven the 45-minute trip upon hanging up and then waited in the drive until the time was right. A moment later, Heinrich ushered his aide onto the veranda where he and Liesl enjoyed the spring breeze over the lake while waiting for Edvin and dessert. Edvin had no sooner sat down when Elisha appeared with his serving tray of tart cherry torte and hand-whipped cream.

"*Guten abend*, Edvin. I haven't seen you for quite a while. Is Werner working you too hard?"

"Good evening to you, *Frau* Koch. Thank you, and no, he isn't. It's just a busy time."

She shook her head. "Please, please, Edvin, call me Liesl. You have become part of our family, and I never had the opportunity to thank you for taking care of my husband in New York. *Danke.*"

Werner was surprised to see his aide blush, even if so slightly.

"It was my honor, Liesl. I greatly appreciate the confidence he placed in me in the States, as well as since our return here."

Werner clapped his hands once. "Enough. Let's enjoy this excellent torte."

They spoke of the warming weather and spring's arrival, as well as mutual friends. Werner had become fond of American bourbon and offered a glass of Pappy Van Winkle to Edvin, who declined. The torte was delicious, but then, that was as expected of Elisha.

Having finished eating, Liesl spoke. "The news about Los Angeles is making its way here to Germany, too. But no one seems to know yet what happened."

Edvin looked to his employer with a questioning gaze. Werner nodded. "Yes, you may speak freely here about it." His aide looked relieved.

"Yes, it is bad. I've been in touch with Zhèng Jian . . ."

Werner smiled. Despite the traditional Chinese name, which often raised questions among the right-wing in the U.S., Zhèng was American-born and Harvard-educated. Werner had recommended him to be President Sidon's chief of staff not because of any leanings toward the Chinese but because the man was loyal to the World Order Council and all of its agenda. The President saw the wisdom in agreeing to the appointment.

". . . and the intelligence they've received so far shows that a dam in the mountains northeast of Los Angeles failed." He proceeded to provide a detailed report on the consequences of that failure.

Werner was a bit confused. He did not know the geography of the State of California very well. Indeed, he had no reason to learn that geography. Still, he could not understand the depth of the calamity there.

"I do not understand, Edvin. You mentioned this occurring in a remote area. How could a flood in a remote area cause the devastation I'm being led to believe?"

"The disaster is two-fold. The loss of the hydroelectric facilities along the river caused others nearby to fail, also. Those facilities all fed into a major high-voltage line into the city. The electrical failure started a domino effect that kept increasing and spreading as a massive demand overload took out electrical substation after substation, as well as a main solar energy farm and several windfarms. Within minutes, the major substations for the city failed. Their three biggest power facilities had to go into emergency shut-down. That included a nuclear power plant. And within minutes, a substation at the Hoover Dam failed, partially affecting Las Vegas."

Werner took a deep breath and shook his head. "So, what is the extent of the power outage?"

"Most of southern California, as well as parts of Las Vegas. There were a handful of microgrids that weren't affected because they were separate from the main grid."

Microgrids? Werner was unfamiliar with the term. "What is a microgrid?"

"A microgrid is a small, localized power grid with its own source of electricity that doesn't rely on the main power grid. These were small native American reservations using a variety of power sources. Curiously, I discovered they are using a new alternator technology, something called the BlueFlux active alternator. It operates at a high frequency and produces twice as much electricity as a standard alternator."

Werner did understand cars, a hobby of his in his younger days. And, as a result, he knew about alternators. Its design hadn't changed since its invention in 1839. So, something new could be of great interest to the WOC. He mentally filed that information for later.

"This whole thing is awful," said Liesl. "Those poor people. I hope they can get things restored quickly."

Edvin shook his head. "That's another problem. These major substations have transformers that cost millions of dollars to replace and take years to manufacture. Also, they are made only here in Germany and South Korea, which means dealing with supply chain issues. With the demand in China and elsewhere, our manufacturers tell me it will take them five years to produce the types of transformers needed in California. The city's department of power and water and other regional companies have some replacements on hand for the smaller substations, but only a fraction of what will be needed. The largest transformers cost over $10 million apiece to replace, and very few replacements are kept in inventory. Restoring full power to the area will take years, not days or weeks, and the damage is likely to be in the hundreds of millions, if not billions, of dollars. The economic fallout will, of course, be much, much higher."

"I thought there were supposed to be automatic safeguards, switches, to prevent this type of cascading damage," said Werner.

Edvin nodded his head. "There are, and utilities have been systematically adding them to the power substations. All I can say is that these switches are made in China by a company called Huīhuáng. Whether they are simply inferior products or were designed to fail, well, I leave that opinion to you, sir."

Werner considered that. Had the Chinese overstepped their agreements with the WOC?

"You said the disaster is two-fold. How?"

"Yes, sir. Fifty percent of the city's water also came from that river through a system of aqueducts. The original aqueduct was built in the first half of the last century, and the second about 60 years ago. Just downstream from the second reservoir's dam that failed, the flood took out the small dam and gates that controlled flow into the first aqueduct. At the same time, a torrent of water descended along the aqueduct destroying miles of it in areas with aging concrete. They've not yet had time to inspect the 230 miles of aqueduct, so there is no estimate yet as to the amount of damage. However, enough water filled with debris made it to the city's purification plant to damage it also."

Werner considered this report. The city would be a scene of havoc by now. Yet, what was the saying? One man's tragedy is another man's opportunity? Power gone, water contaminated, sewage systems inoperable, and more. What a perfect combination to blame for spreading a new plague. And tens of thousands, if not more, of people fleeing the area and potentially taking the virus with them. Forget their planned six-month delay. There was too great an opportunity in this natural disaster to delay any longer.

TWELVE

Pete feared the worst for Los Angeles as he watched the torrent of water surge past his vantage point high on the plateau overlooking the now demolished power plant and control center, as well as the small town of Mesa. While he didn't expect that the water itself would ever reach the city, he knew that the potential loss of power and water would create turmoil in the city.

After years of drought, the rains and snowpack appeared to be answers to the prayers of many. Now, he was reminded of the phrase, be careful what you pray for.

His immediate concern was his family. His wife worked in the city of Bishop just a few miles downstream. Although situated in a dry valley, there was enough of an elevation change that maybe half of the city lay within the mile-wide zone for potential flooding. He would find out shortly.

He did a three-point turn on the road and headed back to U.S. 395. A couple of miles down the highway, he made a right onto Ed Powers Rd and took the back way into Bishop. Rather, into West Bishop. His home and church building were there. They sat about 150 feet above the lowest sections of town, so he expected to find both buildings dry and intact. He was correct.

He had no need to check on the house, so he pulled into the church's lot. Two of the elders, Jim Perry and Charlie

Howell, were already there. He could see them pulling supplies out of the small storage building behind the main building. He drove as close as he could to them and jumped out of his truck.

"Hey, guys. Have you been in town? How bad is it?"

Jim replied, "Yep, the airport's flooded and water followed the creeks up into the business district. Poleta Bridge is gone. Main Street is covered by about a foot of water, and it goes up to about Dwayne's Pharmacy."

Charlie nodded. "The Route 6 bridge is gone, too. I got out of the RV park along the north fork before it got too deep there. Not sure what to expect when I head back."

Charlie worked at the Highlands RV Park, which fortunately was not busy considering all the rain dampening folks' desire to come to the mountains. A month or so from now, the place would be packed.

Pete reflected upon both bridges being wiped out. He wasn't surprised by that, but it made him think about the force of the water that had traveled that far. The river funneled back into a narrow valley after leaving the outskirts of town. All of the water draining the valley would end up there. The odds were good that the aqueduct system was badly damaged. That, too, he expected.

"We're following the disaster plan we discussed and are opening up the church as a shelter. We'll fire up the generator as needed once people start showing up. Right now, we're getting cots and food stuffs set up."

Pete nodded. "Thanks for getting a head start on this. Look, I need to check the power plants along Bishop Creek. And I need to head north to survey the damage to my other power plants. But first, I need to find my family and get them back here. After all's said and done, I might not get back 'til dark."

Jim nodded his head toward town. "Go. We got this covered and more help's on the way."

"Thanks, guys. You're a great blessing."

Pete climbed back into the truck and headed toward the main drag. He thought about his "plan of attack." If the water was up to the pharmacy, he could get close to the bakery where Charis, his daughter worked. She had decided to take a gap year after graduating from high school and had been contemplating college. But after four months of working in a friend's bakery, she found she liked it, despite the early start in the morning and its effect on her social life. Pete Jr. was in his third year at Bishop Union High. The school sat just a couple of blocks north of the pharmacy. His goal was to become the next lead singer for Skillet, once John Cooper decided to retire. Of course, if Cooper was anything like Mick Jagger, Pete Jr was in for one long wait. Pete smiled at the thought of John Cooper at age 80, looking more like Gandalf the Grey with a full gray beard, and using a walker to move out onto the stage.

He found his children first and delivered them to the church. They could help there and walk home whenever they wished. He hoped Pete Jr. had been paying attention to hooking up and starting their home generator.

Finding his wife, Angela, would be more of a challenge. While the bakery and school were on the fringe of the flooded area described by Jim, Angela's new coffee and sandwich shop was right on Main Street near Bishop City Park and sat on the south fork of Bishop Creek. They had scrimped and saved to raise the money to buy an old wine shop and convert it. If Jim's report was correct, the shop would have a foot or two of water in it, and if he knew his wife, she would still be there protecting their investment to the best of her ability.

As Jim had said, the water on Main Street was too deep to safely traverse, even in Pete's 4-wheel drive pickup. Fortunately, he had his chest waders in the truck. He claimed that he kept them there because he never knew when he might have to get into the water at one of the power plants he oversaw. But his friends knew better. The broken down fly rod, fisherman's vest, and a small box of hand-tied fishing flies were the obvious giveaway.   At the edge of the water, he donned the waders and trudged into the dirty water. The shop was about three-quarters of a mile away.

The trek was slow-going. The water was soon up to his knees, and mud settling out of the nearly still water made many places slippery underfoot. He caught himself from falling more than once. As he neared the shop, he saw his wife waving frantically at him from the rooftop of the building. He couldn't hear what she yelled, but suddenly her motions were those of thrusting her palms out in front of her as if urging him to stop and go back. He was at the bridge over the creek and less than 30 feet from the storefront.

Why would she want him to go back? That's when he saw it—the taillights of a small car sitting up vertically in the water—and it dawned on him that maybe the bridge had washed out and he needed to be careful. That realization came a split second too late, as with his next step he found himself with no footing, and the water engulfed his chest and head.

THIRTEEN

As the power went out, Heather's and Olivia's conversation came to an abrupt halt. They looked at each other as if saying, "What just happened?" Only the gray light from the overcast sky lit the room through the window. A second later, the power came back on, but not like before.

"The center's backup generator has kicked on," said Olivia.

The area had been through blackouts before, thanks to wildfires and increasing demand. Critics of the state's government also blamed the push for renewable green energy as unrealistic and a major contributor to the problem. Heather didn't pay much attention to the issue. She could tolerate the inconvenience of a few hours without electricity. Maybe even a day or two. So far, the blackouts hadn't lasted very long.

Still, when she'd first heard those complaints, they made sense. After all, if there's no wind, how do wind farms work? And if the day is cloudy, how much power can a solar farm produce? Plus, what happens at night? With new sales of gasoline-powered cars to be eliminated by 2035, over 63,000 EV cars in L.A. already, and goals to have 80% of cars in L.A. be EV within five years, where was the power going to come from?

They continued their conversation from where the shift

to backup power had stopped them.

"So, do I have some flexibility in which days I work each week if I take this position you're offering me?"

Olivia nodded. "Mostly yes, with a few caveats. We wouldn't want you to work, say, three days in a row, like Mondays to Wednesdays, every week. Also, volunteers can't be expected to pull *all* of the weekend hours, so you'd need to work some weekend shifts, too. Finally, we need the end-of-the-month stats within the first few days of the following month. You've helped with those already, but you would be doing all of that with this job. That means you'd have to be around to get those reports done each month."

This sounded more and more like a *job*. Did she truly want real work? Well, not that she didn't do *real* work when there. She realized that she was looking at taking on real responsibilities with this offer of a part-time position.

"Okay. Like I said, I'm going to have to talk this over with my—"

The power went out again . . . and didn't come back on.

Olivia looked concerned. "Let me ask David if he knows what's going on here." She stood and walked around her desk, heading for the door and David's adjacent office.

Heather stood up as well. "While you're checking on that, I'm going to the little girl's room."

Upon relieving herself of her morning's coffee, she stood up, adjusted her clothing, and pushed the lever to flush. Nothing. *That's odd*, she thought, but upon turning on the water to wash her hands, again, no water.

She hurried back to Olivia's office to inform her of the discovery. She found Olivia frowning at the cell phone in her hand. The woman looked up at her.

"Do you have your phone with you?"

Heather nodded and retrieved it from a pocket.

"Try making a call."

Heather had wanted to call her husband since the power first went out. She looked at the phone as she hit the speed dial. She had no bars, and her phone made no connection with any network. Now she was worried.

"No service. Also, there's no water in the restroom."

"What in the . . ." Olivia's countenance looked worried. "David says the generator runs on natural gas, and the only thing that he can think of that would make it fail is that it's not getting any gas." She stepped over to her window. "I don't see power anywhere. Even the traffic lights are out. This isn't good. I think we need to close up shop here."

As VP of Administration, she could make that call, but Heather knew she wouldn't make that decision on her own. David stepped into the doorway.

"LaToya's not in. I think we need to close down, let people get home." LaToya Hayes was the center's CEO.

Olivia nodded. "I was just saying the same thing. Let's get the word out."

The honks of multiple car alarms sounding off interrupted the conversation. The trio ran to David's office where the window had a better view of the parking lot. A gang of six or so hooded people were attempting to get into the cars. Their clothing hid their genders and skin color. Heather watched as one person smashed a window of a silver Honda Civic.

"Hey, that's my car," yelled David. Instinctively, he reached for his phone but stopped short at the realization that he couldn't make a call. Helpless, they watched as the person successfully hot-wired the Honda and settled into the driver's seat. Three others climbed into the car, and the vehicle drove off. Moments later, a second car started and drove off with the rest of the gang.

David sat on the edge of his desk, looking dumbfounded. He sighed and said, "Well, they won't get far. I planned on getting gas on my way home. Guess that's not going to work now, is it? Getting gas, I mean."

His comment made Heather think about her car. Her husband had filled the tank just a day or so ago, hadn't he? He didn't like her driving into the city alone with less than a third of a tank of gas. If not, did she have enough to get home? Did gas stations have backup generators, and if so, were they natural gas-powered like the one there at the center?

"Where do you live, David?" asked Heather. In thinking about trying to get home, she shuddered at the thought of driving alone with no means of getting help should something happen.

"Woodland Hills."

"I'm in Santa Monica, so I can walk if I have to. Let's get the word out to go home and make sure the doors are secured," said Olivia.

As the trio walked toward the stairs, David looked at Heather. "You live somewhere near the university, right?"

Heather shrugged. "Well, more toward the top of Sepulveda Pass. I was just wondering how best to try to go home. The 405 is stop'n go on a good day. Everybody and his cousins, even second cousins, are probably trying to get home on it right now. I think it would take a miracle to even get within blocks of an entrance ramp."

David nodded. "And all it'll take is one car running out of gas or electricity on it to . . . well, I wouldn't risk it myself. Wow, and think about if this power outage lasts more than a day or so. We're gonna see a lot of abandoned EVs on the sides of the roads. Makes you want to rethink this push toward electric everything."

Heather sighed. David was right about the 405, and Sepulveda Blvd running next to the highway would be as bad a nightmare. She considered taking city streets to the university campus, heading up the mountain past the country club into Sherman Oaks, and approaching her subdivision from the north. Others might think of that, too, which would clog those streets. With Bel Air being such a pricey area, would the West LA police barricade those through streets? If so, her country club stickers could get her through. Maybe. Did she want to chance it? No, wait. Those stickers were on her main vehicle, not the BMW.

"David, what do you think 27 will be like, up through Topanga?"

"That's how I come and go to work every day. It can be busy, but I suspect it'll be a whole lot better than the 405. Actually, I don't live far from the Top of Topanga Overlook."

"I was thinking. If I take you home first and catch the Ventura Freeway back toward my house . . ."

He shook his head. "Forget the Ventura. It'll be a parking lot, too. I'll write out directions over the back streets, past the Encino Reservoir. I think that will be better. Hey, I really appreciate the ride."

"Happy to help. Besides, under the circumstances, I wouldn't mind the company, even if only half way home."

Thirty minutes later, with Olivia satisfied that the center was as secure as they could make it, the trio walked into the parking lot. Olivia's Chevy Bolt EV had its side windows and windshield bashed in and one tire appeared flat. They surveyed the vehicle together. The senseless vandalism had become more common in the area since the Soros-backed DA stopped prosecuting such crimes.

"Looks like that gang was out for more than just stealing a ride," said David.

Olivia sighed. "I know better than to keep anything in my car. I'll have to deal with it later. See you two whenever we get back." She started walking toward the exit from the parking lot.

"Hey, nonsense. I'm going right through Santa Monica. Let me give you a lift."

Olivia stopped and followed the others to Heather's BMW. Only its passenger side window had been damaged, but not completely broken out. With her passengers for company, Heather headed north on Hampton and worked her way toward Neilson Way, which would become Ocean Blvd.

Every intersection posed a risk. Within half a dozen blocks they saw two accidents where one car T-boned another in an intersection. Heather slowed down and used great caution navigating the streets. Upon reaching Ocean Blvd, the traffic became stop-and-go. The line of cars seemed intent on getting onto I-10, so she cut over to side streets to try to bypass the traffic. That strategy worked for a short while, but once they passed the cut-off to the 10, things came to a stop again. The Pacific Coast Highway heading north toward Topanga was a parking lot, too.

Olivia leaned forward toward the front seat. "You can let me off here. I'm afraid if you lose your place in this line, you'll never get back into it."

"You sure?"

Olivia nodded. "Yes. My place is only a few blocks away. I'm good. Thanks for the ride." The woman gathered her things and exited the car, waving as she turned to head east.

The traffic wasn't the only major issue. It was eerie driving through the area with not a single sign of electrical power. Yet, worse was the rampant crime. The stores selling food had already been victimized with windows and doors broken. Heather had no doubt that most of their shelves had been stripped bare. Now, they witnessed people smashing windows to break into stores selling T-shirts and tourist trash. No doubt the police had their hands full with true emergencies, and the lack of a police response gave the thieves a free pass to every store they crawled past in the car. And the power hadn't been out but 90 minutes.

It wasn't yet noon, and Heather didn't want to imagine what nightfall would bring.

FOURTEEN

Shawn started awake with something wet slapping his cheek. As he opened his eyes, his first reaction was to jump back thinking a coyote was sizing him up as a tasty snack, but his body didn't respond. Then he realized it was a dog trying to wake him by licking his face.

The animal grabbed his jacket in its mouth and began to pull. That's when he fully awakened and realized he'd been lucky that his fuzzy reflexes had not made him jump. His body was inches away from a widening chasm that slowly crept toward him. Had the dog not awakened him, or had he jumped up, he would have tumbled into the gap made by the dam's failure—100 feet down into a still-raging torrent of water from the draining lake.

Keeping his legs still, he used his arms and elbows to dig into the wet soil and push away from the opening. The last thing he wanted was to dig in with his feet and trigger a slide that would take him with it. After placing a few more feet between himself and the edge, he finally felt confident in using his feet and legs. He pushed up and scrambled about 15 feet up the hillside. The dog followed.

His heart racing, he sat down, caught his breath, and allowed his heart rate to slow down. The dog sat beside him. He reached over to pet the wet fur of the animal.

"Say, fella, where'd you come from? Wherever it was,

thank you. I'm glad you found me."

He scrutinized the critter and guessed maybe half Husky and half Labrador. He saw a tag hanging from a woven nylon collar that had seen better days. But then, as he looked at his own clothing, they, too, had seen better days, much better. He reached for the tag and read it.

"Really? Tag?" The dog's ears perked up. He shook his head. The dog tag said 'Tag." *Someone has a sense of humor,* he thought. Yet, in reflection, he liked the name. Dogs responded best to one or two-syllable names. The moniker seemed to fit, but he resisted touching the animal and saying, "You're it."

He turned the tag over and saw the owner's name—Rick Webster. His heart sank. Rick was one of the maintenance guys for LADWP. If he'd been working in one of the sheds at the base of the dam, he was likely a casualty.

Feeling stronger, he stood. He didn't dare get too close to the opening, but he needed to see what was left. The cleft in the earthen dam was maybe 75 feet wide and descended in a wedge shape to the original valley floor. The buildings below were gone. There was no sign of his truck or any other vehicles. No signs of life in the area, except for Tag.

He felt his pockets for his phone. Nada. He tried to recall where he'd stashed it and remembered that in his rush from the collapsing building, he hadn't taken the time to fumble with his rain gear and secure it in a pocket. He had tossed it into his truck. Now both were gone. Of course, he had no reception out here anyway.

He considered his options. Well, his one option. The dam remained too unstable, and the water was impassable even if he was able to work his way down the dam to a spot where he might be able to cross over to the other side. Too bad, because U.S. 395 was just a mile away from the other side of the dam. He could expect to get help from someone there.

No, his one option was to begin the trek back to Benton Crossing . . . over 14 miles away. If he could maintain a three-mile-per-hour pace, he might make it before dark. If . . .

And then he remembered the campground was flooded. There would be no campers to assist him, and he couldn't expect day hikers in the area, not with the record snowpack. In reality, the nearest occupied facility would be the Mammoth Yosemite Airport.

"C'mon, Tag. We got a hike ahead of us. Maybe we'll get lucky, and someone'll pick us up once we get to the main road."

He started up the hill along Owens Gorge Rd. As he neared the crest of the rise, the dog suddenly turned back with his ears at full alert. Tag began to bark.

Shawn looked back toward the dam and saw a figure on the other side. The man was waving his arms above his head. Shawn waved back. The man began to yell, but Shawn couldn't make out what he was saying. He was 500 feet away, and the noise of the rushing water below echoed up along the gorge's walls and the dam. Shawn tried to signal that he couldn't hear but wasn't sure that the man understood. The man pointed to a spot behind him. As Shawn's gaze followed the man's arm, he saw that the guy pointed at a vehicle. Yes!

Shawn raised both arms with thumbs-up and pointed to the road behind him. Then he pointed toward the direction that the road would take him. He hoped the man would understand that he had no choice but to start walking. If his message got through, the man or someone else might meet them along the road as he walked toward the crossing. As he looked back across the dam, the man was about to enter his truck.

Either the man would be coming to get them or not. One way or the other, Shawn needed to begin his trek toward civilization. He leaned down and patted the dog on its head.

"Like I said, Tag, we have a walk ahead of us. Off we go."

Pete felt the loss of solid ground beneath him, but it was too late to step back. He gulped in a deep breath just before his head was submerged. But would it be enough?

Under normal conditions, there was a six-foot clearance under the bridge before hitting the water of Bishop Creek's south fork, and the water itself was maybe three feet deep there. Along with a foot of pavement and two feet of water above the pavement, that meant he was dealing with, at most, 12 feet of water. If he had fallen through in his usual work garb, he'd have had no trouble swimming out from under the bridge and surfacing on either side.

But he was in his chest waders . . . and he knew he was in trouble as the waders filled with water and dragged him deeper.

Being underwater was disorienting. With zero visibility from all of the silt suspended in the water, he knew he had to focus on where the water looked the lightest in color. That would be the surface he needed to get to. Yet, keeping his eyes open in that water wasn't easy.

He needed to ditch the waders. Slipping out of the suspenders was easy, but he struggled to bring his right foot up in an attempt to remove the boot. He had to stay calm. Struggling would use up his oxygen too quickly.

Unable to get even one boot off, he did the next best

thing. He pushed the waders down past his waist and then past his thighs until they settled around his knees. They acted much less like an anchor. Despite the resistance of the heavy rubber waders, he began to kick. He raised his hands above his hand and opened his eyes. Yes, the water above appeared brighter.

He began to use his hands and feet together in an awkward breast stroke. A moment later, his hands hit something solid. But what? He was running out of air. He had to resist the urge to take a breath. He focused on the surface he now touched. Concrete. He was still under the bridge.

Unsure which way to swim to get out from under the structure, he began to use his hands to pull himself toward the brightest water. He felt as if he was about to faint. How much easier it would be at that point to succumb to the desire to breathe and let everything go, to enter into the waiting arms of his Lord and Savior. He let go with his hands and felt them drift down along his body.

Suddenly, he felt the need to kick again. He kicked and kicked again.   And again. He opened his eyes. The water grew lighter, and a second later, his head broke the surface. He forcefully exhaled and gasped in the fresh air. Hands grabbed him under the arms and pulled him into a small boat.

FIFTEEN

Aric's class ran late, which was becoming more the norm as the semester wore on. He was hungry and the dorm's cafeteria would be opening in 15 minutes or so. If he hurried, he could deposit his books in the room and make it downstairs before the main crowd formed outside the doors.

As he rushed up the stairwell and out into the hall, he saw that familiar head of pink hair.

"Hey, Toni," he yelled.

The guy, they/them by his preference, turned toward Aric. His eyes widened as he saw who had called him, and he turned back in the direction he'd been heading and bolted. Aric didn't want to waste time chasing him down. Besides, such an action might be seen as threatening, and Aric didn't need such a complaint lodged against him.

Toni—Aric never had learned a last name for him—was now one of the leaders of the LGBTQ+ crowd. The previous fall semester the guy had changed his trademark hair color for purple and actually would speak to Aric if they ended up in the elevator together or someplace else where he wouldn't be noticed talking to the "enemy." However, now, Aric was again the target of their disdain, and Toni had returned to they/them's favorite hair dye.

As he fished his ID out to open the door to his room, he

smiled. One of the members of his Bible club had commented on the LGBTQ+ crowd's use of pronouns. In the Bible, he said, the only entities that identified as they/them were demons. He had a point.

Seeing Toni reminded Aric of the events the day before. He found the police officer's card on his desk and felt like he should call the man now, not later. He'd been learning to rely upon such leadings, so he pulled out his phone and dialed the number that the officer had scribbled onto the back of the card.

"Hello."

"Officer Dickson, this is Aric Afton. You came to mind, so I thought I'd call as you asked. Um, Thursdays are my lightest days, schedule-wise. I only have a morning class."

"Thursday. Have to work mid-shift on Thursday. You know, what are you doing for dinner? Like, right now. I'm off today, and, um, my, uh, wife is out of town. I'd be happy to treat you to dinner. What time and where?"

Aric heard that inner voice say, "Go."

"Well, I was just about to head downstairs to the dorm cafeteria, so I have no specific plans. I'm hungry and ready to eat."

"So, where?"

"Um, Waterfront Warehouse is just down the road. I can be there in ten minutes."

"Perfect. See you there in ten."

Well, wasn't expecting that, Aric thought. He grabbed his car keys, wallet, and phone, donned his jacket, and headed out to the student parking lot. The restaurant was one of his favorites. Its American fare was delicious; he'd never been disappointed with a meal there; and he'd never left hungry. Although not on the water, as the name implied, diners on their deck could see Lake Michigan across the street just past an old fish hatchery tank and the mouth of the Pike River.

On the short drive to the place, Aric felt something else. The man hadn't been quite forthright in what he'd told Aric.

He walked into the restaurant and didn't see the officer. But, he realized, he might not recognize him without the uniform. The host approached him.

"Two, but I don't see the other party yet."

After some back and forth, the host convinced him to be seated and assured Aric that he'd direct the other party to the table. A waitress appeared almost immediately.

"Iced tea, please. Unsweetened."

At the same time as the drink arrived, so did Officer Dickson. The man turned to the waitress. "Riverwest Stein, the 16-ounce, please." He turned to Aric. "You want a beer instead of that tea?"

Aric shook his head. "No thanks. Still have a few weeks 'til I'm legal."

"Ah. I could say I'm your guardian or something."

Aric gave him a funny look.

"Just kidding."

Aric knew all about Wisconsin's confusing drinking laws. They'd covered it in one of his classes. The legal age was 21, but anyone under age could drink legally in a bar or restaurant if accompanied by and with the approval of a parent, guardian, or a spouse of legal drinking age. The proprietor, however, retained the right to refuse to serve the minor. Still, Aric had no real interest in drinking anyway, so he never tried to push the issue.

They both knew what they wanted, so the man flagged down their waitress and their orders were placed.

"Sorry I was a bit late. My brother and his wife live in L.A., and I haven't been able to get hold of them. I wanted to try again before coming here."

The news from southern California was slowly trickling into the headline news, and it wasn't good.

"Sorry to hear that. I hope they're okay."

The man shrugged and nodded. "They'll be fine. They have the resources to leave town if need be. I have a feeling the line of cars exiting L.A. is gonna be a long one, though."

Aric nodded. "Officer Dickson, before we start, can I ask a question?" asked Aric.

"Sure, but call me Dan. That officer stuff is going to get old by the time our meals arrive."

"Okay. So, why didn't you intervene when those people started throwing eggs at us?"

"Fair question. We had orders not to intervene unless it appeared like someone could get hurt. Eggs didn't quite feel threatening."

"So, how'd you know they were going to interrupt our service?"

He shrugged. "Beats me. We just got the call to be there."

"That's still curious. Anyway, what can I do for you?" Aric took a long swig of tea.

"Well, I saw what happened, and I still can't get it out of my head. I mean, you opened up yourself as a target, and as soon as you did, their eggs started breaking in midair. It was like some force field protected you folks at that point."

Aric smiled. "There was. Would you believe it if I said God protected us?"

The man furrowed his brow. "You know, if I hadn't seen it with my own eyes, I'd say that was crazy. But I did see it."

"Do you believe in God?"

"Yeah, basically. Growing up, my folks took us to church. Lutheran. But by college, my siblings and I all drifted away from that stuff."

"Would you say you're a Christian?"

He shrugged. "To be honest, not really, but it's been like God or something has put this bug in my head to find out more. When I saw you yesterday, it was like a light flashing on saying, talk to them, they have the answer you want."

"We probably do, but it might require baby steps to get there." The man had a quizzical look. Aric decided to take a different approach than he'd first planned. "Do you believe God talks to people today?" Before letting the man answer, he continued. "Yesterday, I heard God tell me to show them, the protesters, His love. Not to retaliate, but also not to just ignore them. Instead, He told me to show them His love, and that's when I opened myself up as a target. I believe that's why He protected us. We were following His lead."

The man shook his head. "That does sound crazy. You know, the whole hearing voices thing. I don't know—"

"Well, on the way here, God told me something else. You weren't being truthful about your wife. She's not out of town. She's left you because she wants to see you leave policing, and you refuse to do so. She thinks it's gotten too dangerous, and she cares too much to be at home wondering when she might be the next spouse getting bad news from the higher-ups."

The man's skin paled, and he sat back from the table in such a forceful way that he almost hit the diner sitting behind him at the next table. Aric watched him take a gulp of air as he tried to calm himself. From his reaction, Aric knew that the word of knowledge he'd received was spot on.

The officer leaned back toward the table. "Aric, there's

no way that—"

Aric nodded. "That's right. There's no way I would know that unless God revealed it to me."

Their meals arrived, and they ate and talked . . . for over an hour and a half. The waitress was beginning to glare at them for tying up the table. Yet, Aric wasn't going to cut the conversation short. As long as Dan had questions, Aric would be there to answer them to the best of his ability.

Aric had read about what they called "power evangelism" where people tuned into the gifts of the Holy Spirit. Those gifts—speaking in tongues, prophecy, words of wisdom or of knowledge, healing, and others—were meant to reveal God's glory and power to people who didn't believe in Him. Aric had never expected that one day he, too, might be granted the blessing of experiencing it firsthand. But he had, and he didn't want it to be a one-time thing.

SIXTEEN

Without his phone, Shawn had no idea what time it was or how long they'd been walking. With the clouds, he couldn't see the sun's position, which could have helped give him a rough estimate of what part of the day it was. His time disorientation was compounded by the fact that he had no idea how long he'd been unconscious on the dam before the dog found him. Thus, he had no idea whether they had started the hike at noon, or two, or whenever.

If he recalled correctly, the distance from the dam back to Benton Crossing Rd. was just over five miles, so he estimated that would take him two hours. However, he was exhausted, and the trek had been more than he'd bargained for. The hike had been a steady uphill climb. Not a significant elevation change, but uphill none the less.   Shawn realized there was no way he could keep up a three-mile-per-hour pace. The dog stayed by his side throughout the walk.

"Well, Tag, ol' boy, we might be spending the night out here somewhere."

It got dark in the mountains faster than one expected. Already the day seemed to be waning.

After a short rest, he resumed his walk and Tag followed loyally along. As he followed another curve in the road, he saw something familiar . . . a piece of trash. He had noticed the discarded and broken blue plastic cooler on the way to the dam and made a mental note of the mileage so he could pick it up on the way back to dispose of it properly. He was a little better than halfway to the main road.

The road leveled off a bit. For that, he felt relieved. Once back on the main road, it would be downhill back to the bridge at the crossing. Maybe the worst of it was behind them.

He noticed Tag's ears perk up.

"What is it, Tag?"

He looked about. He saw no animals or other attractions that might catch a dog's attention and kept on walking. Several minutes later, though, he heard it. Tires on gravel. A vehicle approached.

Soon he saw the headlights of a pickup truck. It appeared to be the truck from across the dam. Tag's tail began to wag.

The truck stopped ten feet in front of them, and a man jumped out of the driver's side. Tag barked a greeting and ran to the man who had stooped down to hug the dog and ruffled its fur.

"Rick Webster. Man, am I glad to see you."

"You, too. I didn't know someone was up top when the dam went."

The man walked to the back of the truck and lowered the tailgate. He patted the gate, and said, "Up you go, boy. You're a mess. Not riding inside until we get you cleaned up."

Tag gave his owner a look that said, "What? Are you kidding?"

Rick patted the tailgate again, and the dog relinquished and jumped up into the truck's bed. He walked straight to the front, behind the cab, and lay down.

Shawn glanced down at his torn and muddy rain gear, with his clothing underneath in not much better condition.

He raised his arms to his sides and said, "Do I need to join Tag?"

Rick laughed. "Nope. You get to use Tag's dog blanket. It's already on the front passenger seat. Climb in. We need to be getting back."

Shawn nodded and climbed into the passenger seat. As Rick turned around and headed back toward the main road, he said, "When I saw your name on Tag's ID, I thought you'd become a casualty."

"Almost was. I was working in one of the sheds at the base of the dam when I heard him starting to bark up a storm. I ran outside to see what it was and saw him running up and across the dam. I figured he'd found a rabbit. He loves chasing those things when he's up here with me. I was about to get after him when I saw the top of the dam begin to crumble and give way. He was too far away for me to get him, so I ran for my truck to get out. I was on the other side of the dam looking for him and not expecting to find him when I saw both of you."

"Well, that dog of yours saved my life, too. I was in the shed up top on the phone with your department when the building started to collapse. Ran to my truck but couldn't get any traction. I jumped as it started to slide into the developing crevasse. I think I must have scrambled a bit up the hill, but I really don't remember. Next thing I know, Tag's licking my face and trying to pull me away. The opening was continuing to crumble and coming my way. If he hadn't woken me up, I would have joined my truck, wherever it is."

Shawn looked back toward the truck's bed. He couldn't see the dog.

"I'm gonna have to get him a special treat." Shawn noticed the time on the vehicle's clock. It was still early in the afternoon. "Guess I wasn't out that long. Lost my phone with the truck, so my sense of time was way off."

They rode for a while in silence. Upon crossing the river, Shawn noted the drastic difference from when he'd crossed it early that day. The river was still higher than usual, thanks to the snowmelt, but the flood water was gone from the campgrounds and areas west of the river.

"All of this area was flooded when I crossed here around nine a.m."

Rick nodded. "Not anymore."

"What was it like?"

"Huh?"

"Did you see the dam fail?"

"Part of it. I was focused on getting to higher ground, but I managed to see most of it. Impressive. Truly makes you appreciate the power of water."

Shawn's appreciation of that was limited to book knowledge. In reflection, he wished he'd witnessed it firsthand. That was the kind of knowledge a dam inspector could truly benefit from.

"At first, it looked like any mudslide, but once the water found its pipe through the rock and dirt, the water burst out like it came from a fire hose. And then the hillside practically exploded. I always figured it would be more gradual, a failure like that, I mean."

Shawn knew what he'd been taught about earthen dam failures. However, without witnessing it himself, he couldn't say how this one fit into that.

Rick continued. "Once that water hit the gorge, it backed up into a wall maybe 65, 75 feet tall as it headed downstream."

Shawn didn't want to think of the consequences, but he

had to know.

"Any idea how bad it is? Cell service is lousy up here until we get closer to the airport."

Rick shook his head. "Cell service is gone. No power. I figure once the power went out, the deluge of calls hitting the towers ran their backup batteries down fast . . . if they even had backups." He pointed to a black leather case on the floor between the front seats. "They gave us a radio in case we aren't getting cell coverage up here. I managed to get a call in and talk with my bosses in L.A. for a few minutes. It's bad news. Don't have the details, but the power is out from Bakersfield to north San Diego, as well as part of Vegas. The aqueduct was overwhelmed and badly damaged. Again, no details. It'll take days to survey and estimate the damage there."

Shawn sat back and watched the countryside pass by as he contemplated this report. His thoughts gathered on his wife and kids. Although they were well north of the blackout zone, he hoped they were all together and safely at home. He had no idea how long it would take him to get to them, but he was lucky that he would indeed be able to get back to them. No doubt there were those downstream of the dam who wouldn't be seeing loved ones again.

SEVENTEEN

Aric woke up feeling stoked. He couldn't get over how God had used him with the word of knowledge for Dan Dickson. The conversation afterward had been rewarding, and the officer had agreed to join Aric at church when he next had a Sunday off. However, Aric wasn't naive. He'd been told that before by others who never showed up. He'd believe it when he saw the man walk into the church.

Still, Aric couldn't wait to tell Jess all about it. He rushed through showering, dressing, and breakfast. She had an earlier class than his first one of the day, and he didn't want to miss her.

So, he found himself standing outside the building where her class was held 15 minutes before she typically arrived. As others passed by, he offered a cheery greeting that was mostly returned with less than hearty grunts by students not wanting to be in an 8:30 class.

True to form, Jess arrived, and he saw her walking up the sidewalk a hundred yards away. He ran over to greet her and walk with her. She didn't look all that eager to be there either.

"G'morning. You'll never believe what happened last night?"

She gave him the eye, to tell him she didn't want to play 20 questions. It was too early.

"Seriously."

"Okay. The whole world took the red pill, and we woke up from the Matrix."

"Huh?"

"I know. That movie was before we were born. So, what happened?"

"You know that police officer who was at the egg toss and wanted to talk with me?"

She nodded.

"Well, he invited me to dinner last night." He went on to describe what happened.

"Wow, that's great. I hope he lives up to his promise and shows up some Sunday."

"Me, too. But, I mean, God used me for power evangelism. I'm still amazed. Hey, want to go down to the harbor after classes this afternoon and talk with people."

She took a deep breath. "Let me think about it and see what kind of work load I have after classes today." She looked toward the classroom building. "Hey, I have to run. I'm going to be late. I'll text you. Stay humble."

He watched as she hurried off to her class. *Maybe I should wait to see what assignments I get today, too*, he thought. But he was too on fire for God right now to worry about that.

A group of students walked up the sidewalk toward the building. He walked up to them and said, "G'morning. Did you know that God loves you?"

They all gave him odd looks.

"Whatever."

"Maybe. If there is a God."

"Buzz off."

One of the girls in the group looked at him with a

quizzical look. He focused his attention on her, and motioned her to the side, away from the group.

"You're Amanda, right?" She didn't respond. "God wants you to know that the guy you're seeing has issues and isn't the right one for you."

She huffed and shook her head. "You're crazy. First off, my name's Jocelyn, and second, I'm not into guys. Go take your phony religious stuff somewhere else." She stomped off to rejoin her friends. A moment later, he heard them all laughing . . . at him, no doubt.

The fire he'd felt minutes ago had been doused with a Red Sea-sized bucket of water. He had been flying high for God only to be shot down. That's when he heard that still, small voice inside say, "Follow My lead; don't step out in front of Me," and Jess' prophetic last words echoed in his mind, "Stay humble."

Something awful was in his throat. Pete tried to move his hands to pull out whatever was lodged in his neck. His hands were tied down. He pulled against the restriction. What was happening? Why was he tied down? And what was in his throat?

He began to pull more frantically at whatever held him down. Then, he heard a familiar voice.

"Nurse! Doctor! He's waking up."

His wife? He heard what sounded like chair legs scraping across a hard floor.

"Nurse!"

The voice was farther away. He tried to open his eyes, but something kept them closed as well. He heard footsteps around him and then his mind became fuzzy. He drifted off.

When he awoke, the memory of being tied down seemed like a dream. In that dream, he couldn't see, and he was choking. He slowly opened his eyes. Where was he?

Then he remembered. He had stepped into a void in the bridge and gone underwater. The last thing he recalled before this was breaking free to the surface.

He felt a warm hand on his. "Hon. Hey, it's me. You're okay now."

He turned his face and focused his eyes on his wife. "Where am . . ." His voice was raspy. He tried to swallow but it hurt to do so. Not terribly, but it reminded him of that horrible dream of something lodged in his throat.

His wife held up a plastic cup with a straw extending from it. She put the straw to his lips, and he took a sip. That was better.

"We're at Mammoth Hospital, in the ICU. You almost drowned. Scared me half to death."

"How . . . how did . . ."   He still felt uncomfortable trying to talk.

"How did you get here?" He nodded. "By the grace of God. The sheriff's department had a boat in the water and a helicopter looking for folks stranded by the flood. The guys in the boat saw you go down, helped pull you up, and radioed the chopper. They flew you here. They told me that the timing was perfect because just minutes earlier they were surveying the gorge and Mesa, and a minute later they would have been farther downstream. They happened to be right over the town when the call reached them. And the boat was at the right place at the right time, too."

Pete knew better than to believe in coincidence. When she had said it was God's grace, he knew her to be correct.

"As soon as you got here, they sedated you and put a

breathing tube in. They tied down your hands to prevent you from hurting yourself by trying to pull out the tube when you woke up."

"I couldn't open my eyes."

"They put an antibiotic ointment in them and taped them shut to let it work longer."

Now he understood. It wasn't a bad dream after all. "Water," he whispered.

She held the cup and straw back up to his lips. He thought it funny that at one point he'd been surrounded by water, was about to die in water, and now all he craved was water. Well, that and a large steak.

"When can we go home?"

She laughed. "I told them that would be one of your first questions. Not for a while. They want to do a follow-up X-ray of your lungs later this morning."

This morning? he thought. He felt disoriented. It had been late morning, almost noon, when he'd gone looking for Angela. How could she be talking about *later* that morning? "What time is it?"

"It's just after 5:30, Tuesday morning."

At that moment a doctor entered the room. "Mr. Manning, hi, I'm Doctor Fitzgerald. I'm the ICU doc on duty now. How are you feeling?"

"When can I go home?" Pete felt the need to make sure people were being cared for and that they had everything needed at the church. He didn't need to take up space in a hospital bed.

Angela looked at the doctor. "Told you."

Doctor Fitzgerald laughed. "So you did. Well, here's the deal. You weren't breathing well when you arrived. That's why we had to intubate you, put in the breathing tube. Your initial X-ray looked okay, but we need to make sure it's still that way. We like to give it at least 24 hours between exams because sometimes it takes a while for problems to appear on an X-ray. We'll also do another blood count. You were in some mighty dirty water. If there are any signs of water in the lungs or of pneumonia settling in, we'll want to keep you here on IV antibiotics for two or three more days. If the tests look good, then we'll probably be able to let you go home on antibiotic pills."

"Okay." He resigned himself to accepting whatever they needed to do, within limits. He would be of no value to his congregants and the people of Bishop if he got really sick.

"Any questions?"

Pete shook his head. "Not at the moment. Thank you."

The man gave him a flash of a smile and left the room. As he did so, Pete closed his eyes and said a silent prayer to thank God for His grace and mercy and to ask for health and a quick recovery.

EIGHTEEN

Adam spent the morning doing what he'd said he wouldn't. No, he did not resurrect his program, UltraNet. Still, his actions skirted that issue.

He'd been watching the mainstream news sites, which now included Fox News in his mind since they failed to stand up for election integrity. They had become as woke as CNN or MSNBC. He also watched NewsMax, OANN, and others in the hope that they would have more up-to-date coverage. Yet, it appeared that the government had clamped down on the news out of southern California—both state and federal. He knew the signs to watch for—he'd helped design some of them in a "previous life" in PsyOps—and the reports from L.A. had all the earmarkings of a cover-up.

While UltraNet remained tucked away in virtual security, he'd grown accustomed to knowing what was going on behind the scenes. So, he used his knowledge of various sites to scan them for information. His gut had been correct. The government had put a lid over SoCal. The news reports were just enough to let people think they knew what had happened there, when in fact, the disaster there would have nationwide ramifications.

However, it was a report he found on the WOC website that had him most concerned. He had lived in the shadows for so long that he had few "real world" contacts. He decided he needed to contact Lynch Cully. He placed the call and got Lynch's voice mail.

"Lynch, this is Adam Afton. I know you probably have classes and meetings today, but would you call me at your convenience? Thanks."

He debated calling Aric but remembered that he did have class at that moment. Then he thought of the Colonel, Mike Southworth, and Mike Jurgesmeyer. Adam had teamed up with them briefly to form The Remnant as a means of helping to control the southern border, a task the Sidon administration fought. They had been successful enough that the full force of the weaponized federal police state began looking for them, and they were forced to shut down the operation and lie low.

He called the retired colonel first. The man answered on the second ring.

"Adam, good to hear from you. I was just thinking about you."

"Hi, Colonel. I was wondering if you and Mike J might be available to talk."

"We're already ahead of you. He's on his way here to the house as we speak. I thought of calling you but figured the drive from Wisconsin was a bit long for you to join us."

"I'm back in St. Louis, with my wife and family."

"That's great. I thought I'd heard something to that effect, but I wasn't sure. Anyway, come join us if you want."

"I'll do that. The kids are in school, and Rachel's volunteering at the pregnancy center right now. I can be there in 15."

"See you then."

Adam grabbed his laptop and jacket and was out the door in a minute. And a quarter hour later, he pulled into the drive of the colonel's historic home off a side street in Ferguson, MO. Another car was already parked there, so he backed up and parked on the street in case anyone needed to get out of the garage.

As he walked around the side of the two-and-a-half-story 1904 house to the front door, he noted the couple's award-winning gardens were already well into their spring growth, and the spring bulbs and perennials were showing off their colors. As he climbed the steps to the big porch that spanned the front of the house, he saw that the bullet holes remained there as a reminder of the historic assassination attempt on the new king of England many years earlier. The colonel and his wife, Mary, had provided their home as a refuge for the then-Prince of Wales and his family. They had been in Missouri to give an original Winston Churchill painting to Westminster College when the royal family had been attacked in England. The queen passed away while the prince and his family hid in the very home Adam was about to enter.

The man must have seen Adam walking outside the house. He opened the doors before Adam could ring the bell.

"Come in, come in. Mike's just been filling me in on some of the events in California."

Adam and Mike J exchanged greetings, and the trio sat down in the home's beautifully restored library. The room, with its floor-to-ceiling bookcases on two walls and large fireplace on a third hadn't changed since Adam's previous visit.

"Mary's bringing coffee for anyone who wants it. She's going to join us, too."

Upon pouring himself a cup of coffee, black, Mike J started the conversation. "Adam, I was going to fill the

Southworths in on what's happened in southern California. I've been watching various websites and communications in the state government. I figure you have, too."

Adam nodded. "I have, but, please, go ahead."

"In a nutshell, a dam built for flood control along the Owens River, in the mountains near Yosemite, failed from the heavy rains and record snows. It dumped trillions of gallons of water from Crowley Lake into the Owens River Gorge where it took out four small hydroelectric plants. Those power lines fed directly into a high voltage line going into L.A. and caused a cascade of events that took out five more small hydroelectric plants along Bishop Creek just downstream from the gorge. It also caused flooding in the city of Bishop. As the water continued downstream, it overtopped the dam at the Tinemaha Reservoir causing it to fail and add another few billion gallons of water to the event. The head gates for the Los Angeles Aqueduct system were just downstream from that. They are no more, and the flood destroyed nearly 70 miles of the aqueduct system, much of it from overwhelming the aged concrete or undermining the earth under the concrete." He looked at Adam. "Anything to add?"

Adam shook his head. "Not so far. It does look like a purely natural disaster. The dam was routinely inspected and deemed safe. No one could have forecast the amount of water delivered by those 30 or so atmospheric rivers, plus a snowpack 300% greater than average."

"Right. On the electrical side of things, the instantaneous loss of those power plants caused a cascade event to follow the high-voltage lines into the city. One substation after another failed. Their recently installed safety switches failed to function, and some sources are blaming the Chinese, although you'll not see this reported anywhere. The switches were manufactured by a company called Huīhuáng, which means brilliance in English."

The colonel grunted. "Yeah, brilliant all right. A brilliant way to hurt our power grid. The CCP is following Sun-Tzu, the Art of War. They're going to take us down without firing a shot. First, they release a virus they created in gain-of-function research at Wuhan, all the while buying up our farmlands and pork production so they can feed themselves first. Then came their so-called weather balloons, and now this. And our current government is complicit. The president's family has taken millions of dollars from the CCP."

Adam couldn't refute that. "Currently, the LADWP estimates over 80% of their substations have been fried by the demand overload that resulted. That includes the major substations at the Diablo Canyon nuclear plant, the Alamitos natural gas plant, and the Castaic pumped-storage power plant. Also, major solar and wind farms were affected."

They discussed the costs of and sources for replacement transformers. All of them kept shaking their heads in disbelief at the enormity of the cost and time required for repairs.

Mike J added, "In the entire country, there are only three large transformers in reserve of the size needed for the power plants. Three. And those utilities are refusing to give them up out of fear they might need them and that it would take years to replace them."

Mary looked wide-eyed in shock. "So, you're saying L.A. could be without power for years?"

Both Adam and Mike J nodded. "It will take a long time and power restoration will be scattered and patchy."

At that moment, Adam's phone rang. "It's Lynch." He answered the call. Hey, Lynch, I'm here with the colonel and Mike J. We've been talking about the disaster in California. I'm going to put you on speaker."

A round of greetings followed, and Mary asked about Amy and Joshua, their son. "Well, don't you dare come to St. Louis for a visit and not stop by to see us," she added.

"Adam, I hope you're keeping your word and not using UltraNet," said Lynch.

Adam nodded. "I am. Everything I've learned I've discovered on websites and discussion boards that are technically public but very hard to find for the general layperson." He gave Lynch the Reader's Digest version of what had been discussed so far. "Do your Homeland Security friends have anything further?"

"Well, the national ramifications of this are enormous, so the government is keeping a lid on news reports. But, word's getting out from people leaving the area. Think about it. L.A. is our second biggest city, and the Port of Los Angeles is our second largest port, handling imports from Taiwan, Japan, South Korea, the Philippines, Australia, China, and India. The port was already experiencing slowdowns that affected our supply chain, but now the port is completely non-functional. San Francisco and Seattle haven't the facilities to absorb the load, and costs of goods are going to increase even more than they are now."

Adam added, "And I read where insurers are worried. There's speculation that more than one major insurance company could go bust over claims there."

"That's true. And look at what the stock markets did today. They're down 40% already and the day's not over. That's destroying millions of Americans' retirement savings."

The colonel spoke up. "I have old Army friends in the area. A couple of them have called already, once they found cell service, and according to them, people are leaving the city in droves. The interstates out of town are jammed, but the National Guard is restricting movement for some reason. Plus, many of those people are just abandoning their homes and mortgages. The banks are going to take a monstrous hit. And the city itself is a free-for-all. Looting. Gunfire. Fires, some in areas with no water at all. The police can't keep up and are running out of fuel for their patrol cars. Jungle law rules."

"It gets worse," said Adam. He had waited before speaking up about what he'd found on the WOC website.

"Worse? How could it get worse? Those poor people are losing everything."

"I've been watching certain pages on the WOC website . . ."

Both the colonel and Mike J smiled at his pronouncing it 'woke.'

". . . and they're moving up the WHO international meeting and expect to get approval of the new IHR changes they've been seeking. The meeting is just a month away now."

The colonel looked puzzled. "We've known that was coming for months. Whether or not they agree on vaccine passports, those international health reg changes do the same thing."

"True, but how many people know they've been working on a new enterovirus and will be using it for another plandemic?"

A round of sighs and groans followed. "Are you saying

we're going to have to put up with this nonsense again?"

Lynch, however, concurred and said, "My DHS friend said something about hearing rumors to that effect. He thinks that if that happens, it will be enough to get an emergency meeting of the WHO and pass the IHR changes unanimously."

Adam shifted in his chair. "It's not a rumor. Word went out this morning over various WOC channels. The virus is complete and has already been shipped to L.A. They're going to use this disaster as a cover to release and spread it."

No one said a thing as that revelation hit home. It was a perfect cover—a total blackout leading to sanitation problems. A new "plague" arises, and thousands of people fleeing the area will spread it all across the country, if not the globe. And the National Guard was complicit by restricting the outflow of cars and keeping people in L.A. longer to ensure exposure.

Lynch broke the silence. "That will be enough to get those new regulations passed, and our government will have ceded our national sovereignty to the WHO and their Chinese patrons. A new pandemic could even lead to marshal law being declared in order to avoid new elections next year."

The colonel nodded. "Any legit excuse is all they need."

"These new regulations will restrict international travel to anyone who doesn't have a full vaccination record, right?" The colonel and Mike J nodded.

"But," interjected Lynch. "The wording is such that if the WHO decides you can't enter a store to shop without a full record, you can be legally stopped from shopping."

"And if they succeed in implementing the Central Bank Digital Currency they're already looking to start, then they can shut off your funds. No buying . . . or selling, at all," said Adam.

Lynch's next words came through loud and clear. "Revelation 13:17. The mark of the beast."

NINETEEN

Heather tossed and turned, moaning as she slept. She was distraught over the ordeal facing her and sleep hadn't come easily. It came solely from exhaustion.

A sudden pounding woke her. She gazed about, disoriented. Where was she?

The noise occurred again, and she raised her head and glanced toward its source. Was she still in her car? A police officer stood outside. In his hand, he held his baton and appeared to be ready to break her car's window. She blinked several times, rubbed her eyes, and glanced about.   The sun already appeared over the mountains. Had she really fallen asleep on her steering wheel?

She turned on the car and lowered her window. She still felt lost.

"Ma'am, are you okay? We got a call about a possible dead body in this car."

She shook her head. "Y-yes, sir. I-I'm okay. It's been a horrible . . ." She glanced at the clock on the dash. 9:18? ". . . 22 hours. I left Venice around 11:20 yesterday morning and took a colleague to his home in Woodland Hills after we witnessed his car being stolen. We didn't get to his house until dark. Then, he gave me directions to my house to avoid the Ventura Freeway. I-I got lost."

She began to cry. She had lost count of the car accidents

she'd seen—people hurrying to get home, thinking only of themselves. Several of the accidents led to physical violence, and they'd seen one person get shot by the other driver. And despite the fear they felt of becoming another target, they couldn't move. They were locked into a parade that made slower progress than a snuggle of sloths.

"Where do you live?"

"Windy Hill, off MountainGate."

The man let out a breath. "Wow. You really did get lost. You're in Reseda."

Reseda? She knew the name but couldn't recall ever going through the neighborhood.

"Can I see the directions you were given?"

She handed the paper to him.

"Ah. You turned the wrong way on Reseda Blvd. You went north, not south. But how did you end up on this street?"

"There was an accident blocking the road, and I thought I could just go around it on a side street. Then that road was blocked, so I turned again. Got totally mixed up. It was early morning at that point, dark, and I was exhausted, so I parked. I thought I'd just rest a bit and try again, but I guess I finally fell asleep."

"What about your car's GPS system? If your car runs, they still work in a blackout."

"We bought this used. The navigation system was an option the original owner didn't get."

The officer took his pen from his shirt and began to write on the paper she'd given him. After a minute, he handed it back to her. "Here. This should get you home. Do you have enough gas? You won't find any between here and there."

She nodded and looked at the fuel gauge. "I think so. Still

have half a tank."

"Good. Go straight home. The governor's ordered the National Guard in and travel's going to get more restrictive as they arrive and set up."

"Thank you, officer."

She felt better now. Plus, it was light outside. She'd be able to see familiar landmarks as she neared her home and where she shopped. She felt a bit embarrassed, too. She was a native Angeleno, having left the area only to go to Stanford—where she met her husband—and to travel. Yet, she knew very little about navigating around the greater Los Angeles area. She relied heavily on her GPS systems to get places, but this wasn't her usual vehicle. To make matters worse, her phone had died, and that power cord was in her Range Rover as well.

Per the directions given to her, she found her way back to Reseda Blvd. and headed south. In contrast to the previous day with its wall-to-wall traffic, the roads appeared barren. Well, void of moving cars anyway. Abandoned vehicles were strewn across the landscape. Many were left right in the traffic lanes where they died. And many were EVs. They would have to be towed. At least with a gas-powered car, the owner could tote a container of gas to the vehicle and expect to drive it away.

As she continued, she was not surprised to find several intersections partially blocked by cars disabled in accidents. She wondered how many of those she personally witnessed the night before. Driving on was like navigating an obstacle course.

Entrances to the Ventura Freeway were barricaded. At times, she could see those traffic lanes and they looked like a used car lot. No wonder the ramps were blocked. It would take days, maybe weeks, to remove all of those cars from the freeway.

Ventura Blvd, which the officer had directed her to use, was another American Ninja Warrior course that she had to work her way through. She found her travel through this neighborhood eerie. The shops, restaurants, and businesses there, instead of being busy with midweek customers, were nearly void of activity. Windows were shattered, doors broken. At one grocery, she saw a woman with a cart full of baby formula and diapers running from the store. At an electronics discount house, two men fought over a large-screen television. She wondered if one of them was the store manager and how the thief expected to use the device without power. She passed a gas station where a man knelt over the opening where the in-ground tanks were filled. He was using a hand pump to fill multiple red, plastic gas containers. She suspected he had already filled his SUV.

As her gaze returned to the road, she saw a man and woman running toward her, directly in front of her. The man appeared to be holding a handgun. She veered into the opposite lanes and floored it, narrowly missing an oncoming car—one of only half a dozen vehicles she had seen moving that morning. In her rearview mirror, she saw the carjackers rush that car, but that driver wasn't intimidated and hit the man rather than stop.

It was at that point that Heather realized the woman was very pregnant. As much as she wanted to get home, she couldn't ignore the thought that maybe the couple needed help. Certainly, the man did now. She screeched to a stop, put the car in reverse, and backed up to where the woman was kneeling over the body of the man and crying.

As Heather exited her car, the woman turned her gaze

on her and reached for the gun. Fear etched her face.

"Hey, don't need the gun. Would you please put it down?"

The woman shook her head.

"Do you need help?" She paused. "Sorry. Your husband certainly does."

"W-w-we were trying to get to the hospital. My labor pains started an hour ago." She grimaced as another set of muscle spasms hit her. "Our car ran out of gas back there. We tried flagging down the few cars we've seen, but no one would stop."

"Well, waving a gun at folks doesn't help."

The woman looked at the gun in her hand. "My boyfriend was mugged and robbed yesterday while trying to get home. He insisted we take it from our apartment."

Heather nodded. She knelt next to the unconscious man and put her fingers on the side of his neck. There was a pulse. "We need to get you both to the hospital. Help me get him into the back seat."

Together they managed to get him into the car, and Heather did her best to keep his neck stable. She had seen that on numerous medical dramas on TV. Then they climbed into the car.

"Which hospital?"

"Northridge. It's north on Reseda."

Heather waggled her head. "That figures. I just came from that direction."

The woman groaned and grimaced again.

"How far apart are your contractions?"

"They were ten minutes apart when we left. Now, I really don't know, but they're faster."

She backtracked the four or five miles she had just

traveled and continued north on Reseda Blvd. She noticed that the woman's pains were barely three minutes apart. With no traffic and no stop lights, they made good time, even while running the obstacle course of abandoned cars. Two miles farther, she saw the hospital and pulled into the area where ambulances unloaded.

She jumped out of the car as the woman struggled to do the same. Heather ran inside, surprised to see that the automatic doors worked. Inside the place was dim, but functioning. Somehow, their backup generators continued to work. A nurse came up to her.

"I have a woman in labor. Pains are about three minutes apart. And her boyfriend is in the backseat, victim of a hit-and-run as they were trying to get help and a ride."

Heather followed as several staff members rushed outside with one pushing a gurney and another a wheelchair. As the woman was wheeled past her, she grabbed Heather's wrist.

"W-what" your name?"

"Umm, Heather."

"I like that name. My little girl now has a name. Thank you." The pain hit her again, and she grabbed her belly.

Heather didn't know what to say.

One of the nurses also came up to her, and said, "Thank you. Since the blackout, we've been seeing the worst of what people can do to each other. It's refreshing to see someone go out of their way to help a stranger."

Heather felt embarrassed at recalling that she had sped up to go past these people. Still, she thought she was about to be carjacked and pulled over after realizing the woman was pregnant. Would she have done so if the woman hadn't been so obviously with child?

Standing alone next to her car, she realized she never got the woman's name. Well, she wasn't going to try to track her down now. She was likely already in the facility's birthing center. She got into her car and for the third time that day traveled along Reseda Blvd. Now, even the abandoned cars seemed familiar.

Several minutes later, having passed the point where she'd picked up the couple, she noticed a local U-Haul facility. Their rental selections had been scant for months, thanks to all of the people leaving the area for less green pastures—less green in the sense of reasonable energy policies. Lower taxes and housing prices elsewhere also drove the exodus. Today, the rental lot was empty. Even the sign advertising cargo carriers was marked through with "Sold Out."

After 20 minutes of driving, she found herself in more familiar territory. She was close to home. Compared to Reseda, turning onto N. Sepulveda Blvd was another story. The northbound lanes were packed with cars, both abandoned and moving, while the southbound lanes were largely open. The message was clear. Everyone wanted out of L.A. No one was driving *into* the city.

Almost home. She turned onto Mountaingate Dr. and headed for the entrance into their gated community of Windy Hill. She passed the country club and noticed cars parked all along the road, even on the sidewalks. Then she saw the entrance to the neighborhood. Cars filled both sides of the street leading up to the unmanned gatehouse, in front of the closed gates.

She shook her head. It hadn't occurred to her. *Of course. No electricity, no gates*, she thought. She felt surprised that no one had forced the gates open, but then, her security-minded neighbors more likely felt that safety behind the closed gates was better than the inconvenience of parking their cars outside the community.

She found a place to park, secured her car, and walked the hundred or so yards to the gate. There was a man-gate there as well as the main ones for cars. She never used it. She had never needed to. Upon walking up to it, she discovered it had an electronic lock.

She surveyed the borders of their community. Where there wasn't a tall masonry fence, there was an eight-foot tall metal fence ending in spikes at the top. Even if she succeeded in climbing to the top, which she was not too confident about doing—what if she slipped and impaled herself on one of those spikes? So, now, how was she going to get in?

TWENTY

Werner's driver picked him up at the usual time and drove him to the Munich office, where he found a stack of briefs already sitting on his desk. *Edvin must have been up late*, he thought, *to have put this together since the day before.*

A moment later, his secretary entered with his customary cup of organic coffee. He preferred kopi luwak coffee made from coffee cherries ingested and defecated by palm civets in Indonesia. Recently, two men had perfected a chemical method for duplicating the fermentation process that occurred during the bean's travel through the animal's gut. That was much more appealing than thinking about coffee made from civet feces.

The top of the stack held a one-page brief on the spring elections in the U.S. the day before. He read through the information. No surprises there. Of course, with the acceptance of mail-in ballots and the use of various electronic voting machines, their ability to control the elections was assured. Expectantly, there would be those states which would fight for election integrity, but the numbers were against them in upcoming national elections.

Also expected would be a groundswell of support to bring back President Graham. That would never be allowed, and their friends in the mainstream media would help drive down his popularity ratings. The result would be the same as the midterm elections—a great red wave that ended up being hardly a ripple.

He smiled and nodded in approval that a liberal judge in Wisconsin had been elected to their supreme court. That bode well on two counts. First, her stand on abortion was in line with that of the WOC. For decades, abortion had served well in controlling the minority classes, and now they could add one more state where that remained an option after that ridiculous ruling by the U.S. Supreme Court to toss out Roe v. Wade. He remained amazed that the blacks in America continued to aggressively support the political party that once tried to prevent their attaining equal civil rights and still sought to reduce their numbers by eliminating their babies.

On the second count, she was progressive in her thinking about criminal justice. The move toward defunding the police in the U.S. was a slow one, but one needed to further destabilize the country and prevent anyone from trying to restore its "superpower" status.

The next few briefs detailed business transactions requiring Werner's decisions. On one he made a note asking for more information. On two others, he signed off on the projects.

A knock at his door caught his attention. The door opened, and Edvin's head popped in.

"*Guten morgen, mein herr.* Is now a good time? I have that special report you requested I not put in writing."

Werner nodded and waved him into the office. His aide took his usual seat across the desk.

"I have the final report on the enterovirus. The gain-of-function work was completed on time, and they estimate that it will cause an acute flaccid paralysis in roughly 50% of those who contract it."

Such paralysis was once diagnosed as polio before the mid-1950s when the American Medical Association split the polio diagnosis into over a dozen other categories. Of the great polio scares of that time, fewer than 1% of the cases had ever been caused by the wild polio enterovirus. And while the true polio virus was a member of the broad enterovirus family, its status as the poster child for vaccinations remained a valuable commodity for their agenda.

The non-polio strain they were using was a coxsackievirus like the one that caused hand, foot, and mouth disease—highly contagious and evident by an obvious rash. The rash alone could be promoted to make pariahs of those infected. By increasing its ability to infect the central nervous system and produce paralysis, the fear of "polio" would cause people by the tens of thousands to rush to get the newest mRNA vaccine. Never mind that such paralysis was 100% survivable with full recovery. Vaccine hesitancy would be a thing of the past.

His aide continued. "The virus has been shipped to Los Angeles and should have arrived there by now, but I don't yet have confirmation. The plan is to first release it within the homeless camps closest to the sewage treatment plants so that patient zero tracing points back to the failed plant. I believe the LA Sanitation plant in El Segundo near LAX is first on the list. There is a homeless camp on what they call Dockweiler Beach across the street. It is closest to the airport as well. That will be followed by a plant in Anaheim, north of Disneyland, with its homeless camps along the Santa Ana River Trail."

"Very good, Edvin. They can launch it as soon as they are

able. What about population control? Has the state moved in their National Guard?"

Edvin nodded. "They have and as soon as they arrived, they closed down all traffic on the major thoroughfares. No one in or out of the county for the past 12 hours."

"Excellent."

"They are using the guise of needing to clear abandoned vehicles from the roadways before allowing normal traffic flow again. Not that there is any normal traffic flow. Everyone who can is trying to leave the city."

Werner clapped his hands together. "Perfect. Just what we want, but only after the virus has been released and a case or two arise to show the release successful."

"Yes, sir. They say it could take a week to open the interstates and several more to open other freeways."

"Also, send word to our friends there to stop all outbound traffic intermittently after that. They can use the reason that the unaffected areas where people are going need time to absorb the influx of people."

Werner smiled. This was moving along better than planned. The longer they can keep people in L.A., the more who will get infected. Reports of the new virus and its spread will be primetime news by the time of the upcoming WHO meeting. The member nations will be eager to pass the new IHRs.

TWENTY-ONE

Heather couldn't believe she had slept in her car for a second night. Her idea of roughing it was an all-inclusive in Puerto Vallarta or the Caribbean. And she really wanted a shower, but just the thought of standing under a cold stream of water without the benefit of their on-demand electric water heaters made her shiver. How in the world the homeless in Venice survived was beyond comprehension for her, but she had grown more empathetic in her time at the shelter. And yet now, they were probably better prepared for living through this disaster than she.

The sun topped the mountains in the east as she stood once again outside the gate. She had walked the perimeter once again without finding an easy way in.

"Hey Heather, you want in?"

She raised her hands in victory. "Yes, Walt. You're a godsend."

One of the men from the neighborhood stood on the other side of the gates with a portable generator. Just what the doctor ordered, so to speak, since the man was a general surgeon.

"It took a few of us to figure out how to power these things. Give me a minute to get it running."

"Great. Have you seen Dennis? Is he home?" She had been worried about her husband as he had been scheduled on a job site on the south side of the city. Without cell phone communication, she had no idea where he was or how he was doing. She didn't like that.

As Walt pulled the cord on his generator, he shook his head. "Don't know. Haven't seen him. Is his car here somewhere?"

Heather had to admit that she hadn't fully surveyed the cars parked nearby. She did know that it wasn't anyplace close to the entrance to the community.

"I haven't seen it."

A moment later, with the generator running, Walt had the man gate open, followed by both car gates. With them all open, he shut down the power to prevent them from closing.

Heather walked through the gate and right up to the man. She hugged him. "Thank you, Walt. Now we just need to get these cars moved out of the way."

He nodded. "Working on it. I've been letting folks know we'd get them open today, so if you see anyone as you walk home, tell 'em the gates are open. With a bit of luck, we'll have this parking lot cleared in a few hours, and you can get your car back to the house before lunch."

Heather thanked him again and began her half-mile walk to their house. She saw a handful of people watching her through their windows and waved. She pointed toward the entrance and yelled, "The gates are open!" A couple of them gave her a thumbs-up, while others came to their front doors and asked her what she'd said. She repeated her information and walked on. She glanced back at one point and saw two neighbors heading toward the gate.

As she neared her home, she thought about how unchanged it looked. And yet, life as she knew it had changed drastically.

Standing at her front door, she again became flummoxed. They had an electronic deadbolt. Despite its being battery-powered, without their WiFi functioning, she couldn't unlock the door. Yet, it didn't concern her. Her husband knew the importance of being prepared. The side door to their garage required a standard key, which she never carried with her, but they had hidden a spare outside.

As she walked around the side door, she heard the faint thrum of a gas engine. Someone had a generator running. She glanced around and recognized that the noise was coming from their next-door neighbor's house. She walked to the property line and realized the generator was running inside their garage.

She panicked at the thought. Sure, running it outside the house ran a risk of someone taking it, especially under the circumstances, but didn't they understand the risks of running it in their garage?

She ran to their front door and began pounding on it. No answer. She ran around to their kitchen window and knocked loudly on it. She waited. Still no response. Their backyard was enclosed. She hoped the gate was unlocked. She ran around to the other side of the house, found the gate partly open, and rushed to their back patio overlooking their pool.

She rushed up to the large, plate glass sliding doors that offered the occupants an enviable view of the cityscape. However, this time it provided her with a ghastly view of the interior. Both bodies appeared lifeless. She was tilted over on a couch, while it appeared that he was trying to get to the sliding door and didn't make it. Both had complexions of cherry red. She had read that such was the case in carbon monoxide poisoning.

She tried the door, but it was locked. She looked about for a way in. Their patio furniture, which she had envied when they first bought it, was aluminum and not likely to break the safety glass. Then she saw what she needed—a 12-inch spherical, stone planter. She tried to pick it up, but it was too heavy. She tipped it over and ripped out the plantings and half the soil. Now she lifted it, carried it to the door, and heaved it with all her strength against the door. The glass shattered but did not break out. She repeated the action, and this time the glass fell out of its frame. As she reached in to unlock the door, the stench of exhaust caught her off-guard. She thought carbon monoxide was a silent killer. Surely, they would have noticed the smell of the engine's exhaust, but maybe they had been overcome before the smell became obvious.

Her first priority was to open all the doors and windows to ventilate the room. Then she ran to him. His eyes stared into open space. Unlike the man hit by the car, he had no pulse. Sadly, his wife didn't either.

She took a deep breath and headed to the garage. As often as she'd been in their home, she made a wrong turn at one point and ended up in a study. Tears welled up in her eyes as she noticed the photos of their grown children and grandchildren. She opened the window in that room as well, took a deep breath of clean air, and found her way to the garage. There sat the offending machine. She found and pressed the button to open the garage door before taking time to figure out how to shut down the generator and then doing so.

She stepped outside and sat down on the short retaining wall adjacent to the drive. She began to cry. How could things get worse? Her comfortable life seemed a distant memory. The ordeal of getting home. Seeing accident after accident, a man being shot by another, a man being run down by a car, and now this, friends and great neighbors dead. Where was her husband? She wanted him home. Now.

TWENTY-TWO

Shawn had drifted off to sleep after passing Benton's Crossing a day and a half earlier. Web, as his new friend liked to be called, had been kind enough to let him.

It was only after arriving at the Mammoth Yosemite Airport that the enormity of what had happened started to come into focus for both of them. The power was out throughout most of southern California. Water shortages, if not total outages, were being reported throughout the metro area. Communications were down except for emergency personnel. The National Guard was mobilized. A federal disaster was declared. The airport itself was told to be aware that many celebrities might be flying in via their personal jets to find refuge at the ski resorts. Shawn had shaken his head at the last comment. Nothing like decrying climate change from one's private jet.

The airport personnel at first looked at him as being a homeless drifter coming out of L.A. and tried to move him outside. But when he explained that he was the dam safety engineer, had been at the dam when it failed, and had lost his truck, his phone, and nearly his life, they quickly moved to help him. The airport director arranged a private office for him with a land line to make whatever calls he needed to make.

On his third attempt, he reached his wife who broke

down crying upon hearing his voice. She knew that he was going to that dam and thought him dead when she hadn't heard from him and his phone kept going to voice mail. They arranged to meet near Lake Tahoe at the Enterprise Car Rental as he could get a car there at the airport and drop it off at Tahoe. The spot was about a two-hour drive for him and three hours for her. That would give him time to find some clothes and take a shower, which he really needed. Even Tag didn't want to be around him.

He also phoned his office but got no answer. That didn't surprise him. After such a colossal dam failure, he felt confident that every engineer and able-bodied person in the office was out inspecting dams that could be affected by the rain and snowpack. He left a detailed message, explaining that he had lost his truck and phone and would be in touch again ASAP.

Someone on the airport staff rummaged through the unclaimed baggage and found him a change of clothes. They were definitely a step up from his usual, but while he would look nicer, he would still smell overly ripe. They arranged for him to shower in the maintenance department shower room, which was typically used only for emergencies such as solvent or AVGAS spills. At that point, smelling like aviation gas would be a step up, too, like the wardrobe.

By the time he arrived in the Tahoe area, he was exhausted. He didn't want his wife to drive through the mountains again in the dark, so they found a nice room and spent the night getting reacquainted.

Now, it was Wednesday morning, and the hard part was still to come—paperwork.

Pete was champing at the bit to get out of the hospital. His doctor had insisted on one more day and one more X-ray. They told him there was a suspicious spot when comparing the images of the previous two days. When they showed him the X-ray images on the bedside computer, he saw no difference. Plus, he had no fever, cough, or shortness of breath. He felt fine.

Yet, when his wife had an emotional outburst, stating that if he died at home from pneumonia, she'd never let him live it down, he looked at her askance. She never did catch the humor, or perhaps the absurdity, of what she'd said. And he wasn't about to point it out. Happy wife, happy life.

As he returned to his bed from the radiology department, his doctor was already there and waiting for him. And he seemed to be smiling . . . as much as the gruff, old country doc ever did, anyway.

"Good news, Pete. X-ray looks clear."

Pete figured that doc hadn't actually looked at the film, but that the radiologist had called him with a report. That's the only way the man could have beat him to the room.

"We can let you go home, but remember, you were in some pretty filthy water. Any sign of a fever or cough, don't wait to come back here. And shortness of breath is often a later symptom, so if that starts, don't think you should wait for it to worsen before coming to the ER."

Angela gave him her "look." He'd seen it often enough in 25 years of marriage. *Happy wife . . .* He repeated mentally.

"Got it, doc." He smiled. "And if I forget, Ang here will quickly remind me."

She nodded. "You got that right, buster." She turned to look at their family doctor. "Don't worry Doc Carter, he'll toe the line."

Pete nodded and held up three fingers on his right hand. "Scout's honor."

The older man guffawed. "Whatever you say, tenderfoot. Need to work on that swimming merit badge."

Pete raised his brow in surprise. The doc had a sense of humor. Who would have guessed?

Angela punched him in the arm before some dad joke came out of his mouth. Not that any came right to mind. They always seemed reserved for sermons.

"Okay. Your discharge papers are signed. The nurse will wheel you out as soon as they process things."

Pete frowned. "I don't need to be wheeled out. I—"

Doc Carter shook his head. "Sorry. Hospital policy." The doctor offered a subtle wave goodbye and turned to leave the room.

Pete started to pull off his hospital gown only to realize he wore just boxer briefs and a tee-shirt underneath. His wife grinned as she lifted his clean trousers and shirt above her head and danced away from the bed. "Grrrr. . ." He remembered his mantra, *Happy* . . .

TWENTY-THREE

Aric walked out of the classroom building following his early afternoon forensics lab class and headed for the dorm. His foray into power evangelism the day before had been disappointing. He had felt confident that the word he'd had for the girl he approached was correct. True, maybe God hadn't exactly told him to approach her. Maybe he *had* stepped out before God, but still . . .

He saw the girl farther down the street talking with friends outside the athletic building. At the same time, he saw Chris, Jess' brother, walking up the hill from the student parking lot. He ran across the street to meet him.

"Hey."

Chris nodded in greeting. "I thought you had class this afternoon. Where're you headed?"

"It's an hour-long lab on forensics. We're done."

"Got it. What's up?"

Aric nodded his head toward the group of female students where he spotted the girl. "Those girls over there. The one with the gray hoodie and torn jeans. Do you know her?"

"Yeah. We were in the same high school here in town. She's another local. Name's Amanda. She's been dating a guy in my business admin class, but I heard things are kind of rocky there. Why? Should I let Jess know she has competition?" He grinned.

Aric shook his head. "Nope, your sister's solid with me." Yet, he was confused, too. Why had the girl reacted as she did? Why had she denied her name was Amanda, called herself Jocelyn, and said she was gay? He didn't get it.

He debated telling Chris his reason for wanting her name. But then, he realized that of all of his friends, Chris would be the most understanding and insightful.

"Did Jess tell you about my dinner with the police officer?"

"She did. That was amazing."

"Well, yesterday morning, Amanda was walking to class with some others—guys and girls—and I felt like I had a word for her. I asked her to the side . . ." He went on to describe the encounter. "Why do you think she'd lie to me like that?"

His friend shrugged. "Dunno. Maybe she thought you were going to hit on her. Maybe the boyfriend was in the group, and she didn't want to seem interested in what you were saying because he might have interpreted it wrong. Maybe the whole idea that God had a message for her freaked her out."

Aric thought about those reasons. They all made sense.

Chris continued. "And maybe God wanted to use that to slow you down, keep you humble and open."

There was that word again, humble. Out of the mouths of two or more witnesses. Wasn't that what the Bible said? *Message received, Lord,* he thought.

"Hey, I gotta run. See you around." Chris rushed off to class.

Aric continued down the road toward the dorm. As he passed the group of girls, he looked at Amanda, smiled, and nodded a greeting. Well, the smile was more of a knowing smirk. She blushed and turned away to face the girl next to her.

He continued to the dorm but as he neared the doors, his phone rang. Dan Dickson, the officer.

"Hi, Dan. What's up, sir?"

"Hi, Aric. Look, I was planning on calling you about meeting you at church this Sunday, but ends up I'm taking some personal time off to go to L.A. My, uh, brother and his wife are there, and no one in the family has been able to get in touch with them."

"Wow. Sorry to hear that. I hear that nothing good is happening there. I hope they're okay."

"I'm sure they are. They have the resources to leave, which is why I'm concerned. They would have contacted one of us by now if they were able to leave and made it to someplace with cell service."

That made sense. "You flying?"

"No. Ran into a problem there. There are plenty of flights *into* Fresno and Bakersfield, but none out for weeks. Seems everyone is leaving. Not going there, just leaving."

Can't blame them, thought Aric, but he didn't want to say it.

"So, I'm borrowing a buddy's full-sized van and driving, via Bakersfield. I'm told the National Guard has closed off the interstates and main freeways, but I'm hoping they live far enough north and that with my police ID, I can get to their home. With the van, we can at least get their most valuable things out."

"Well, I'll certainly keep you all in my prayers, and I'll get my friends to pray, too."

"Thanks. That's, um, that's actually why I called you.

After our time together, I've come to value prayer more than I ever have."

"You got it. So, when do you leave?"

"Within the hour. Have three long days of driving ahead of me. I need to get gas, and I bought half a dozen 5-gallon gas containers. Gonna fill them, too."

Aric felt the urge to tell the man what Adam had told him the night before. But was this just him responding to something his brother told him or was it God? Then, he recalled the admonitions for watchmen to sound an alarm. If a watchman failed to alert someone to danger, the "blood" of that person was on the watchman's head. If he sounded the alarm and the person ignored him, then that person bore his blood on his own head.

"Hey, look, be careful. My brother is *very* well informed, and he told me there's a plan to launch a new viral pandemic in L.A. It's already been released. He called it an enterovirus and it can cause paralysis, like polio."

The man laughed. "Your brother's a conspiracy nut, I take it." He continued to laugh.

"Not really. He tends to think of conspiracy theories as spoiler alerts. All I'm saying is, be careful."

Aric shook his head upon hanging up. Had he just stepped ahead of God again? But then, this wasn't a word from the Lord. It was a warning from his brother, and Adam had resources few knew about.

TWENTY-FOUR

As Heather sat on the retaining wall near her neighbor's garage, she saw the first of the cars moving in from the gate. It was Mr. Iverson, an elderly man living a few doors down and across the street with his wife. The couple was nearing their eighties, still played 18 holes of golf three times a week, and attended all of the MountainGate Country Club events whenever they weren't gallivanting off to visit kids and grandkids. She hoped to have that kind of energy in 40 years.

She jumped up and ran, waving, to the car. The vehicle stopped, and the passenger side window lowered.

"Heather? What's wrong?"

After wiping the tears from her eyes, she said, "The Littels. I-I think they're dead. They were running their generator in the garage."

He nodded slowly. "Walt's still by the gate. Let me go get him."

He turned the car around in the drive and drove off back toward the gates. A minute later, he returned, and Walt jumped from the car before Mr. Iverson continued to his own home. Heather ushered him into the house and to the living room. She explained her actions in finding them as they walked.

Within two minutes, he confirmed her conclusion, shaking his head. "We don't want to move them, but we should probably cover them up. Who knows how long it might take to get EMS or police here? Think you could find a couple of sheets?"

Heather found a guest bedroom and cried at seeing it set up for visiting grandkids. She pulled the covers off the two twin beds and ripped the top sheet off each one next. Back in the living room, she handed one to Walt. She covered her while he covered him. As they did so, a shadow crossed over the room. Startled, Heather looked up to see Mr. Iverson standing in the doorway of the glass door she had broken.

"I called 911."

She gave him a quizzical look and reached for her phone in the back pocket. He shook his head.

"No. Cell service is still out. We have a land line. At our age, we can't trust wireless in an emergency. We're definitely old school. Police and EMS will be here, but no idea when."

"Well, no rush. Don't want to seem callous, but they're not going anywhere," said Walt.

She flashed him a look of displeasure but realized he was right. The police had more pressing matters facing them.

"I'll keep an eye out for them out at the gate. By the way, Heather, you ought to be able to get your car into the community now."

Together, they unlocked the front door for easy access and closed the garage door, watching it slowly descend on its backup battery. Then they slowly walked back to the main gates.

"Sorry you had to stumble onto that."

Heather could only offer a slow nod. "We need to figure out how to let their kids know. I know one son lives in Seattle with his family. Not sure about their other kids."

"If we can find some numbers, the police can handle that."

"Okay, I'll go back and check his study, see if I can find something."

"Their cell phones will probably have that info, but if they're still on their bodies, don't disturb them. Let the police do that."

She agreed. She'd enjoyed enough crime dramas on TV to know that much. Besides, the last thing she wanted to do anyway was touch a dead body.

A few minutes later, she sat in her car in their driveway and watched as their garage door creaked open on its battery. She pulled in next to her Range Rover and glanced across to the empty third bay of the garage. Her thoughts— and worries— went back to Dennis. Where was he? Was he okay?

Finally! Once that wheelchair stopped outside the hospital's main door, he jumped out of it and raced to the car ... all of 15 feet away under the portico. His wife hadn't had time to climb out of the car to help him, not that he needed any. The 40-minute drive home was largely quiet.

"Do you want me to detour to any of the power plants on the way?" asked Angela.

"No, hon. I don't want to tie you up with that."

"No, seriously, I don't mind. It's not like I can cook, clean, watch TV, or surf the internet at home."

She had a point.

He shook his head. "That's okay. I need some things from home and the office in Bishop before going there. And it's likely to take me all afternoon."

At home, true to his word, he gathered what he needed,

climbed into his truck, and drove first to the church. The place seemed full. He hadn't expected that since the waters in town had receded. More correctly, the waters had followed gravity's beckoning call. With the city's elevation of just over 4,000 feet, the waters continued to move down through the mountains and didn't stay long. He had heard that Owens Lake was again full of water. That hadn't been the case in over 80 years when the water diversions into the aqueduct system had caused the lake to dry up and become a mineral salt flat.

He found Jim working in the kitchen making peanut butter and jelly sandwiches.

"Hey, Jim."

"Pastor, welcome back. You gave us all real scare."

He nodded. "You weren't the only ones. What's with all the people here? I figured they'd all have headed back to their homes now that the water's gone."

Jim shrugged. "Nothing there to go back to for most of 'em. I mean, their homes might be intact, but here they have company, food, and toilets."

Pete smiled. Portable outhouses weren't exactly toilets, but he could understand. "Good thing we got those for emergencies."

Jim looked up. "Say, the sheriff was looking for you."

"Oh?"

"Wanted to thank you. Your early alert saved over a dozen lives. Congrats."

Pete could be thankful for that. At last count, almost three dozen had lost their lives and others remained unaccounted for.

"Oh, and there were two men here asking for you."

"Did you get any names?"

Jim shook his head. "Didn't offer any. They were driving some kind of rig with a 20-foot container on the back. They just asked for the pastor, not for you by name."

"Did the container hold disaster relief supplies? That could really help us."

"They didn't say. Rather, they *wouldn't* say. We asked 'em. Just that they needed to talk with you privately first."

That struck Pete as mighty odd.

"They said they'd be back around supper time." He paused. "Another thing. When they drove off, the truck barely made a noise. It sure wasn't a diesel engine."

That added to the mystery. Pete made a mental note to be back by supper time.

"Look, I need to go and detail the extent of the damage and work on my report for the department. I'll shoot to get back here by five, five-thirty. Anything I can do while I'm here?"

Jim shook his head. "Got it covered."

Pete wondered about these mysterious visitors as he drove toward his old control center. And a truck that made no sounds? That sounded like an EV. However, to have any range and be able to climb the grades into the mountains with a load on the back would require a ton of batteries. His thoughts raised more questions than answers.

As he descended into the gorge and Birchim Canyon, it took only a moment to realize his report would be brief. Everything was gone. Leveled. Where two-story homes once stood in the canyon, even foundations were rubble. The road leading to the control center ended abruptly into a steep gulch formed by erosion from the torrent of water.

He climbed out of the truck, snapped a few photos, and returned to the vehicle. Next stop, Middle Gorge. As with the control center, everything was scoured clean. He did notice a pickup truck, or what was left of one, flattened against one rock wall of the canyon. It looked like it had been flattened for reclamation by a compacter at a salvage yard.

He shook his head and muttered, "Hope no one was in that thing." Against his better judgment, he climbed down from the truck and descended along the remains of their washed-out road. He took his photos while doing so. Upon getting as close as he could, he saw that the driver's door had been ripped off. While he couldn't cross the high water to inspect it more closely, he was able to determine that the cab was empty. As he wondered whose pickup it once was, he noticed the bright yellow safety vest and helmet strapped to the passenger seat.

Shawn Westhope. He had been informed that the dam inspector would be there that day. *"Lord, I pray that he got out in time and is safe,"* he thought quietly.

His inspection of the Upper Gorge area yielded no surprises. Three power plants. Three total rebuilds. In his mind, the millions required for the task kept rolling higher, like dollar signs in Scrooge McDuck's eyes. *Where did* that *dated reference come from?* he thought.

As he anticipated, the inspection of the Bishop Creek turbines took more time. There, the turbines and facilities were intact. The damage had been to the adjacent substations and their transformers. He itemized what would be required for replacement and felt frustrated by his inability to inquire online about spares at the equipment depot. He also suspected that his area would be on the long list for such replacements. It could take years.

He checked his phone. 4:45. He needed to get back. Again, his mind wandered to his mystery guests.

TWENTY-FIVE

After learning about the WOC's plan to launch another pandemic, Adam set about trying to find more information. What he discovered bothered him even more.

He checked the time. Lynch would be home from the college by now, but he might have plans for the evening. The colonel always seemed to be ready to talk, but the retiree did not have the level of connections that Lynch had. He decided to reach out to the professor.

"Lynch, do you have a few minutes to talk? I've been following up on what we discussed the other day."

There was a pause, but Adam thought he heard muffled voices in the background.

"Amy tells me we have about 15 minutes until dinner. Shoot."

"Okay. Have you ever heard of or read the Deagel forecast?"

"Can't say that I have."

"The Deagel Corporation was founded by a military contractor well positioned in the Deep State. The company was an offshoot of U.S. military intelligence. Anyway, in 2014 they did an analysis that forecast massive global population declines, with the worst being in the U.S., U.K., Germany, Canada, and Australia. That analysis stated that the U.S. population would fall to 99 million by 2025."

"Wow. Our population now is what, 336 million? That's quite a drop in the next couple of years."

"Well, that's where it gets interesting. That current population number comes from the U.N., which keeps pushing the dangers of overpopulation. The U.N. says the world will top eight billion people this year, and says we can't feed that many, that we're running out of resources, and so on."

"Good point. If I'm hearing you correctly, we shouldn't trust their numbers."

"Right. The interesting part is a group called the COVID Blog. They've been tracking excess deaths and birth rates since the COVID jabs started. They acknowledge they can't get reliable data from China and India, but they've been following reports in those countries of trucks overloaded with bodies heading toward crematoriums working 24/7. They estimate the world population has actually *dropped* by a billion people since the vaccines started."

There was a pause on the other end. "Had to let that sink in. And they just started another pandemic? Excess deaths will really skyrocket."

Excess deaths were the number of deaths above what would be expected. Most of the time, it was calculated by averaging the death rate for the previous five years and comparing that average to the current mortality rate. The issue first came to light in Indiana when a state insurance auditor sounded the alarm in 2020 that there had been a 40% increase in excess deaths since the beginning of COVID. Subsequent analyses revealed growing numbers of deaths since the jabs began with those deaths being concentrated in the 24 to 55 year age group.

"So, that Deagel forecast appears to be more than

prophetic. It seems that the Deep State used them to calculate the results of their depopulation plans."

"Where can I find that analysis?"

"That's another interesting thing. They took it off the internet in March 2021. You won't find it unless you copied it before that."

"Not even with UltraNet?"

"Hey, I'm being good. I put that to rest. I called because I hope you have some ideas as to how we can fight this."

"I'll have to think about that and pray about it." There was another pause. "That was Amy. She needs me in the kitchen. Look, there's something else I need to think and pray about. Maybe I was premature in encouraging you to abandon UltraNet. In a fight like this, maybe we need that edge."

Adam raised his brow. Did Lynch really just say that? His mouth almost began to water at the idea of getting back in the saddle and letting his baby loose on the WOC. The phrase, *Old habits die hard,* came to mind.

Pete glanced at the clock in their community room, which was the primary location of the shelter they provided—almost six p.m. He would be expected home. His wife had him on call to grill since none of their other appliances worked, and they needed to work on foodstuffs from the fridge and freezer before they went bad.

Angela had made a point of not letting anyone freely open either appliance and of using their small gas generator intermittently to power them and keep things cold. Still, their supply of gas was limited until he was able to make the three-hour run north to Tahoe to find an operating gas station. And that assumed they had power. He'd only heard secondhand reports about how extensive the blackout was.

Two other elders had taken over for dinner duty. They, too, were expected to grill for the people there at the church.

"Larry, if those two mystery visitors show up, send someone to get me at home. Otherwise, I'll be back after dinner."

"Got it, Pastor Pete. We'll be here." He smiled as he flipped the grilling tongs in his hand.

Thirty minutes later, after a meal of burgers and baked beans, Pete sat back and smiled. It was like camping in their favorite mountain campground, without the discomfort of sitting on the ground or some log. He hadn't heard from the church, so he assumed the men had not shown up. Maybe they wouldn't, and that would be disappointing. He'd been speculating all day about the purpose of their visit earlier.

After the five-minute walk back to the building, he saw the earlier mentioned truck sitting next to the church. Curiously, it seemed nosed up close to their electric supply and meter. Even more amazing, as he walked into the community room, the lights were on, the kitchen was fully functional again, and people were singing praise songs to CD recordings. He saw two strangers sitting with Larry and Dean and headed their way.

Dean raised his hand in a wave as he approached. "Hey, Pastor Pete, they're here. We invited them to eat with us before sending for you and look what they did." He waved his arms around the room.

Pete extended his hand to both men. "Hi, I'm Pete Manning, or Pastor Pete as most call me around here. And you are?"

The two men looked at each other. The older one spoke

up. "Umm, nothing personal. Please understand that. Under normal circumstances, we would love to make your acquaintance and more. We love meeting and fellowshipping with other believers. But these aren't normal times. We'd like to keep our identities secret, as much to protect you as us. Call us Thing 1 and Thing 2, or whatever."

Pete didn't like the sound of that. That hinted at something illegal. Really? The old "more to protect you than us" gambit?

"Gentlemen, I appreciate that, but honestly, that sounds fishy to me. If we can't know who we're dealing with then we'll need to pass. Thanks. Hope the food was okay."

Larry furrowed his brow. "Um, Pete, I have this feeling you need to talk with these guys. Seriously."

That caught Pete off-guard. Larry was one of the more prophetic men in the congregation. In the past, his "intuitions" had been spot-on. He hadn't expected him to support these two. He weighed Larry's comment into the mix.

"Okay, but my elders need to be in on it, too."

Thing 2 spoke this time. "Well, that's okay, as long as they're willing to take a risk."

Risk? thought Pete. "What if *I'm* not willing to take a risk?" His recent stay in the hospital resonated through his mind.

Thing 1 nodded. "Fair enough. Let's go someplace private to talk, and we'll lay it out to you. You can decide then."

That sounded fair. Pete nodded. "Okay, if you're done eating, my office is this way."

Thing 2 grabbed another brownie and stood up. They all followed Pete to his office. Larry grabbed two more chairs from an adjacent room and closed the door.

The older man, Thing 1, started the discussion. "First, let me give you a little background. We're with a start-up green energy company owned by Christians who have a heart for missions. What we've developed is so disruptive to the current powers-that-be and Big Energy that we've been operating in a very low-key way. We haven't wanted to attract any attention because, to be honest, previous developers of disruptive technology tend to mysteriously die."

Pete nodded. "I can understand that. I remember reading about a guy who developed a car that could run on water, and he was found dead." Now he was beginning to understand the mystery . . . and the risk.

Thing 2 spoke up. "Actually, there've been two of those, and a third one thought he'd found backers for his company, accepted their funds, and the investors ended up being a front for Big Oil and shelved his work to never see the light of day."

"There are more examples, but I think you get the picture," said Thing 1. "So, what we're about to offer you presents a risk. Our work won't be in the shadows anymore, quite literally. The state, feds, military, Big Energy, they will all come wanting to know where this technology came from. If they think you know, they won't stop trying to extract that info from you. They'll use whatever means they think necessary, all under the heading of national security."

"And if we do know your names and tell them, then they go looking and find you and—"

"And we're locked away or killed, and this life-altering technology will never help anyone."

Pete continued. "The point I was going to make is it

sounds like the risk is on both sides here."

"True, but if you don't know who we are or where we came from, and they realize that, you'll be safe. Or maybe I should just say safer."

Pete and Dean nodded. "Point taken. So, what kind of tech are we talking about?"

"Okay, but at this point, anyone who doesn't want to take the risk needs to leave the room, and everyone staying needs to agree that what we say from this point on doesn't leave this room. We're beyond the point of requiring written non-disclosure agreements but still want your word as Christians not to go spreading this around. Again, part of this is for your safety. You never know who might be listening."

No one left the room, and all agreed to the terms.

Thing 2 spoke. "You saw our truck out there, right?" They all nodded. "Would you believe it's all-electric and requires no recharging? Not only is it still running while we've been in here, but it's also powering your building." Three sets of eyes went wide. "Theoretically, in a car, instead of parking it in the garage to recharge its batteries, you could plug it in to help power your house. But it makes more sense to downsize the motor to fit the EV."

Thing 1 nodded. "Not saying where we came from, but you can drive that truck across the entire country and back, and do it all again, without needing a recharging station. Now, there is one battery in there. It's made of graphene and requires zero lithium. It's used only to restart the motor when needed."

As an electrical engineer, Pete was now thoroughly engaged. How was this possible?

Larry laughed. "I can tell from Pete's face that you've got him hook, line, and sinker. He's the supervising engineer here for LADWP. Has an electrical engineering degree from UCLA."

Think 2 smiled. "Well, take your electrical engineering textbooks and manuals and throw them all out."

"We won't tell you how this works. Again, for your protection."

"Sounds fair enough," said Pete. "So, what's your offer?"

"That container on the back has four units in it that should be able to power most of your city. Maybe all of it from the number of trailer homes we saw as we drove around. We'd like to give the unit to you, the church."

"Give it to us?" asked Dean. "Why?"

Pete wondered the same thing. "Yeah, why us and what would it cost?"

"No cost to you. In fact, the unit is already paid for."

This made no sense.

"So again, why us?"

"Are you familiar with a church in the city called Destiny in Christ?"

Peter nodded. "Sure. It's a big church with an elementary school and a senior living center. The pastor there and I went to Bible school together. He wanted to do the big urban church thing, and I chose the, well, more of the itinerant preacher route. He, uh . . . well, I shouldn't say anything more."

"No, go on. I think it plays into the story," said Thing 1.

"Well, lately, he drifted into more of a love-and-acceptance kind of doctrine that's not fully biblical. He started losing his more conservative members. I've always been more the repentance and God's grace lead to salvation type of preacher."

"Yeah, big on repentance," said Larry.

Pete smiled as Dean chuckled.

"Go woke, go broke," said Dean.

"Or face God's judgment, perhaps?" asked Thing 1. "They purchased this unit to power their church, school, and assisted-living center. We were halfway there when we got a call from the pastor. Vandals defaced and then burned down his church and school shortly after the blackout hit."

All three men frowned. "That's awful," said Pete. He could barely imagine the heartbreak of seeing one's lifework go up in flames. Yet, he also knew that increasing persecution of the church was ahead for all of them.

"Since they no longer have a use for it, I asked what he wanted to do with it. Since we already had it configured and were en route to him, we weren't going to be able to refund his money. He asked that we give it to you."

Pete's eyes widened. "Really?"

Thing 1 nodded. "I think he knew that its power generation could make a difference for the whole town while giving your church a real boost."

"Did he actually say that? I mean, we were good friends in Bible school, but not so close in the last few years."

"Not in those exact words, but yeah."

They discussed other details, such as how the church could become the power provider for the city, charging much lower rates than LADWP, and using those funds to benefit the community. Of course, that route would likely entail legal challenges from LADWP and state regulatory issues. And it would require smart meters to monitor power usage at each home or business. Or they could offer the power for free, particularly during this immediate crisis.

Finally, they discussed practicalities. This was right up

Pete's alley.

"Where's the town's substation? It would be easiest to hook it into that."

"Gone. The three power plants within the gorge were wiped clean and the Bishop Creek plants had their substations fried by the demand surge. But their power goes downstream into LA. We get, well, got our power from the Bishop Power Plant at the end of the gorge."

"Is there a nearby trunk line we could tap into? As I said, this unit was configured for three buildings, not a small city. It won't put out the voltage needed to travel long distance."

"I know just the place," replied Pete.

TWENTY-SIX

Heather had tried to keep an eye open for the police and EMS, but two nights of sleeping in her car held other plans for those eyes. She had opened the windows in their home to try to capture as much of the breeze coming up through the pass as possible. The sound of car doors slamming woke her, and she noticed flashing lights dancing through her kitchen. She heard knocking at her front door and opened it to find a police officer.

"Ma'am, I'm Officer Coleson. I understand you discovered the couple next door. Could you step next door and walk me through it?"

Dusk settled into the northern suburbs of L.A. Under normal times, it would have been an ideal time to grill out and socialize on the patio. Normal times. That seemed a distant memory, despite the blackout having occurred only two and a half days earlier.

"I didn't want to use the garage door battery and our electronic lock on the front door wouldn't work without WiFi. Well, actually, I couldn't remember the combination either, so I walked around to get the hidden key to a side door, That's when . . ." She proceeded to tell him what had led to her discovery and how she broke the glass on their patio door. She offered as much detail as he requested. She mentioned getting her medical neighbor involved and covering the bodies to give them some dignity while waiting for EMS. The idea of the sheets also keeping the insects away creeped her out. He thanked her, both for her detailed account as well as for being a good neighbor and checking on them.

"Oh. Just a second." She ran to the man's study and collected an address book she had found earlier. She handed it to the man. "I flagged the couple's kids. They need to be notified."

He nodded. "We'll take care of it. Thanks."

She stood off to the side of their driveway watching the EMTs load the bodies into their ambulance. Tears again fell.

"Hon? Heather? Wh-what's going on?"

The sound of that familiar voice brought a flood of relief to her mind. She turned and ran to her husband, grabbing him hard. She didn't want to let go. "I've been so worried. Where have you been?"

"I need a glass of wine for that story. What happened to the Littels?"

Without going into detail this time, she told them they had been running their generator in the garage and had died of carbon monoxide poisoning.

He shook his head. "Sad. They were excellent neighbors. With the level of education in this neighborhood, I would never have expected that." As the ambulance drove away, with the patrol car following, he led her back into their home.

"I really need a shower."

"No water, either," she replied. "There are wet wipes."

"Ugh."

She looked him over. Despite the two-day stubble, which she thought looked kind of sexy, he didn't appear too worse for wear. But some things were missing, and she noticed his "shoes."

"What are you wearing on your feet?"

In fact, on closer inspection, those weren't his pants or shirt either.

He popped open a bottle of Cabernet and filled a glass halfway for her, but to the rim for himself. He shook his head.

"And where's your car?"

"I had to walk home."

"What?!"

"Yeah. Walked."

"And your shoes wore out?"

He laughed and shook his head.

"We were at the work site in Santa Ana when the blackout hit. At first, we didn't think much of it. California is California. Earthquakes, wildfires, and blackouts. Part of our everyday lives." He shrugged. "Anyway, we kept working on some details of the project and realized after a couple of hours that this wasn't likely to be a short-term inconvenience. So, Chet and I decided to call it a day and head home. We get to the parking lot and see some punks siphoning the gas from our cars. They got away and left us nothing."

He took a long drink of wine.

"Chet lives in Irvine, so walking home for him was a snap. I tried to call for an Uber. No cell service. That's when I realized things were serious. At least there was still water there. So, I started walking. Tried hitchhiking but no one would stop. Then I noticed how crazy things were getting. Cars careening through intersections. Fights. It was like folks in the city took crazy pills or something."

Another long drink. Heather could see him finally starting to relax.

"I was north of Disneyland and trying to avoid the homeless camps, but those folks were out on the streets in droves. I was stopped at knife point. Two guys. Took my laptop, cash, and watch."

That's what was missing—his $6,000 Tag Heuer. At least he hadn't been wearing the $40,000 Phillipe Patek. He never wore that one to work.

"I kept following the 5, but it was getting late, almost dark. So, I took a clue from the homeless I'd seen and found a safe place to sleep. Not that I got much sleep. Every noise had me jumping. The next morning, I hadn't walked another two miles when I was stopped again, at gunpoint this time. I explained that I had been robbed the day before and all I had left was credit cards, which wouldn't work in a blackout. He took them anyway, along with my blazer. At least he didn't hurt me."

The third drink drained the glass.

"I made it through downtown and past Skid Row unscathed. Figured I would follow the 101 as a shortcut. Go up to Universal City and get Ventura Blvd to come west. By then, the 101 was a parking lot of abandoned EVs. I was making good time. Saw lots of small groups breaking into cars, but they didn't seem interested in me. I must have jinxed myself in thinking that because when I got to Hollywood Dell, three young guys stopped me. I told 'em I'd already been robbed, twice, and didn't have anything of value. Showed them my empty wallet. One guy grabbed it, took my ID out, and flipped it back at me. Then the bigger guy told me to strip down. He took my pants and shirt and left me his. The third guy took my shoes and left these things for me. At that point, I looked truly homeless and wasn't bothered. From that point on, others on the street avoided me."

She tried not to laugh. In hindsight, he made it sound like something of a comical adventure. But most of all, he hadn't been hurt. For that she was grateful. He had made it home in one piece. The old, misfit clothing could be tossed in the trash.

"Maybe I need to spray you with Lysol or something." He filled his glass again. "And you can sleep in the guest bed. Don't want bedbugs."

He squirmed at the thought. "Yeah, I wondered if I might have been better off walking home in my underwear and barefoot." He took another drink from his refilled glass and sighed. "Now I'm feeling hydrated."

She went into the kitchen, opened a cabinet, and pulled out two boxes of crackers. She made a quick forage into the fridge, pulled out an opened packet of vintage white cheddar, and made two plates of crackers and cheese. The refrigerator still felt cool, but that wouldn't last much longer even if they never opened it. When she returned, Dennis wasn't there.

A few minutes later, she heard a gas engine on the back patio. She stepped to the door to see that Dennis had claimed the Littel's generator and hooked it into two outlets in their home. He turned on several lights but only some of them had power. He took one of the heavy-duty extension cords and tried it in other outlets until all of the lights came on.

"There, now we have power to both sides of the service panel."

Then he turned off the majority of the lights.

"Don't want to overwork the generator, we need it most

for the fridge and freezer."

She looked at him aghast. "Did you just steal the Littel's generator? That just doesn't seem right."

He nodded. "I know, like an undertaker stealing expensive jewelry from the dead."

"Exactly. You're a tomb raider."

"Whoa, they can't use it. Why not take advantage of it? They'd probably agree, considering. Besides, it's temporary. I'll put it back once we figure out what we're going to do and where we're going to go." He gulped down a cracker with cheese. "And forget the wet wipes. I'm going to take a dip in their pool to clean off."

He had a point about the generator. And the pool? She hadn't even thought of that. She would join him.

He had stripped off the vagrant clothing outside and sat back on the couch with his wine. "So how have your past few days gone?"

She opened a second bottle.

TWENTY-SEVEN

"Let's go see the penguins, Daddy. I love the penguins."

Adam smiled. How long had he hoped for a day such as this? To have Rachel at his side and both kids running and playing around them, excited to see one animal after another at the zoo. His mind went back to that day five years earlier when then-one-year-old Carolyn was kidnapped at a park in Washington. He had descended into an alcoholic hell that tore apart his marriage.

And yet, now, on a beautiful spring day in St. Louis, all had been restored. And how appropriate was it that it was Good Friday? In two days, they would celebrate their first Easter together since that fateful day five years earlier. Indeed, God was the expert at restoring all things, and Christ was coming soon to do just that. Sooner than most people would suspect. As in the days of Noah, they would be surprised by His coming and shocked to find themselves under His judgment.

"Okay. Do you remember the way?"

"Of course, Daddy." Grace, as she was known today, began to run past the Lakeside Café and to the path toward the polar bears and penguins.

"Stay close!"

She slowed down. Arthur, now eight, stayed next to them.

"Can't we get something to eat first? I'm hungry."

Adam looked at his wife. "He has a point. It's almost noon, and we ate breakfast around 7:30."

She nodded. "Okay. I'm up for lunch."

"Let me take Grace to see the penguins for a few minutes while you two get food. What do you think she would want?"

Rachel gave him a what-do-you-think look, and he laughed.

"Of course, chicken nuggets and fries. I'll take a brat and fries, and a root beer."

"Got it."

Adam rushed to catch up with Grace and gave her one chance to change her food order. She didn't.

The penguins were now housed in what could only be described as an isolation chamber. The threat of avian flu remained high, so they were separated from the crowds by glass. Grace seemed mesmerized watching them waddle, slide into the water, and swim.

After ten minutes he said, "Your mom's probably got the food by now. Let's go."

She nodded and worked her way slowly toward the exit. He expected more of a protest. That she didn't, pointed to her being hungry, too.

As they rounded the lake heading back toward the café, his phone rang. It was Lynch.

He saw the other two sitting outside with the food and pointed Grace toward them. She ran to join them while he answered the phone.

"Hey. Happy Resurrection Day."

"You, too. Hope you have great plans with your family. I know this one is a milestone of sorts."

"It is. We're at the zoo right now. Getting ready to eat."

"You're making me homesick. The zoo was always one of my favorite places in St. Louis." There was a pause. "Anyway, I've been thinking about our last conversation."

"Okay. Which part?"

"UltraNet."

Adam smiled. He hadn't understood that he was having withdrawal from his program but in a sense, he had been. It had become a craving that required hard work to resist.

"I know you said you would stop using it and that you've been good about keeping your word. But I think that as long as you're not using it for personal gain or to cut corners to indict people like you were doing, we could use all the ammunition we can get to fight the Deep State's push to depopulate the world and bring totalitarianism to this country."

Yes! he thought. To hear his "accountability partner" give him the go-ahead to use the program was like a sugar rush flooding his body.

"Okay, that's reasonable. Anything I find, I'll pass on to you and you alone. You can distribute the info as you believe right."

"Fair enough. Keep me posted and enjoy the day at the zoo."

"I will. Have a great weekend. Give Amy and Joshie our love."

Adam watched Grace enjoy her chicken nuggets, but then, he realized she hadn't yet met a chicken nugget she didn't like. Arthur, too, engulfed his double cheeseburger like a pro wrestler wrapped around his opponent. Where did that kid put all that food? Adam worried about what kind of world would be left for them should Christ tarry.

Maybe someday he'd be able to tell them about UltraNet.

After all, Grace was an instrumental part of it. His motivation for developing the program had been to find her, and it had. Without UltraNet, the family outing they now enjoyed would never have materialized.

TWENTY-EIGHT

Pete shouldn't have been surprised to find an available boom truck in the department's lot in Bishop. After all, they weren't dealing with downed power lines or toppled towers. He signed out the truck, to the curious stare of the linesmen sitting there waiting for something to do. From what he'd learned, they were going to have a long wait. The supply chain for their needs had a lot of broken links.

He met T1 and T2, as he'd come to call them, at the predesignated spot right on the edge of town. They had lowered the container into the perfect location, too. These two had done this before it seemed. Now, all he had to do was provide them with wires. Maybe he should have shanghaied one of those linesmen after all. Line work, while he had done some in the far past, was not exactly his forté.

He raised his bucket to the nearby tower and inspected the connections there. He wanted one specific set of cables. He found what he was looking for and rechecked his work to make sure. Measure twice, cut once, was a saying his dad had ingrained into his mind long ago. He'd regretted not doing so more than once over the years.

Upon disconnecting the lines, he dropped them to the men waiting below. Finished, he lowered the bucket back into its place on the truck and joined them.

The far end of the container had its doors open. Finally,

he was going to get to see what was inside.

Wrong! All he could see was a solid wall with a control panel.

"Shoot! I thought for sure I was going to get let in on the secret sauce here."

T1 smiled as he shook his head. "Nope. Trust me, you're better off right now by not knowing."

Pete wondered if he could narrow the options down some. "I saw the warning sign on the back door that said 'Caution: Hydrogen inside.' Is it some kind of advanced hydrogen cell with those graphene batteries you mentioned?"

T2 laughed. "Won't work. He's impervious to playing 20 questions. The warning label is just what it says, in case somebody was to decide to cut or drill into the container to open it."

T1 nodded. "Don't want anybody blowing up in a hydrogen fireball. By the way, you should know that we've already programmed the system for this specific GPS location. Any attempt to move it and use it elsewhere without our reprogramming it will render it useless. Plus, we'll know about it. It communicates with our offices via satellite, so we can monitor it."

"Wow. You guys think of everything."

"We try to. Software control is one of our strengths. When, or should I say if, you folks rebuild your hydroelectric plants in the gorge, we can double your output. That goes with your Bishop Creek turbines, too, when you work to get those substations back on line."

That took Pete back. To double their output would be amazing, but how? The engineers at the department had worked for decades to squeeze everything they could from their turbines, and now these guys just show up and say they can double it?

"How? We've worked on those things for years."

They both smiled. "Like I said, take your electrical engineering textbooks and throw them out."

T1 said, "Our engineers are working on quantum drive for space travel right now."

"Really?"

They laughed and gave each other a fist bump "Got 'im," said T1.

Pete blushed.

"Just kidding, but we are serious about your turbines. And when it comes to rebuilding your plants, using our equipment to build microgrids eliminates the need for transmission lines. No acres and acres of solar panels that don't produce at night or giant wind turbines that kill birds, clutter the scenery, and are useless on still days. Not to mention becoming landfill nightmares when decommissioned."

"We mentioned we all have hearts for missions. Imagine systems like this to bring power to the third world. We plan on tithing these to missionaries around the globe."

Pete pondered that as he watched the pair feed the lines into custom-made, heavy plastic conduits to insulate them from where the connection within the container was made to the outside. The insulators were supported by steel towers that rose about ten feet above the container to raise the lines out of reach by most typical means of access.

T1 noticed Pete watching them. "Just an added precaution. To keep the lines away from innocent hands."

The men finished their connections and then cross-checked each other's work.

"We need to run some tests. Where's the first building that this line feeds?"

Pete pointed toward town. "Just down the road, and then it branches off. The small gray house."

"Okay. We'll talk with the owner if he's there and let him know we're running tests and that his electric might go on and off for a while."

Pete nodded. "Actually, the owner's a she, en elderly woman from our congregation. Her name's Judy Kirk, and if she offers you pie, don't turn her down." He smiled.

"Got it. Ask for seconds," said T2.

Pete laughed. "So, when do you think we can go live with this?"

"Maybe dinner time or a bit later. Also, start telling people to spread the word. We want everyone to turn on their lights at eight p.m. All of their outdoor lights, too. We want to test this unit to the max and see what it can do. We've never done a small town before, particularly with a unit configured for a different purpose."

Pete thought about that and figured eight would work. Official sunset was around 7:20 and twilight would end about 25 minutes later. With the mountains, the town got dark a bit faster. So, even with the clear skies they were seeing, eight should be dark enough for a good look.

"And we want to take some drone footage at dark of the town glowing in the midst of the blackout."

"Future PR?" asked Pete.

"Yep, gotta take advantage of it."

Pete nodded. *That you should,* he thought. *If this works.* He still wanted to know what *this* was and how it worked.

"Anything else I can do here?" he asked.

Both men shook their heads. "We've got it. If all goes as

expected, we hope to be back at the church by dinner."

"After some pie," added T2 with a grin.

Pete returned the boom truck, signed it back in, and drove to the church. Charlie was managing the place when he arrived.

"Hey, Pastor. Glad you're here. You've got visitors coming in a little while."

"Oh?"

"Yeah, some anchor from Fox 26 in Fresno is doing a big piece on the blackout. A guy named Chance Picard."

"Chance Picard?"

Charlie laughed. "Yeah, never heard of him, but with a name like that he was either a struggling actor at some point or his folks were Star Trek fanatics."

Pete laughed. "Okay, so what's the deal?"

"He's flying in with his team and someone from the dam inspection department. They want to do an aerial tour of the Owens River gorge and the damage that was done. They want to interview you."

"Dam inspection department? Did they say who?"

"Shawn somebody."

Pete felt a wave of relief. The man was alive. "Thank God. I knew he was up at the dam that morning. I found his pickup truck flattened against a rock face at Middle Gorge. I thought he was a goner."

Charlie echoed his sentiment. "Thank God is right. They'll be here about four."

Four? That didn't give Pete much time.

TWENTY-NINE

Heather worried about her husband. That first evening and the next day, all seemed fine. They mapped out their options. He had a brother in Wisconsin. She had a sister in Denver and a brother in Nashville. But neither one wanted to burden a sibling. They had the wherewithal to go anywhere and stay for an extended time, but in reality, they truly desired to leave this crazy state for good. Dennis had wanted to finish this one last project before making that commitment.

Today, however, Dennis wasn't feeling well. Having slept on the streets for two nights couldn't have been good for him. He got a cold every spring like clockwork, so between that and his adventure home, she might expect him to come down with something.

Yes, he had the usual symptoms of a cold—runny nose, congestion, cough, fatigue, and low-grade fever. But something about this illness struck her as odd. That was the weakness he complained about. He could barely get out of bed to go to the john, and his breathing was becoming more labored.

Yes, she was worried. She wanted to go to the Iverson's home to call EMS, but Dennis was insistent that they not be bothered. This was simply his annual cold, and he'd be fine. And once he recovered, they'd be on their way.

He had been irrationally insistent as she thought about it. He said he had started his customary zinc supplements, which always seemed to diminish his symptoms. But she checked. The one bottle they kept on reserve hadn't been opened. Then he started talking to someone in the room when only the two of them were there. She kept feeling the urge to go to the Iverson's, but she didn't feel comfortable leaving him even for the time it would take to walk there and ask *them* to call EMS for her.

She emptied the last of the gasoline on hand into the generator and turned it on. They would only run it briefly, to keep their food from spoiling, but unless she siphoned gas from one or both of her cars, even those times would soon be gone. She had never siphoned gas from a car. How did one do that?

Then what? With him sick and no gas to get away, he could die on her. The thought brought her to tears.

"Dennis? Please wake up. I need to know how to siphon gas from our cars. Dennis?"

She shook him gently. He seemed limp, and his breathing was worse. That was it. She was going to bother the Iversons.

She opened the front door and ran down the street. She pounded on the door and waited. No response. She knocked again. Still nothing. She tried to peek into the garage. Had they left town, too? All the windows into the garage were obscured. She couldn't tell. She tried knocking on the back door but saw no signs of life in the house.

Did she dare break in? No, she couldn't bring herself to do that.

She'd been gone too long, so she bolted back toward their house. As she approached the home, she saw a van ease down the street and pull into their drive. Her first thought was *Oh good, help is here.* But then fear hit. A van. Were they scouting the neighborhood and saw the open door?

Instead of running to the vehicle to seek help, she now approached with caution. A man exited the Chevy, but she couldn't see his face since he faced the house, not her. At least he wasn't wearing a hoodie to try to hide. He must have heard her because he suddenly turned toward her.

The emotional roller coaster of her week took another downhill plunge as relief again flooded her entire body and tears began to stream down her cheeks. She ran to greet her brother-in-law Dan and let his arms engulf her in a hug.

"Heather? What's wrong? Are you okay? Where's Dennis?"

"I-I . . . Oh, Dan . . . He's sick. I-I c-can't wake him up."

"Show me."

She grabbed his hand and led him into the house and their bedroom. Dennis lay still, but she didn't think his breathing had worsened in her absence.

Dan did a quick check of his brother and looked at her in alarm. "We need to call 911."

She began to sob. "We c-can't. No power, no cell service, no water, no 911. We were planning to leave but he got sick."

"That explains why no one heard from you two. C'mon, help me get him into the van."

Together they carried Dennis to the van and laid him across the back seat. Heather noted gas cans in the back, along with food and one carry-on bag that she assumed held his personal gear.

"W-we should leave the gas here. It'll make the van a target in any parking lot around here."

He gave her an incredulous look. "Really? It's that bad?"

"Worse."

They hurried to carry the gas containers through the house and into her garage. She made sure the generator was off and followed Dan to the van. The only hospital she knew how to get to was the one where she had taken the pregnant lady and her boyfriend, so she gave Dan directions to get there. She debated directing him to the 405, but all traffic in both directions appeared to have been stopped by the National Guard. *Why?* she wondered. Wouldn't they want to allow people out or let residents in to claim belongings? She missed being kept up-to-date by the local news. Her reliance on the internet had become an albatross around her neck.

As they drove, she recounted both her and Dennis' stories of leaving the city after the blackout began. He kept shaking his head in disbelief but kept noticing the broken windows and doors of the businesses they passed while avoiding abandoned cars.

"We're used to brief blackouts here, but I think what threw everyone into a panic was losing *everything* and not being informed about what happened. I still don't know what caused this."

"The government put a lid on it here . . . to keep people from panicking, I think. As usual, their best intentions were the exact opposite of what was needed. The rest of the country has a pretty good idea what happened. In fact, as I drove here, it was pretty much the only thing being talked about on radio and TV." He went on to explain about the dam failing near Mammoth Lakes and the results of that. "Some of the talking heads are saying it could take years to fully restore L.A.'s power grid and months to rebuild the water system that was lost."

Now Heather understood. L.A. was about to become a

ghost town, and she and Dennis would be part of the mass exodus.

As they neared the hospital, Dan asked, "When exactly did Dennis get sick?"

"Just yesterday, like I said."

"And it progressed this quickly?"

She nodded. "Why?"

"Not sure. Something I was told right before I left Wisconsin."

They cleared a first stop by some National Guard soldiers, pulled into the ER, and asked for help. Two paramedics from a nearby ambulance came to their assistance first, followed by a nurse from inside. Heather explained what was wrong, when her husband's illness started, and how quickly he had deteriorated. The three healthcare workers gave each other concerned looks. Heather noticed.

"What? What's wrong?" she asked.

"We can't really say yet, but this is the fourth case like this just this morning," said the nurse. The woman pointed Heather toward the ER registration desk. "Ma'am, please go register him and have a seat in the waiting room. The doctor will find you there if she has more questions or information."

Heather did not want to leave Dennis' side but acquiesced. What choice did she have?

Dan found her in the waiting room and sat down next to her. An aide stopped by and handed them both masks. Dan shook his head but complied.

"I'm not in healthcare, but even I know these things won't protect anyone from a virus."

Heather gave him a look. "But everyone says they do.

Please don't get us kicked out."

"Hey, I'm wearing it. See. Don't like it, but I'm wearing it. Just please don't tell me you wear a mask in your car when you're driving alone."

She thought she detected a grin under that paper as if he was trying to be funny.

"Um, yeah, sometimes. Actually, all the time until a few weeks ago."

That settled one question. She would not be happy living close to her brother-in-law.

She saw a woman in scrubs and a white coat enter the waiting room and glance around. "Heather Dickson?"

Heather raised her hand and the woman she assumed to be the doctor approached. Before Heather could stand up, the woman sat down near her.

"Hi, I'm Doctor Douthat. Can you give me the details on when your husband got sick and what's happened since?"

"I-I told the nurse already."

"I know, but I like to hear it directly."

Heather repeated the story and answered the handful of questions asked by the doctor. At the end, the doctor stood. "Thank you. We'll keep you posted."

"Do you have any idea what it is? I was told there are three others with a similar illness."

"Not yet. We're still trying to figure it out."

Dan leaned toward the conversation. Heather had noticed that he had been listening closely.

"It's an enterovirus."

"Excuse me. You are?"

"Dennis' brother."

"How do you know that? Are you in healthcare?"

He shook his head. "No, ma'am. I'm a cop from the

Midwest and one of my sources told me to be careful here, that an enterovirus had been purposefully released here using the power outage as a cover to start a new pandemic. You folks are in for another wild ride, doc. Be prepared."

"Dan!" Heather couldn't believe what she heard coming from her brother-in-law's mouth. When she saw the doctor's brow furrow above her mask, she became embarrassed. "I'm sorry, doctor. I-I don't . . ." She scooted one more chair away from him.

"I see," said the doctor. "Well, I'll be back when I know more." She turned and left the waiting area.

Heather turned toward Dan. "I can't believe you told her that. What do you think you're going to achieve with a story like that?"

"Save some lives, maybe. Dennis', in particular."

He proceeded to tell her about the egg-throwing protesters and the college kid he'd come to know. He related to her how that same kid called out his lie about his wife and had been completely on target, down to the reason for his wife leaving him. Heather wasn't aware that Helen had left him. She liked Helen. He continued to tell her about the warning about the virus.

"I arrive and find my brother fighting for his life after walking through downtown L.A. for two days to get home. First thing that came to my mind was this kid's warning. So, now can you understand why I said it, why I might take this young man's warning seriously?"

She had nothing to say, but he was correct. His statement made more sense now. It was crazy maybe, but more understandable.

An hour later, the doctor reentered the waiting area and walked straight to them. This time, both Heather and Dan stood to talk with the woman. "Your husband is doing better. We didn't have to put in a breathing tube. We're using something called Bi-Pap. It's a step down from full ventilation and is used a lot for sleep apnea. We used it a lot with COVID, too. He's doing well with it so far."

"Why does he need it? What's causing this?" asked Heather.

"He's developed something called acute flaccid paralysis. It's like polio—"

"Polio?" Alarm bells rang inside Heather's head. All she could envision was Dennis being destined for a wheelchair for life.

"No, no, not actual polio, just something kind of like it."

Heather could see heads turn toward them at the mention of polio.

"We usually see a full recovery from this type of AFP. I think he'll do well."

"So, what caused it?" asked Dan.

The doctor looked straight at him and said, "A non-polio enterovirus."

THIRTY

Shawn arrived at the Fresno Chandler Executive Airport at the requested time. He found it a bit surprising that he could simply drive in and park in front of the airport's administration building but took solace that actually getting onto the flight line required more effort. He underwent a brief security check inside the building—very brief, as all he had with him was his wallet and phone. His state employee ID also helped smooth the way.

A staff member escorted him out to the tarmac and all the way up to a party of people already waiting there. Shawn had expected they would take off promptly, but the helicopter had not even powered up.

He greeted the group and introduced himself. Extending his hand, he said, "Hi, I'm Shawn Westhope."

He had no idea which man was Chance Picard, but from the name, he gathered it was the taller of the three men, the one with chiseled features, broad shoulders, and perfectly coiffed hair for the camera. His wife would have commented positively on him given any chance to do so.

Instead, the middle guy extended his hand. "Nice to meet you. I'm Chance." He pointed to the taller man. "That's Chris, our pilot, and this is Chad, my camera man." He nodded toward the third man.

They shook hands.

"I figured we'd be ready to go." Shawn kind of wanted to get this over with, so the delay was a minor disappointment.

"We did, too. Slight delay. Flight control informed us that we need National Guard clearance to fly over any part of the blackout area. We thought that was only over L.A. itself. So, we're waiting. Chris has his preflight check done and our gear's on board."

Shawn's gaze was drawn to the sleek lines of the aircraft. Bell 407 was stenciled on the cowl over the door.

"Nice aircraft."

Chris nodded. "They are. Love flying this baby. Seats six. 133 knots max airspeed, and a range that should get the job done today without any problem."

"As soon as we get clearance, we'll take off and head over the mountains to Bishop to get one more passenger," said Chance.

"Oh? I didn't realize there'd be one more."

Chance nodded. "You probably know him. Pete Manning."

Shawn smiled. "Sure do. Great guy. I hear he saw the water coming and sounded an alarm that saved a bunch of people."

The reporter's brow rose in surprise. "Really? We hadn't heard that. Chad, let's remember to get something about that."

After about twenty minutes of chit-chat and a quick tour of the chopper, a man emerged from the admin building and waved at Chris. They had their clearance. An hour later, they landed in the parking lot of a church.

As they powered down, Shawn saw Pete walking toward them from a truck at the other end of the lot. After introductions, Pete said, "Glad you could land here. The airport is still pretty muddy even though the water's gone now."

Chris replied, "Saw that as I made my approach there. Shawn suggested your church."

Pete smiled. "You had me running in circles. I was on my way to the airport when I saw you turn away. I followed you back here."

"Glad you did. We had no way to reach you," said Chance. "By the way, sorry we're late. We needed clearance by the National Guard."

"Chance, we better get going if you want good light," said Shawn.

The two engineers sat facing aft with Chance in between. Chad and his gear took up the forward-facing seat. A few minutes later, they lifted off and headed toward the dam.

"Today I have with me Shawn Westhope, a senior dam inspector with the state, and Peter Manning, supervising engineer for LADWP's Bishop control center. Thank you, gentlemen, for joining us." Both men smiled and nodded. "So, Shawn, I understand you were at the dam when it collapsed. Can you tell us what happened?"

Shawn outlined the three ways an earthen dam can fail—overtopping, seepage, and structural failures. "Although the dam was close to being overtopped, I can't call that the cause. I'd say it was a combination of the other two. There were signs of seepage in the section of the dam that held its spillway, and my educated guess is that the seepage formed a pipe that followed the concrete of the spillway. As such, the additional water from all the snowmelt that found its way into the spillway, finally found that pipe and also caused both the soil matrix around the spillway and the spillway itself to collapse. As you can see out the window there, that's where that wide gap in the dam is seen."

Chad was busy recording video of the dam. "Got it." He turned his attention back to Chance and Shawn.

"Now you were actually on the dam at that moment, weren't you?"

Shawn nodded. "I was. Almost didn't make it." He went on to relate his experience with the collapse.

"Wow. That's an experience I don't think any of our viewers will ever want to have." Chance paused and then said, "Okay. Chris, take us down the gorge, as close as you can get. As if you were on a sightseeing tour."

Now it was Pete's turn. Shawn watched as Chance interviewed Pete. They passed by the previous location of the Upper Gorge plant and neared the Middle Gorge plant's remains. Shawn was impressed by Pete's estimate of a 75-foot wall of water and could believe that possibility considering that the gorge narrowed dramatically downstream from the Upper Gorge plant.

"Chance, I think Shawn's going to find a point of interest coming up."

Chance replied, "Oh?"

"There, over there." Pete pointed toward something metallic pinned up against the rock wall. Chad turned his focus toward the object.

Shawn shook his head in disbelief. "Oh wow, my pickup. That's a great testimony to the power of water. Glad I wasn't in it."

As they left the gorge and flew over Bishop again, Pete pointed out where the town had been flooded. Shawn, too, was amazed at the extent of flooding considering the dry plain on which the town sat. They continued downriver. Shawn pointed out the dam at Tinemaha Reservoir and spoke on how it had failed because of being overtopped. The destruction at the headgates of the aqueduct system shocked them all. Soon they were over Owens Lake. None of them had been born yet when that lake had dried up.

"Folks, here you're seeing the rebirth of Owens Lake. A hundred years ago, steamboats once plied the waters here, and then the aqueduct came along. It took so much water from the river that Owens Lake dried up and became a mineral flat." He provided another minute of narrative.

"Need to turn back here, Chance," said Chris. "Unless you don't want enough fuel to get home." He laughed.

Twenty minutes later, the aircraft settled down in the church parking lot again. The local sheriff sat in his car off to the side, waiting for them. Other cars sat there as well. As they powered down, the sheriff was joined by ten or more people and approached the group.

Pete looked at them and asked, "Wayne, what's this?"

The man smiled. "Well, Pete, we have something for you. Mr. Picard, if I might talk with you for a moment."

The newsman looked surprised but also curious. A moment later, he motioned for Chad to quickly retrieve his camera. Once set up, he stepped aside, next to Chad, and allowed the sheriff to have center stage. The officer stood next to Pete and all of the others filled in behind them.

"Pete, as sheriff of Inyo County I would like to present you with this Certificate of Appreciation for your actions on April 3rd, 2023. Your quick thinking saved the lives of all of those standing behind you, as well as several others we couldn't get hold of in time to join us. And I, personally, am among this group. We wish we could get you more than this piece of paper and our handshakes, but know that we are eternally in your debt." He handed Pete the certificate and shook his hand, followed by the handshakes and hugs of those in the group. The tears in Pete's eyes acknowledged his appreciation of their gesture. Even Shawn had to dab his eyes a couple of times.

"Thank you. I honestly don't know what to say."

A woman with an older boy and girl came up to him and held a group hug. Shawn had never met Pete's family, so he had to assume that this was his wife and kids.

The sheriff clapped his hands several times to get everyone's attention. "Folks, on a different note, we have to thank Pete for one more thing. Pete, we have no idea how you did this, but thank you for bringing power to the town. Word's gone out. We're gonna celebrate at eight o'clock."

Chance walked up to the sheriff and Pete. Shawn edged closer, too. How could Pete have brought power to the town? That would require a massive diesel generator and fuel. Where? How?

"Sheriff? What's this about power?" asked the reporter.

The sheriff nodded. "Somehow he's gotten hold of a generator to give us all power."

Pete shrugged his shoulders. "It wasn't me. And we're still not sure it will power the entire town. That's what we want to test at eight."

Chance looked at Pete. "Can we get this on record?"

Pete looked unsure but finally offered a subtle nod. Chance set up the interview and Chad began to record.

"So, Pete, tell us how you are planning to bring power to the town. It appears everyone is expecting something to happen at dark."

"Chance, I can't take the credit. A church in downtown L.A., Destiny in Christ, had ordered this generator to power its buildings, but then vandals burned down the church and its school a few days ago. The generator was already on its way, and the folks at Destiny in Christ asked that it be delivered here. We spent the morning hooking it up to the grid. We hope it will power the whole town, but it might not. I see it as God blessing our church with it, and our church blessing the whole town with its power."

"You say 'we.' Who delivered it and how is it powered?"

"I can't say."

The newsman's eyes shot up in surprise. "You can't say? It's some kind of secret?"

Shawn wanted to know the answer to this as well.

Pete waggled his head. "No, truly, I can't say. I have no idea who made it, where it was built, or how it's powered. The mystery men who delivered it would only tell me that it's powered by God. There's no fuel source that I can determine—no diesel, solar, or wind, and yet I know it's creating electricity. Judy Kirk's been baking pies all afternoon as it was tested." He laughed.

"So, what's happening at eight?"

Pete nodded. "We asked that everyone in town turn on all their lights, especially outdoor lights, so we can send a beacon of thanks to the heavens."

"Thank you, Pete." Chance looked about. "What time is it? The sun's starting to set. How long do we have." He hurried to the pilot. "Can we wait until eight, maybe get some aerial footage of whatever is about to happen?"

Chris shrugged. "Not wild about traversing the mountains at night, but we can do it. It's already 7:30."

Shawn turned as Pete announced, "Hey, Judy's here. Who wants pie?"

A woman unloaded nearly a dozen pies from her car and handed them to various people to carry into the church.

That's when Shawn first noticed that the church had power. He'd heard Pete explain that it was a mystery, even to him, and of all the people there, he would have expected Pete to understand the how and why.

For the next twenty minutes, Shawn enjoyed pie . . . really, really, good pie. That presented another mystery to him—where did this woman sell her pies and why had he never heard of them?

At 7:50, Chris rounded up their group. Pete came up to them and asked, "Would it be too much to ask that I join you for the aerial view? I know it means letting me off again before heading home." Chris approved the request, and soon they hovered a thousand feet above the town.

As eight o'clock hit, Chance looked at Chad. "You're getting all of this, right?"

"Sure am. Look."

Down below, lights began to show. Chris was the first to say something. "I don't believe this."

A minute later, Chance turned to Pete. His questions came through everyone's headsets. "You said two mystery men delivered this power source, right? And they told you that the system is God-powered? And you said the whole town is set for power, not just a selection of homes?"

"That's right."

"So, can you explain what we're seeing?"

Pete shrugged. "I can't see it from this seat."

Chance turned his monitor to show Pete. Pete raised his hands toward heaven and said, "Lord, I praise your Holy Name. Thank you for this miracle amid the darkness."

Shawn motioned to see the monitor, too. His eyes widened as he saw that the lights of Bishop formed a bright white cross.

THIRTY-ONE

Like everyone he knew, Aric was glued to social media and conservative news portals. "God's Good Friday Miracle: A Light in the Darkness of California," "God's Power Lights Up Bishop," and "A Light in the Darkness: God Brings a Modern Message of Hope to Ravaged Southern California" were but a few of the headlines following an 11 O'clock News report on Fox26 in Fresno. He searched for anything new on the event, amazed that there was still no credit being taken for the mysterious power source.

The response to the reports followed the usual lines. Social media was abuzz with it and Facebook quickly labeled it as possible misinformation. Twitter saw tweets on the topic start great wars of words, with most naysayers resorting to ad hominem attacks on anyone who called the report credible. Many on the left called the whole thing a hoax and that the video had been staged. Those on the other side accepted it as a miracle. The mainstream press avoided the topic altogether. Fox News limited its coverage to a single article. Yet, Newsmax, OANN, and The Epoch Times gave it extensive coverage.

Aric looked at the clock and realized he needed to hurry. Easter Sunday in any given year was busy at church between out-of-town family visitors and those Christmas and Easter "Christians" coming for their semi-annual fix. He had promised to help with ushering and wanted to be there an hour early to help set up extra chairs.

As he arrived at the building, however, he saw that he had underestimated the need. The church's small lot was already half full. He parked a block away on the street.

Jess greeted him just inside the door.

"Glad you're here. Dad wants the downstairs classroom opened up and chairs set up for the overflow. The main sanctuary is already filling up."

"What? Going to be a lot of disappointed people if they can't get into the main hall."

Jess laughed. "Maybe some of them will learn to be on time."

Their congregation was known for arriving about ten to fifteen minutes after the service started on any given Sunday. To do that today would relegate them to the basement.

With the aid of half a dozen other young adults, all of whom reserved seats upstairs first, they opened the sliding partition that divided the room into two and set up two sides of seats with a middle aisle to mimic the main hall. One of the associate pastors wheeled in a large-screen TV and set it up in the front. At least those downstairs would not be limited to just the audio of the service upstairs.

He and Jess walked back upstairs to find the main hall nearly full . . . and they still had a good thirty minutes before the start of the service. They started to talk with some of the new people they didn't recognize. It soon became evident that the story out of Bishop, CA, had impacted people in profound ways. By the time the service started, they had talked and prayed with three couples who wanted to know more about God and the Christian faith.

As the music continued, Aric directed the latecomers to the basement. Several minutes later, he walked downstairs to see what kind of seating remained available. The place was full. He looked for Jess back upstairs.

"Jess, the basement is full. We're going to exceed our occupancy limits. What do we do?"

"I-I don't know. Let me find my dad."

A couple of minutes later, Pastor Larson followed Jess to the front lobby. "I hear we're full to the brim. That's great."

Aric nodded. "But what do we do with the people still trying to get in? We don't even have chairs to set up outside."

"Umm, get the audio team to set up speakers outside. Tell people we'll be having an 11 a.m. service, too."

A second service? Aric wondered how that would play out.

By 10:45 it appeared that no one was leaving. The musicians switched out with the second praise and worship team to take a short break. As 11 a.m. rolled by, praise and personal prayer became the focus of the morning. More and more people joined in on the lawn. No one wanted to leave.

Aric saw firsthand the results of God Himself doing power evangelism. It made his two small efforts seem minuscule. His thoughts centered on the revival that had erupted at Asbury University in Kentucky. Were they now seeing that Holy Fire spreading to Kenosha? If so, might they see it on their own campus? The thought of that happening excited him.

As had become his custom, Pete rose before dawn on Easter Sunday. While they did not offer a Sunrise service, he personally held one in preparation for the day to come. In prayer, he asked for strength, discernment, and the words to speak to his church. In addition, he asked for a double dose of wisdom because the press had already descended upon the city of Bishop.

T1 and T2 had reappeared after the helicopter flew off and the crowds left the church. They, too, had been surprised by the cross of light. They reassured him that it was not of their doing, but indeed a miracle of God. They recorded the whole thing via drone. After showing him their video, they left. They hadn't expected the television news team to catch the lighting celebration, but upon learning about it, they knew they needed to disappear. Pronto.

Pete had not thought it wise for them to leave and to try to traverse the mountains in the dark. Yet, after seeing a dozen news vans arrive by nine a.m. the next morning, he knew they had been right to do so. By noon, another dozen had arrived. Not only had God's message of hope become the news of the day, but curiosity about a generator powered by God had become a focus for the curious.

To the best of his knowledge, no one had yet tracked down and discovered the container. That took some of the pressure off. The news crews stuck close by the church, and Pete found himself fielding questions all day Saturday. It became annoying at times. He had an Easter Sunday service to finalize. He ultimately resorted to working at home, not in his office. It was the only way he was going to get his sermon done.

On Sunday, he arrived at the church at eight a.m. to find his elders busy setting up a stage and chairs outside.

"Hey, Pastor Pete. Have you heard what's coming?"

The comment took him by surprise. "Uh, no. I mean, I know the news crews are here. Is there something else coming?"

"The sheriff's department came by to inform us that a line of cars is coming to Bishop from the south and another from the north. I have no idea how anyone coming from the south would know about this, unless they're all coming from Bakersfield, not L.A. Communications in L.A. is still in shambles according to the sheriff."

That made sense to Pete. There was no direct route from Bakersfield thanks to the mountains. Pilgrims would have to move south from Bakersfield to Mojave, near Edwards AFB, and pick up U.S. 395 north to get to Bishop. Folks out of L.A. would also have to take that route, but like Charlie said, how would they have known about the miracle?

"Route 395 is jammed in both directions, and folks are asking for directions to the church. The department is holding them off until we can get set up here. I asked them to give us until nine."

Pete didn't know whether or not to feel intimidated but felt confident that God would not let him down. "At least the weather is going to be great."

Charlie laughed. "Did you think God wouldn't have thought of that after His light show?"

Pete smiled. "No, He wouldn't, would He?"

By 9:45, the remainder of the parking was packed, as were nearby fields and streets. This was going to be an Easter service for the records. Revival was coming to the Sierras.

THIRTY-TWO

Werner couldn't escape it. Every news source he turned to for the past week covered the alleged "Miracle of Bishop." He had expected that of the misinformation carriers of the U.S. but even the U.S. mainstream media had caved. They had found themselves losing too many readers and viewers to continue to ignore it.

Yet, what truly astounded him was the high level of coverage in their European media. In the U.K., the Mirror started covering it, followed quickly by the Daily Telegraph, Daily Mail, The Sun, the Times, and the Metro—all feeling circulation pressure to join the fanfare. Le Monde and Le Parisien followed suit in France. El Pais and El Mundo led the way in Spain, while Corriere della Sera informed the Italians. He was ready to congratulate Die Zeit, his favorite weekly in Germany, as well as their Munich paper, Süddeutsche Zeitung, for not following the center-right Bild, until they did.

Karl Marx had written, "Religion is the sigh of the oppressed creature, the heart of a heartless world, and the soul of soulless conditions. It is the opium of the people." Werner sought to free man of its self-imposed oppression and to free men's souls to become all that nature intended them to be. Once freed, men would no longer need a mythological higher being in which to find solace. They would no longer need religion to bring comfort to the hurt. They would find all of that within themselves.

The World Order Council was formed with that goal in mind, but to succeed they needed to free the earth, too. Overpopulation, climate change, dwindling resources, food scarcities, and man's inhumanity to man had overtaken the globe. How would they support a new world order capable of freeing man's soul without dealing with such issues? And how could they succeed without the guidance of men like himself?

So, Werner looked beyond the "Miracle of Bishop." The whole thing had to have been carefully constructed, an elaborate hoax. Or perhaps the news team had concocted the video for ratings. Either way, Werner saw it as serving his purpose. While millions focused on the ruse, they remained blind to the spreading virus emanating out of L.A.

A knock on his door preceded its opening.

"Sir, I have your update from Los Angeles."

"Come in, Edvin."

The young man came into the office and sat down opposite Werner. He handed Werner a written brief, as per usual.

"The brief details the highlights and known stats. There is a 36 to 48-hour delay in our people reporting to us because of the communication issues there. I asked them to remain in the shadows so that they do not arouse any suspicions."

Werner nodded.

"As you can see, the virus has established a strong foothold. EMS is struggling to keep up with demand, as are the police. Fuel remains a problem for them, despite gasoline tankers supplied by the National Guard.

Acknowledging that and the reporting delay, as of two days ago we had over a hundred confirmed dead in the homeless camps and surrounding areas. Interviews with survivors in the camps say the people got sick and too weak to breathe, which points to the enterovirus and its paralysis. Our people have started spreading the polio scare."

"So far, good. What about local hospitals?"

"First, sir, you should know that we are beginning to see an exponential rise in cases."

Werner nodded again.

"As for the hospitals, the first few cases were reported as unknowns, but someone at one hospital in the northern suburbs figured out that it's a non-polio enterovirus. They communicated that to other healthcare facilities, and now they're starting to treat patients with ventilation support. No deaths reported to date there."

Werner frowned. "That is not good. That goes against our need to use the fear of polio to push the vaccine that our pharmacy friends will say is in the pipeline."

Edvin nodded. "We've asked our media people to begin the rumors of a polio resurgence. Perhaps we can get ahead of this."

Werner hoped so, too, but feared that the truth now coming out about COVID from the PfenRich data dump and making its way through conservative channels might produce a "fool me once, shame on you, fool me twice, shame on me" scenario. Fifth-gen PsyOps required gullibility and believability for success. With COVID they had had the element of surprise to create a fear of the unknown and had pushed the vaccine on an unsuspecting populace. Now, there were too many skeptics, as well as thousands of families affected by vaccine injuries who would not be fooled again.

"Perhaps, but let's accelerate the plan. Have the virus introduced in Texas and Florida. We'll see how our conservative friends there deal with it. Oh, and let's release it in Singapore and Hong Kong. After the first couple of dozen cases, ask our friends at the CDC to produce a tracking report to link those cases back to L.A. Once we show it spreading quickly, we can stir up the fear factor in the media. And ask the CDC to implicate polio, too."

Edvin made a few notes on his device.

"Edvin, what do you make of this event in Bishop, CA?" Werner wanted to hear his aide's perspective on the supposed gift from God.

"Sir, I think it is a clever hoax timed perfectly for the Christian holiday. However, there are those within my own family who believe it to be true. One cousin goes so far as to say the mysterious men must have been angels."

Werner chuckled. "We all have *those* family members, don't we? The crazy uncle or off-their-rocker cousin."

Edvin smiled. "Yes, sir. It would seem so."

"What about this so-called God-powered generator? Have we any information on it yet?"

This was twice in less than two weeks that Werner had heard mention of power technology that he had no previous information on. He prided himself on being up-to-date and knowledgeable on green energy, and yet, this "God machine" made him look ignorant.

"Yes and no. The leader of the church to which it was donated has informed authorities that he was told that it is GPS dependent and that moving it will disable it without being reprogrammed by the company. We are told that there is also a hazardous warning label about hydrogen inside, so it would seem that cutting into it could be dangerous."

"What company is it?"

"We don't know, and he doesn't know."

"Or so he claims."

"Yes, so he claims."

"So, ask our friends in military intelligence to take it and him, under the guise of national security. We need to get it open, see what's powering it, and reverse engineer it if it looks promising."

THIRTY-THREE

Over the Easter weekend, Heather wondered if she would ever see this day. As the nurse wheeled Dennis out of the main entrance of the hospital to the waiting car, Heather reflected on how just a week earlier, Dennis' condition had deteriorated to a point where the doctors fully intubated him and placed him on a ventilator. Her husband could blink his eyes to communicate yes and no, but otherwise seemed fully paralyzed. Unlike using ivermectin or hydroxychloroquine for COVID, no one had yet to find a similarly effective treatment for this enterovirus, and it became a game of simply waiting it out and supporting a patient's breathing.

And waited it out they had. After two days of full ventilation, Dennis was able to return to the Bi-Pap machine and quickly recovered from there. Now, ten days after it started, they were heading home. Sort of.

Dan sat in the driver's seat of the Range Rover waiting for them. As they neared the vehicle, he jumped out of the car and ran around to the other side to help. With Dennis inside, he had started back to the driver's side when the nurse stopped him.

Heather overheard her say, "Doctor Douthat wanted me to thank you and your friend again for the heads up on the virus. None of them had ever seen polio or even non-polio flaccid paralysis. They might still be scratching their heads over this had you not mentioned the enterovirus. They let other area hospitals know as well. Your comment has probably saved dozens of lives already."

"I'll let my friend back home know. I thought it sounded a bit crazy when he told me, but, well, he's told me other things in the past two weeks that were dead on, so I figured it wouldn't hurt to mention it. Glad it's been helpful."

The nurse nodded and turned to take the wheelchair back inside. Heather looked at him.

"I think I'd like to meet this young friend of yours."

"Well, seems like you're going to get that opportunity."

She nodded. They had spent the previous day packing valuables into the van, which was parked in their garage for safekeeping. Upon arrival home, they would complete their packing into the Range Rover, fill both vehicles with the gas in the spare cans, return the generator to its rightful home, and leave.

The National Guard still had most access into the city closed, so they would have to travel north first. Fortunately, that fit their plans. Their goal for the day was to get to Stockton, but they wouldn't be alone.

Hundreds of people were now leaving L.A. daily, and they, too, could only go north or east. Each part of the city had its specific evacuation routes, which some would find frustrating. If you lived in the northern suburbs and wanted to go to, say, Texas, you would have a circuitous route via I-5 north ahead of you. If you lived in the southern neighborhoods, you would find yourself on I-10 going east even though your destination might be Portland or Seattle.

Of course, no one wanted to go to Portland either. Nor San Francisco for that matter. Even major chain stores and restaurants were abandoning those cities.

An hour later, with vehicles packed, Heather and Dennis in their Range Rover followed Dan in the van as they joined the slow parade on I-5 north. Maybe they'd make it to Stockton by dark . . . and maybe they'd find rooms there. Gauging from the line of traffic they joined, the odds weren't in their favor.

Pete began to wonder whether or not the power supplied by the mysterious container was worth all of the fuss. Yes, it was great to have power again. People were so accustomed to it and the modern conveniences electricity made possible that they took it for granted . . . until it was gone. Having those niceties restored after being told it could take years for power to come back to the city was indeed a blessing.

However, sometimes blessings had a flip side. Whereas the stream of curiosity seekers over the holiday weekend appeared drawn by either an interest in Christianity or in seeking something, anything, supernatural, the parade of people since then seemed drawn by the container itself.

First came his own bosses wanting to know how it worked and what role did he play in its development. They felt convinced that he had developed a new technology on their time and nickel, and they wanted, almost demanded, the rights to it. They brought up the hydrogen warning and asked about what was inside that warranted the alert. They asked about the label they found that said: "M-Cube." He hadn't noticed it before, and as far as he knew, the M stood for mystery, just as the two men remained a mystery. He debated with them for the better part of a day before they believed that he had nothing to do with its development, hadn't the faintest clue as to how it worked, and didn't even know how to turn it on or off.

The next day brought investigators from the state. Other than not demanding rights to the tech, their questions were an echo of those the day before. And Pete's answers were the same as the day before. He began to think he might need to record it and run it on autoplay. Then came federal Department of Energy bureaucrats, UCLA engineers, scientists from Los Alamos National Laboratories, and more. Same questions. Same answers.

The scarier ones were men who never identified themselves but drove vehicles that seemed to point to Big Energy. Their questions more pointedly aimed at identifying the people behind the container's development. Their probing conjured up T1's and T2's warnings about suddenly and unexpectedly dying. Their questions also resulted in unsatisfactory answers.

The most interesting group was a band of five researchers from Arizona State University. While their questions were little different, Pete had overheard them talking about magnetic induction and more. However, he also heard them say they were years away from being able to generate electricity. They actually looked deflated at having been "scooped." Since Pete had no inkling as to how the container worked, all he could think was maybe, maybe not.

Charlie came rushing into Pete's office at the church. "Pastor Pete, I thought you should know some men are trying to mess with the container. They don't look familiar, so I don't think they've been here with any of the other groups so far this week."

"Mess with it how?"

"I think they're trying to disconnect it. They've got a trailer and forklift, too. Probably wanting to steal it."

Pete shook his head. He opened a desk drawer and retrieved his 9mm Glock. He typically carried it to deal with rattlesnakes and coyotes when he was out in the field. He'd never use it on a person, but then, he had never faced someone who might do him harm, and he wanted to be able to defend himself.

"Charlie, head over to the sheriff's station and let them know we might have some rustlers. Then grab a couple of guys . . ." He told the man what he wanted them to do.

Five minutes later, he pulled up near the container. Sure enough, there were four men there with one man on top of the container examining the lines coming down into the generator. He stood a short distance away, and they had yet to notice him. None of them seemed armed, but then, that's why they called it *concealed* carry.

"I don't think I'd mess with those lines unless you've figured out how to turn it off first."

All of the men started at his voice, and two quickly produced handguns. Pete wasn't about to escalate the problem by producing his weapon.

"Whoa, no need for guns. Just saying you'd better turn it off before trying to disconnect it. You know, like turning off a breaker at home before replacing a receptacle or switch."

"Who are you?"

"Peter Manning, supervising engineer for LADWP and pastor of the church that owns this. Right now, you're trespassing, not to mention risking getting electrocuted. And if you somehow manage to get this on that trailer of yours, you'll be facing felony theft charges in a county where you tried to steal their electricity. Wouldn't expect any leniency."

They looked at each other, and the man on top looked worried.

The older man with a gun pointed it at Pete and said, "Turn it off."

Pete shrugged. "If I knew how, I would. I've been wanting to figure this thing out ever since it was given to us. But like I told over a dozen government officials, engineers, and scientists this past week, I wasn't given instructions on how to operate it nor any kind of manual. I was told simply that moving it would disable it because it's locked into these GPS coordinates."

The man looked at the guy on top and said, "Disconnect it."

The guy looked back, shook his head, and replied, "You come up here and do it. You're the one with the most experience."

Pete heard two, maybe three, cars stop on the road a short distance away. His reinforcements had arrived. But he didn't look toward them. He didn't want to give their arrival away.

Pete shook his head in disbelief when the older man climbed the ladder and took a pair of heavy-duty cutters from the first man on top. Was he really going to try to simply cut the wires? What kind of experience did this guy have? Whatever it was, he was about to have a new one. Perhaps his final, earthly adventure.

The first man scrambled down the ladder and hit the ground just as the older man touched the first cable with his cutters. The man was thrown five feet into the air and a good 15 feet from the container, landing flat on his back.

At that moment, three sheriff deputies, Charlie, and three others appeared surrounding the men. All were armed. As the deputies moved in to handcuff the men, Pete rushed to the older man. He didn't expect him to be alive, and he wasn't surprised to see that he was correct in his suspicion. The man's hands and one foot were charred from the electrical burn. During training, he'd been shown pictures of the inside of a body that transmitted a high amperage current. Pictures were sanitized. He didn't need to see the real thing. The smell alone was enough to make you toss your cookies. He turned away.

As the sheriff himself arrived, Pete looked up toward him and shook his head. "I warned them."

The sheriff shrugged. "Nobody ever said criminals were smart." He looked about the area. "That said, you folks might want to add a tall fence and razor wire around this thing. You know, liability issues."

Pete nodded. "Good point. I guess our church is considered the owners of this thing, even though we've never received a title or bill of sale or whatever that would show us as owners."

He made a mental note to look into that as soon as possible. Too bad the electricity from the container hadn't restored cell service. Contacting the few fencing companies that served the area would take some effort without phones.

Pete waited with the sheriff until the local EMS arrived to transport the body to the morgue at Mammoth Hospital. Then they parted ways. He hated sitting on his Glock, so per his usual routine, he removed it from his waistband and placed it in the glove compartment. After doing so, he headed home.

He was roughly halfway there when a black van sped

past him in a no-passing zone. He was about to blast his horn in disapproval when the van suddenly swerved to block his way. As he screeched to a halt, three armed, masked men emerged from the van and rushed his car.

The surprise of the maneuver caught him off-guard. Before he could lock the doors, put the truck in reverse, or retrieve his gun, one man pulled him from the car and pushed him to the ground. A second covered his head with a black cloth bag, zip-tied his wrists together, and pulled him to his feet. A moment later, he was pushed into the van. He heard the other men hurry into the vehicle and the doors close.

As the vehicle sped away, he could only think, *This only happens in the movies. What in the world is going on?*

THIRTY-FOUR

Adam had been almost giddy upon "unpacking" UltraNet from its hiding place on the Dark Web two days earlier. He thought it appropriate to resurrect his program over the Easter weekend but that's where any resurrection comparisons ended. Still, in a secular sense, it was as if he'd found all the Easter eggs and stashed away all of the candy for himself.

The goal of relaunching the program was simple—to find evidence of the globalist agenda that one would never see reported. Over the course of the week, there had been much in the news about document leaks of Top Secret/SCIF analyses of the war in Ukraine, of the battle of Bakhmut, and of several allied and enemy countries. Allegedly, the documents had been released by the leaker to help make an online video game more "realistic." Yet, how would an Airman First Class have access to such highly classified materials, much less be able to remove them from the sensitive compartment in which one could view the documents?

Perhaps there was truth to the story, but Adam first suspected much of it was a smokescreen designed to take away attention from other behind-the-scenes activities. He liked to believe that to be the case until he realized that no smokescreens were needed. The mainstream media fell lockstep into pushing whatever agenda the Deep State wanted it to promote. Nothing more. That made the document leak story more likely to be one of "this is what happens to you if you don't toe the line." The alleged airman might not even exist.

Well, he wasn't about to fall in line with the others. He wanted the truth, a rare commodity in today's world.

The truth was that the Deep State wanted uniformity and compliance. To get that, they needed control of the government to be able to weaponize the entire system against those who resisted. Peaceful protesters on the wrong ideological side were criminals, while violent protests that burned cars and destroyed property were "mostly peaceful," and the perpetrators would never see a courtroom. Those who claimed that the 2020 elections were stolen would be castigated or imprisoned for insurrection. Likewise, the Deep State demanded control of the children, and if parents were to get in the way, they would be labeled terrorists, censored on social media, vilified, and if need be, arrested and jailed.

Upon first relaunching UltraNet, he found numerous reports on all of this. The conservative press was only showing the tip of the iceberg.

He had promised Lynch that he, and he alone, would receive the information Adam discovered. After a few texts, they agreed upon a time for the call.

"Hey, Lynch, still a good time?"

"Sure is. Now that your program has been back in business for a week have your cravings been satisfied?" He laughed.

"Getting there." Adam joined the laughter and realized it had been years since he'd been so freely able to laugh.

"So, do you have anything earth-shattering for me?"

"For some people, maybe, but probably not for you. I do have one bit of excellent news, however."

"Oh?"

"Does the name Edvin Bergstedt mean anything to you?"

"Not at all. Who is he?"

"He is Werner Koch's executive assistant, and . . ." He paused, wondering if he had a drum roll recorded somewhere on his phone.

"Aaaannd . . ."

"I found his email and phone accounts and have cloned them so that anything and everything he receives or sends, I'll get a copy."

"No, you won't."

The immediacy of Lynch's reply caught him as much as the negativity of it.

"What do you mean? It's perfect. We'll know everything the big man himself learns and does."

"Which is illegal. You can't legally clone the man's accounts without his permission, and I seriously doubt he'll give it to you. Even if you don't make use of the phone account for personal use, which is fraud, tapping into the accounts and sharing that information is like illegal wiretapping. We're not doing this the-ends-justifies-the-means thing. We have to be above reproach."

Adam felt his balloon pop . . . at 10,000 feet . . . and crash to earth with him in it. He was sure he'd found the ideal source for information.

"So, you don't want to know that they're planning to release their enterovirus in Florida, Texas, Singapore, and Hong Kong? Or that they've tried to steal the mystery generator in Bishop, California, and have kidnapped the church pastor there?"

He heard Lynch release a long sigh, followed by a longer pause. Adam felt frustrated.

"You know something, Lynch, I don't know what you expected. You became my accountability partner about using UltraNet, and I honored your advice about that. I refrained from using it until *you* brought it up and gave me the go-ahead to use it under certain circumstances—not for personal gain or to gather evidence to be used to indict someone. I've lived up to that standard, but now you're telling me the method I'm using is illegal. What did you expect UltraNet to do?" He paused. "This is what it does. It finds information, information that's not exactly publicly available on the internet or in your hometown, local newspaper. If they existed anymore."

After a moment, Lynch spoke. "Sorry. I guess I didn't fully think this through."

"From what I've found, it looks like our forewarning about the virus in L.A. has saved dozens, if not hundreds, of lives. Do we sit on this info and let people die in Texas, Florida, or overseas? Do we not alert the authorities in Bishop that the pastor there has been kidnapped?"

"Adam, this is a moral quandary I've wrestled with before. I guess I'm still wrestling with it. I've been in law enforcement for so long that most of me still says follow the law. And yet, part of me asks, what if the law itself is immoral? Now, I'm not saying that laws against fraud or invasion of privacy are immoral. They're not. But if breaking laws like those against wiretapping saves lives, what would God have us do?"

Adam's frustration eased. He saw the dilemma facing his friend, and honestly, he hadn't grappled with that himself.

Or maybe he had and had arrived at a different answer.

"Didn't Jesus kind of address that when He took a coin and asked whose likeness was on it, and then taught us to give to Caesar what is Caesar's and to God what is God's? Wouldn't God want us to save life and help those in trouble, even if it meant breaking one of Caesar's laws?"

He heard Lynch take a deep breath and slowly release it.

"Not quite the same thing, Adam. To me, the Bible also teaches us to respect the privacy of others. It's not so clear-cut. Some laws, like those allowing abortion, are clearly immoral from a biblical perspective. The Nazis made it legal to kill Jews, gypsies, and homosexuals. Again, such laws are immoral, no matter what you might think about certain groups. Standing up against such laws would certainly be biblical. Yes, I believe that God wants us to save life and to help those in trouble, but . . . but wiretapping laws are not so obviously immoral. Where is the line drawn?"

Yes, Adam realized he had come to a different conclusion. He wasn't looking to invade the man's privacy. These people were set to kill thousands again, and what he sought was information to prevent that. If he could save lives, help people, and fight for the freedom God had established this country to be a model for, he didn't care where the information came from.

"Lynch, we'll need to discuss this further, but right now I have this information, and I need to act on it. It would be great if you would, too."

"Agreed."

As they hung up, Adam realized that Lynch's puzzle was one that he, too, now needed to solve. Like that enterovirus, the uncertainty that faced his friend was contagious. He just hoped that, unlike the virus, it wouldn't paralyze his efforts.

THIRTY-FIVE

"Pete, you okay? Pete, wake up!"

Pete awoke groggy and dazed. Where was he?

"That's it, Pete. Wake up."

He felt someone shaking his left shoulder. He looked in that direction, and at first, his vision was blurred. He tried to focus on the two people standing there but they kept switching places and moving.

What time was it? He remembered heading back home in the early afternoon. Then what? Something strange had happened, but what?

The two people to his left slowly merged into one. A man. In uniform.

"Pete, you okay? We got a call that you'd been kidnapped. What happened?"

After a few moments, he recognized the man as the sheriff. And he was still in his truck. Or was it that he was *back* in his truck? If so, how? And it was now dusk, not afternoon.

He tried to talk, but his mouth felt like dry sand. He had had a bottle of water in his cup holder. Was it still there? He looked about. It was. With a shaky hand, he grabbed it but fumbled with the cap.

"Here. Let me help."

The sheriff took the bottle, untwisted the cap, and

handed it back to him. "Man, looks like you've been drugged. What happened?"

Drugged. That was it.

He took a mouthful of water and swished it about in his mouth to get rid of the sand. The fluid was so warm, he almost gagged on it, but he managed to get it down. Then he guzzled over half of it, quickly, to overcome the warmth.

"Sh-sheriff, I *was* kidnapped. R-right after leaving you at the container."

"What happened?"

"I-I was heading home, and a black van passed me and swerved to a stop in front of me. Two, maybe three men got out and rushed my truck. Two of them pulled me from my seat and put a black hood over my head." He downed another drink. "They dragged me to the van and threw me inside. The last thing I remember is a sharp stabbing pain in my right shoulder."

He pulled up his short sleeve and scrutinized his shoulder. Sure enough, there was a needle mark. He showed it to the sheriff.

"After that, I don't remember anything until you woke me up. It all happened so fast and was so unexpected, I had no time to react." He gave the officer a questioning look. "How'd you know to look for me?"

"We got a radio call. Someone managed to call us on our frequency to tell us of a pending theft of the container and that you'd been kidnapped or were about to be. We checked the church and your home. Your family was worried 'cause you missed dinner. I figured to try the roads between our last meet and your house, and that's when I spotted your truck here."

Pete shook his head. "You mentioned being drugged.

That's what I feel like, but I can't recall anything."

"Which can also be from being drugged. Are you hurt anywhere else?"

Pete twisted about in his seat and motioned the man to step back. He climbed down from the truck and almost toppled into the dirt. Wow, were his legs wobbly.

"Other than still feeling the effects of whatever they gave me, I think I'm okay." He felt around his arms, chest, and thighs. "No obvious pain."

"Let me see your hands."

Pete complied and held them out toward the sheriff. The man looked over his hands and inside the web spaces.

"Another needle mark here." He pointed to the web space between his left index and long fingers. "I guess they hoped you wouldn't find it here. The puncture mark, that is."

Pete shrugged. "And I wouldn't have either. Whatever they used, it's wearing off pretty fast now. I-I think I'll be fine."

"You sure? I can take you to the hospital."

Pete wasn't about to make that trip. His gut growled.

"I'm sure. I think I need to eat something. Then I'll feel better."

The man nodded. "Okay. You're sure you can't remember anything else?"

Pete shook his head. "Nothing, but if I start to remember anything, you'll be the first to know. I think I can safely drive home now."

The officer nodded again. "Okay, but I'm gonna follow you home."

Pete climbed back into his truck, started it up, and slowly drove home. As he pulled into the drive, the sheriff tooted his horn and continued down the road. Pete waved back. He was hungry, but what he really wanted to do was crawl into bed and sleep.

Werner had a busy schedule ahead of him that day and headed into the office before dawn. He hoped to review the finalized business transactions to be signed that day without any interruptions. As he walked through his outer office, he was surprised to see light coming from Edvin's office. He knocked gently on the door, and his aide opened it.

"Sir, you're in early today."

"And apparently you came in even earlier. Did you go home last night at all? You didn't sleep in your office, did you?" He felt concern for his aide as well as a bit of consternation. He needed Edvin at his best for the day ahead. Yet, had he been working him too hard?

The man nodded. "Yes, sir. Made it to bed early last night so that I could come in early today. It's almost nine p.m. in California, and I wanted a full briefing from our people there so I could report to you at our usual morning briefing."

Werner's mind had been focused on the upcoming business transactions. However, the mystery device in California had interrupted his thoughts on more than one occasion. He wasn't particularly fond of mysteries and wanted answers to this one.

"Are you prepared to report now? If you can brief me now, I won't be disturbed later."

"Yes, sir. I'm afraid it's rather short and has provided no real answers."

That was not what Werner wanted to hear.

"Go ahead."

"Here? Or shall we move to your office?"

"Here is fine. Nobody is present to eavesdrop."

"Yes, sir. Well, in a nutshell, we are no closer to knowing about the mystery device. The team hired by our people in Bishop was inept. The leader is dead—electrocuted—and the rest of the team was arrested by local law enforcement. They had nothing with them to incriminate us."

Werner frowned. The news itself was disconcerting, but what bothered him most was that their people there had hired such incompetent fools. Perhaps those who said that the term "military intelligence" was an oxymoron were correct.

"And the electrical engineer who is a church pastor?"

"Our man with the state investigators was part of a team that interviewed him earlier in the week. He had told them he knew nothing about the generator other than two men had shown up at his church to give it to them, and that they set it all up. He was told the generator was programmed to work only at those GPS coordinates. Moving it would render it useless. He stated he had no idea what was inside, how it worked, or even how to turn it on or off."

"That's hard to believe." Hard to believe in more ways than one. The man had to know more than that. But more importantly, what kind of device could continue to generate electricity without any energy input?

"I thought so, too. So, I instructed our people to take whatever measures needed to extract what he knows."

"Whatever measures? Was that wise?"

"We chose to use drugs, nothing that would physically injure him. They first sedated him with midazolam and took him to an isolated area. Once there, they hooked him up to a polygraph and then administered sodium thiopental."

Werner knew better than to believe in a truth serum.

There was no such drug that could compel someone to tell only the truth. Yes, various barbiturates, such as Pentothol™, and benzodiazepines, such as midazolam, sedated a person to a point where their mind was unable to fabricate a story within the short amount of time needed to fool an interrogator. But they did not guarantee the truth. They worked to make the person chatty. As such, the person tended to tell the truth as they knew it.

"Between the drugs and polygraph, he told the same story. He never wavered in what he told them. They took him back to his truck to sleep it off."

Soldiers and spies were trained to withstand drugs during interrogation and to pass a polygraph. It could be done. However, with his brief understanding of the man's background, Werner saw no way that this electrical engineer could do it.

"So, we're back to point zero. We know nothing about this container, how it works, or who made it."

"Yes, sir. I mean, no, sir. We still know nothing."

This was not a promising way to start his day. He frowned in dissatisfaction.

"Sir, on a better note. The virus has been released in Dallas, Orlando, Singapore, and Hong Kong as requested. The word from Los Angeles is that deaths there continue to be limited, occurring mainly in the homeless camps. And cases are now being reported from San Diego, Bakersfield, Fresno, and Las Vegas. Our friends in the media are tracking this and beginning to report concerns about polio returning as a major health threat. By the end of the week, the CDC will make a statement that it is investigating this new outbreak."

Werner smiled. The WHO meeting was but a month away. By then, the momentum of the new contagion would be such that the public would clamor for the passage of the new regulations.

THIRTY-SIX

Aric reread the two prophetic words given at church over the previous two weeks. The first was an answer to prayer, his prayer regarding his vision.

> Your prayers rise up before my altar like the incense I ordained for My temple in days long ago. As I watch from the heavens, those prayers are like beacons, lights calling those who are lost to come to Me. Continue to strive for the lost. Do not let My lights go out, but instead, let them intensify.

The lights he had seen in his dream dotting the U.S. at night were indeed those of people praying. Specifically, they were prayers for the lost. And yet, the second prophetic word seemed just as important, and it tied right into the dream he had had just as well.

> You sing of longing for revival.

> Look around. Across the globe, the fire of renewal has already begun. In many countries, it began years ago.

Millions in the Middle East, China, India, Africa, and South America are coming to Me.

Why? Because of desperation and difficulties. They hear of and see the light of My Kingdom and that My yoke is easy and My burden light. It has been persecution that drives them to want what I offer them.

Look around. Within your nation that fire of renewal began within My young people, just as it did 50 years ago. A time for jubilee. What you see and hear about now is that fire growing and spreading, just as it did 50 years ago.

Now, look within. Revival doesn't come from the outside. It comes from within. Look to your own hearts. Are you ready? If it's revival you seek, **you** must be the one to spread the Word. **You** are My hands, My feet, My voice to those around you. How can those around you believe if they have not heard?

Be firm in your faith and bold in your proclamations. Time is short. I am coming.

While many pastors taught that the charismatic gifts ended with the 12 apostles, that made no sense to Aric and was not considered doctrine in their church. After all, the Bible taught that God was the same yesterday, today, and forever. Why would His Holy Spirit act one way millennia ago and a different way today?

Aric believed this prophetic word to be authentic. It aligned with biblical teaching. And time *was* getting short. A Bible chronologist whose blog he followed had shown that there were 41 jubilee cycles between Adam and Abraham and 41 cycles between Abraham and Jesus. Today, mankind was in the 41st cycle since Jesus . . . with only a handful of years left in that cycle. The precise date was hidden, thanks to alterations in the Jewish calendar by the Sanhedrin over 2,000 years ago.

Other things pointed to Christ's soon return. In the Book of Revelation, John described an acceleration of climatic events preceding the Lord's return—wars and rumors of wars, drought, wildfires, pestilence, and more. The war in Ukraine threatened to become a nuclear war. China challenged Taiwan's air defenses weekly. Drought had devastated California until recently. Now the Midwest suffered drought with the Kansas winter wheat harvest being the worst it had been in decades. Wildfires continued in the west, as well as in Greece, Australia, and various other countries across the globe. Over a thousand wildfires had started in Canada since the beginning of the year, burning millions of acres of timber. As for pestilence, one needed only to look at what COVID had done to people all over the world, as well as to the economy and businesses. Now, a new pestilence had been released.

Other prophetic images issued within the seven seal and trumpet judgments were possibly on the horizon. Russia, in its war with Ukraine, had received clearance from other Black Sea countries to allow passage of its submarines armed with nuclear torpedoes. The goal of such weapons was to eliminate major ports, but the consequences poisoned the waters. That, in turn, killed the aquatic life. And waters turned to blood evoked modern-day images of red tide algal blooms. Thousands of fish had already turned up on beaches in Texas where the algae's toxins were killing them. Likewise, algal blooms along the West Coast, while not red, had already killed hundreds of short-nosed dolphins and seals whose food sources had ingested the toxins and transmitted them up the food chain.

What men called climate change had been seen as God's judgments throughout history. Such were the depictions in the Book of Revelation.

In addition, 2 Timothy 3:1-5 taught:

> *But understand this, that in the last days there will come times of difficulty. For people will be lovers of self, lovers of money, proud, arrogant, abusive, disobedient to their parents, ungrateful, unholy, heartless, unappeasable, slanderous, without self-control, brutal, not loving good, treacherous, reckless, swollen with conceit, lovers of pleasure rather than lovers of God, having the appearance of godliness, but denying its power. Avoid such people.*

If any scripture described the current state of society, this one did. This was fitting of Revelation's prostitute clothed in scarlet and riding the beast.

So, Aric took the prophetic word to heart. He and his friends were Christ's hands and feet on the earth, and it was up to them to spread the Word. Eagerly, they took time at the end of each day on campus to set up a table outside the dorms to talk to other students and hand out free Bibles. On weekends, they moved to the Kenosha Harbor to do the same.

As Aric stood with two others from his Bible group, one of the guys looked to their right and said, "Uh-oh, trouble."

Aric glanced in that direction and shook his head. So far, they'd had no problems threatening their endeavor. They knew that was unlikely to last, and now it appeared that that time had come.

A group of LGBTQ+ activists known throughout the campus was bearing down on them, and the looks on their faces were pricklier than usual. What surprised Aric most was that pink-haired Toni was among them. He knew the guy didn't have the chutzpah as an individual to confront them, so he must have found strength in numbers. Aric now wondered if this group had also been involved in the egg incident.

The guy in the lead of the group walked up to their table and promptly flipped it over. "Take your hate literature somewhere else. We don't want it on our campus."

"Your campus? It's our campus, too, you know," replied one of Aric's friends.

Another member of the group, a lesbian displaying a distinct butch vibe, grabbed a Bible from the ground and began to tear it apart.

"Hey!" yelled the third member of Aric's trio. Aric used his arm to restrain his friend.

Aric looked squarely at her and said in a calm voice, "Take them all. Tear them all apart. That doesn't cancel the truths in the words written inside."

The woman glared at him.

"We're not here to judge anyone, but all will be judged. Are you prepared for that?"

The woman and another whom Aric assumed to be her partner stepped toward him and spit on him. He shook his head.

"What? Didn't like that?"

"Would you? You complain that we're promoting hate on campus, but who's showing the hatred and spitting on people?"

The partner moved even closer and slapped Aric across the cheek. He refrained from laughing at the meager effort, and instead turned his head and pointed to his other cheek. She seemed to grin and wound up to hit him full-fisted, but he caught her swing midway and stopped her hand dead in the air. As he squeezed her fist, she began to scream.

Ms. Butch moved in head butt him, but he stepped aside in time, and she fell headfirst to the pavement. Her face bloodied, she stood up and began screaming.

"He assaulted me! Did you see that? He assaulted me!"

Aric sighed. This certainly escalated quickly. A crowd had already formed encircling them. He noticed a few cell phones pointed toward the altercation and assumed video was being recorded.

"Look out!"

The warning came in time for Aric to notice the guy who had flipped over the table lining up to round-kick him. However, Aric deftly avoided the roundhouse kick, used his hand to add to the guy's momentum, and watched him as he took a violent fall. Unlike the woman, though, he landed on an arm on the curb. Aric could hear the bone snap before the pain registered on the guy's face.

At this point, security came running and split up the groups. As the activists were herded away for medical attention and questioning, they continued to hurl accusations at Aric and his friends. Aric, on the other hand, took a few photos of the overturned table, the torn Bible, and other damage before starting to clean up.

Security Officer Ryan Krueger watched over them as they did so. For that, Aric was grateful. Ryan was a friend and would give them a fair shake.

With their stuff gathered and ready to put away, members of the Bible club took over to deal with it. Officer Krueger led the trio to the security offices to give their statements.

Aric had a bad feeling about the whole incident. Yes, Officer Krueger would be fair, but he had a job to do. Plus, the Dean of Student Affairs would make any final decisions. He and the dean had some history.

Aric knew he had simply defended himself. He had even turned the other cheek, although the Bible didn't say what to do *after* turning that cheek. He smiled at the outcome and the fact that the many on-scene videos would corroborate his story. Even if individual student videos fell short, they had made a point of placing their table right in front of a dorm security camera.

Then the Lord caught him up short. Okay, okay, maybe he hadn't fully followed Jesus' intent for that teaching.

THIRTY-SEVEN

Heather didn't want to complain. She understood that she was in no position to do so. After all, her brother-in-law, Dan, had gone out of his way to drive to L.A. and assist in evacuating them. Had it not been for him, Dennis might not be with them and she could still be stuck in Bel Air. Dan had not only come to get them, he had taken an unpaid leave of absence to do so.

Now, they were situated in his home in Kenosha. That was awkward with his wife staying elsewhere. Plus, by Heather's standards, the home was small. After several days there, the walls were closing in. She would escape to the harbor area and walk along the lake, but even that could not compare to the ocean.

Dennis seemed content, but it had been his childhood home, a familiar place. Although both boys had inherited the house jointly, Dennis had turned his share over to Dan. With his business and home in Bel Air, he had no need of the property, nor was he going to make his brother buy out his share when he had more money at his disposal than Dan would make in his lifetime.

"Honey? I'm going for a walk by the lake." No answer. "Dennis? Where are you?" She checked the bedroom they were using, followed by the kitchen, the basement, and back yard. Climbing the basement stairs seemed to take more effort than it should have. She stepped out into the yard and called, "Dennis?" Still no answer.

Now she felt a bit worried. He would have told her if he was going out. She noticed the side door to the detached garage ajar. She walked to the building and eased open the door.

However, as she leaned inside to look for Dennis, she became lightheaded. She tried to stand back upright but found little strength to do so. Her energy seemed to have been sapped from her in an instant. At the same time, her skin began to feel clammy as if she now had a fever. Her mind raced back to her husband's first symptoms. Had she caught the enterovirus that had afflicted him? He had had cold symptoms to start. Plus, it had been over two weeks since he had come down with the illness. She thought she had been spared.

"Dennis!" Her voice sounded raspy.

She fell to her knees. Where was her phone? Where was Dennis? She had left the phone in the kitchen inside the small fanny pack that she took on her walks. Could she make it back to the house?

After great effort, she found herself in the kitchen reaching for her pack on the counter. After four attempts, she snagged it and watched it fall to the floor. She managed to open it and retrieve her phone. She dialed 9-1-1.

"9-1-1, what's the nature of your emergency?"

"Help!" It came out as a hoarse whisper. She struggled to take a deep breath and forced her next words. "Help! . . . Off . . . icer . . . Dickson . . . home."

Aric had finished dinner with Mitch and his friends from

the football team and now settled in at his desk for an evening of study. He found such studies getting harder to focus on with the warming weather and just a few weeks left in the semester. Yet, having but a few weeks remaining for the term also meant finals were fast approaching.

His criminology courses were going well. He had little concern about those finals. However, he had signed up for a religion class, thinking it might be interesting and recognizing he'd likely get an alternative perspective from that taught at church. Whew. Alternative was an understatement. Alternative lifestyles. A substitute Jesus. The flipside of biblical morality. He wondered whether his professor had actually read the Bible at any point in his life. His challenge throughout the course had been to divert what was being taught back to what the Bible taught. His final would hold the same demand but with short notice.

As he tried to think about potential questions on the exam and refocus them on the Bible, his phone rang. CallerID revealed Officer Dickson as the caller.

"Hey Dan, welcome home. Hope your trip went well."

"Hi, Aric. It proved to be a bit of a challenge. Getting there went smoothly." He proceeded to tell Aric about his brother's ordeal and to thank him for the alert about the enterovirus. He also passed on the doctor's thanks about the virus.

"I'll let my brother know. He'll be glad to hear the warning saved some lives."

"More than some. Coming home took twice as long. It took us three days just to get out of California. The traffic leaving the state was worse than Chicago at rush hour, to give you some comparison. But, hey, that's not why I called."

Aric sensed that something was wrong.

"What's up?"

"My sister-in-law, Heather, is in the ICU right now, on a ventilator. From what's been reported, they suspect it's the enterovirus. She had no cold symptoms or other complaints. The paralysis just hit her like a train, sudden and severe. She managed to call 9-1-1, but if my brother hadn't found her in the kitchen and started mouth-to-mouth resuscitation before EMS got there, I'm not sure she would have made it. The doctors suspect a mutation of the original virus, but they won't know for sure for two, three days."

Aric had no medical training, but this didn't sound good. A mutation that gave no warning before the paralysis hit was not a good thing. And if he recalled correctly from the COVID mess, most viral mutations became more contagious with each round of change. However, each mutation was also supposed to become less severe. This one didn't appear to be so, if the doctors' suspicions were validated. The combination of greater severity and higher contagiousness would be trouble.

There was only one thing Aric could offer the officer. "Dan, can we pray for her? I'll get my friends to do the same." He heard a sigh of relief on the other end.

"That's why I called. Thanks."

Aric closed his eyes to be able to focus on God. "Lord, we come before You on Heather's behalf. You know what's happened to her and what *will* happen. We call on You now to bring healing to her body because You are our ultimate healer and Your Word says that You bore the lashes, the stripes on Your back, to bring healing to our bodies. We ask that You give the doctors and medical staff wisdom and discernment on how best to help her and that You give her husband, plus Dan and the rest of her family, Your peace, that peace that passes understanding because we don't understand how we can remain so calm when all is falling apart around us." He continued his prayer for another minute and said, "Amen. Thank you, Lord."

There was a moment of silence on the other end and then Dan said, "Thank you, God . . . and thank you, Aric. I wouldn't even know how to pray."

"That's the thing, Dan. Prayer doesn't need to be elaborate and lengthy in words. It simply needs to be sincere. God already knows what you need. In fact, while we're on the phone, I'd like to pray with you about accepting Christ. The Bible says that today is the day of salvation. You never know what might happen if you put it off."

There was silence for a minute on the other end. "Aric, thank you for the offer, but . . . well, I don't think I'm quite ready for that yet. However, I'm off this coming Sunday and would like to meet you at your church."

Aric wasn't going to push the man. He was available if Dan needed him. "That would be great, Dan. You already have the time and place, so see you then."

THIRTY-EIGHT

After dinner, playing with the kids, and the kids' bedtime routines, Adam dove headlong into his work. UltraNet had shown him that the real disinformation during COVID had come from the government and those agencies supposedly entrusted with protecting us.

The majority of those who allegedly died from COVID actually died of untreated bacterial pneumonia. So, those numbers again reflected that many so-called COVID deaths were of people with positive tests who died *with* COVID but not *from* it. The CDC had withheld this information.

The CDC had held a conference in Atlanta the previous week for 1,800 members of its staff from all across the country. Ten percent of the attendees became positive for COVID while there and 99.4% of those had been vaccinated. There was no data for 20% of the attendees or for unvaccinated individuals. However, since the conference was for CDC staff, Adam thought it reasonable to assume that most, if not all, were vaccinated. Still, they had a superspreader event and did not warn anyone outside of their own staff. Where were the news reports on this?

He also found data to suggest that Big Pharma was experimenting with the lethality of their vaccines. Three different batches of the mRNA vaccine could be identified by their lot numbers. Each group shared the same three letters in the alphanumeric sequence. One group had minimal, if any, adverse reactions associated with it. A second group consistently had moderate adverse reactions reported, while the third suffered severe reactions. Sadly, 47% of those receiving vaccines from the third group died. A fourth group appeared to function like a placebo. On a graph, each group's trends appeared linear, and there was no scatter between those trend lines which pointed to the fact that these were not simply random findings.

While trying to stay within the parameters he and Lynch had agreed upon, UltraNet was finding a lot of hidden data on COVID and the planning that went into it, but not much on the latest plague. That's what he needed. COVID was, in a sense, old news. If they were to save lives, he needed up-to-date data on the enterovirus. He retuned his search by stretching those parameters and soon the results were more rewarding.

Of the current outbreak of SEERS-23, as it was being labeled by the press, the CDC planned to push for new, emergency vaccine development by labeling this virus as a new polio. *Push* for a vaccine? There was no need to develop a new vaccine. It was already waiting in the wings and had been well before the virus was released. As for the new SEERS-23 "plandemic," they acted as if this was as unexpected as the dam failure and L.A.'s problems, when, in fact, they were complicit with the WOC and WHO in its release. They had already prepared "tracking" reports for the outbreaks overseas that would link those new cases with being spread by travelers from L.A. Yet, those virus releases predated the arrival of anyone from L.A. Would the press investigate that timeline? Unlikely.

One bit of information from Edvin Bergstedt's files

caught his attention. The man had been tasked with leading the re-creation of AlterNet. That confirmed to Adam that the WOC was behind that renewed effort, which he had foiled some months back. Bergstedt was now tasked with coordinating the SEERS-23 pandemic response. From Adam's perspective, their playbook hadn't changed.

Fear was a standard in the PsyOps program, so they had simply replaced fear of the unknown with fear of the known. What was more dreaded than polio? The famous images of patients in iron lungs filling a gymnasium or Franklin Delano Roosevelt in a wheelchair again claimed top billing in nightly newscasts. Of course, no one reported the fact that the gymnasium photo was a staged photo op—few hospitals at that time had more than two or three iron lungs, or that FDR's paralysis was the result of Guillain-Barré syndrome, not viral poliomyelitis. Again, the truth was masked.

Adam also found the report on the attempted theft of the mysterious power generator and the subsequent kidnapping of one Peter Manning. The man was not only the supervising engineer of the Bishop Control Center for LADWP but also a well-respected pastor. As the latter, Adam knew better than to suspect the man of lying about the generator. But for the godless WOC, no one could be trusted on their word. They had kidnapped the man and plied him with drugs, only to find out he had been telling the truth all along.

And then it happened. As he sought more information, he somehow had tripped an alert on the man's system. In an instant, he was shut out of the man's network. More importantly, he found his own search being backtracked. He quickly shut down his search before his program could be traced on the Dark Web and his location determined.

He stood and began his old habit of pacing. How? And as important, who? No one on that AlterNet team had the skills to foil him. Only one person he knew had such skills, but "Seth," whom he now knew as Dr. Caleb Wahlburg, was on his side. Wasn't he? Adam couldn't believe that Seth would turn to the WOC. No, there had to be a new nemesis on the scene.

THIRTY-NINE

Two weeks had passed since his abduction, but the hassles continued. Two more teams from the state had come to ask questions. One more from the federal DOE. And a dozen teams from various universities and research laboratories. Had the control center remained and had Pete been required to work his full day, he wouldn't have been able to keep up with all the lengthy interruptions.

He sat in the office at the LADWP facility in Bishop finalizing his equipment requests and preliminary budget requirements. He rubbed his eyes at the numbers appearing before him.

"Hey, Q!"

He yelled to an adjacent room where several of his men now "worked"—if work consisted of playing cards, backgammon, and penny-a-chip poker. At least LADWP kept them on the payroll . . . for now. At first, the higher-ups hadn't wanted to, but Pete and several other supervisors had successfully lobbied on their staff's behalf. After all, if they were all furloughed, with their experience, they could find work elsewhere with ease. Then, when the time came to begin rebuilding, there was no guarantee they'd come back. Where would experienced workers come from then?

"I'm beginning to see double. Could you run these numbers and double-check me?"

Quentin nodded as he entered the room. "Sure thing."

A couple of minutes later, he took a deep breath and shook his head in disbelief. "Wow. Folks downtown are going to faint upon seeing this."

Pete nodded. The eight-figure estimate for repairs and rebuilding was not going to be well received in this time of cutbacks, supply chain problems, and environmental surveys that sometimes took decades to complete before building could even begin. In truth, the environmental impact statements required today could cripple the rebuilding of these plants and delay them into the distant future. Such studies hadn't been required when these plants were first built, but now, the river ran wild again, and Owens Lake had water. Despite L.A.'s power and water needs, the environmental lobby was not going to step back and look the other way.

As they discussed rebuilding, the power went out. The two men looked at each other with surprise. Pete's thoughts, however, went directly to the idea that the generator was being hijacked . . . perhaps successfully this time. After all, the power was out. That meant the generator had been disconnected somehow.

He jumped up and ran from the building. Once in his pickup, he sped to the site where the generator sat. Upon arriving, he was shocked to see it being loaded onto the flat bed of a truck. Not just any truck. T1 and T2 were back. They had disconnected the generator and were halfway into moving it back onto their remarkable EV truck.

As Pete approached, T1 saluted with two fingers to his forehead. "Hi, Pete. Took you longer to get here than we expected."

Pete was perplexed and angry. "I don't get it. I thought

this belonged to our church. You can't just take it back."

"Sorry to have to do this. We had no way to communicate with you since the cell system remains down."

Pete frowned. "You could have come to me at the church. I'm there pretty much every afternoon these days."

Both men nodded. "But it wouldn't have changed the outcome. The timing maybe, but not the outcome," said T2.

As T2 continued to secure the container onto the truck, T1 climbed down, tossed a custom-made tarp to his colleague, and walked over to Pete. "First, let me reassure you that this still belongs to the church. You'll get it back, but here's the deal. I told you it was configured for a different use and that we monitor it remotely. Well, if you continue trying to use it for the whole town like we're trying to do, our tests show it's going to fail within a month or less. We know what we need to do to keep it running. If we take it now, we can do that at no cost to you, but we can't do it in the field. We have to take it back to our facility. Yes, there's a cost in manpower and some materials to us, but we're willing to absorb those costs and write them off as research, which this little experiment has been in many ways."

Pete had no counterargument to that.

"Second, we know that a man was electrocuted while trying to steal this. We're truly sorry about that loss of life. We hadn't foreseen that possibility. Because of this, we need you to develop a secure enclosure for the container for when we return it to you. That's for your sake and ours. Neither of us wants that liability. That said, we have an idea for a safer connection setup. We'll make those changes while we have it, too. You, on the other hand, can take some time to decide the best location for this and get the enclosure ready for us."

Pete had already contacted several fencing companies to

secure bids. T1 was correct, however, in that this location was not as ideal as he'd hoped. It had worked well on short notice, but Pete preferred having it on the church property and some new lines would be needed to make that happen.

"Finally, we hadn't expected what happened on Good Friday. The Lord surprised *us* with that one, too. While we're pleased with the spirit of revival that seems to be spreading across the continent because of it, the downside has been intense scrutiny, and, well, the search for us has scared us a bit. We're hoping that removing this container will reduce the curiosity and let us stay out of the limelight a little longer."

Pete nodded. It was as if these men had been reading his mind. "I wouldn't mind getting the curious off my back, too. I have my own work to do without facing a thousand questions almost every day. So, when do you think you can bring this back? The people here are going to be asking."

T2 joined them next to the truck. "The reconfiguration will take about a week, and the new connection setup, maybe another week. Travel time has to be added, and we'll need to move at night now to avoid detection. Pictures of the M-Cube have shown up on social media, so we need to stay off folks' radar."

T1 looked at Pete. "Really, that's the minimum. The bigger question is when can we bring it back without attracting attention to it again? That could be weeks."

Pete sighed. He had grown accustomed to having power again, as had everyone he knew in town. This was going to be a big disappointment, but he had little choice.

"You have my cell number, should that system get back up and running. But here's a land line where you can reach me, too. If I'm not there, leave a message as to when you're calling back, and I'll make sure I'm there."

T2 extended something in his hand toward Pete. "Found this attached on top. GPS locator is my best guess, but it's not ours."

Pete raised his brow. "I think you're right. Looks like someone wants to keep tabs on this container."

The two men nodded. T1 said, "Probably best to leave it right here after we move out."

Pete thought about that. Only two locations could go unquestioned—their current spot or the LADWP depot. "Yeah, maybe. But if one of my guys is headed to the equipment depot downtown, I might give it to him to stick on the building there."

The trio laughed at the suggested subterfuge.

FORTY

Heather sensed something familiar, and yet, not familiar at the same time. The smells, the sounds, the roughness of the bed sheets . . . all were like those when Dennis was in the ICU for the virus. And yet, she knew he had been discharged from the hospital in California and they were now in Wisconsin. Was she simply dreaming about those things, somehow reliving them?

No, what was unfamiliar was the sense of air being pumped into her lungs. That air forced her chest to rise and fall. It was an external force, not the intrinsic, automatic use of her diaphragm and chest wall to pull air in and breath it out. No one paid much attention to breathing because it was so, well, so normal. You didn't have to think about it. It was spontaneous. And yet, now, it wasn't.

She tried to take a deep breath. Her body didn't respond. The same rhythmic in and out of air continued.

Then she recalled her struggle to get to her phone. Her body had become so weak. And with that recollection, she realized she was in a hospital, on a ventilator just as Dennis had been. She didn't panic at that thought. Like him, she would recover and be released, at some point.

She felt a touch. Her left hand had been engulfed by someone's hand. She tried to reciprocate, but her hand didn't respond. Had a finger moved? Maybe a flinch?

"Hon? You waking up? I'm here."

Dennis was with her. She found that she could open her eyes, but she was unable to turn her head to face him. A moment later, his face appeared in front of her.

"Hey, there you are. You're in the hospital. I found you before the ambulance got there. You weren't breathing very well, so I started mouth-to-mouth like we learned that time from the Red Cross. The paramedics said that . . . well, I won't go into that. I am so glad to see you waking up."

She didn't like the sensation of the tube going down her throat, but she knew better than to resist it. She had learned that much watching Dennis fight it in the hospital a few weeks earlier. Still, as she continued to wake up, her gag reflex increased with her level of consciousness. In short order, she could no longer control her response to the tube. She began to gag.

"Nurse!"

She heard some commotion and sensed others in the room. In a moment, she again faded out of consciousness.

Aric had been down this road once before. After the encounter with LGBTQ+ activists, he wasn't surprised to get a summons from the Dean of Students. What did surprise him was that the meeting was to take place in the college president's office. He sat outside the woman's office with his laptop in hand. On it, he had a compilation of videos showing the altercation of three days earlier.

His palms felt a bit sweaty. Rebecca Collier had become the college's first female president a year earlier. That was after the incident with his old roommate and his previous "visit" with Dean Schmitz about alleged hate speech involving things posted on their dorm room's door. However, she had been present when the mayor awarded him the city's first award for courage. And yet, he knew enough about her past to be worried.

She wasn't married. It was rumored that she was a lesbian but kept that lifestyle quiet to get and keep her current position. Yet, he had no confirmation of that and didn't want to get into an argument about her possibly being biased, should it not go well for him. *That* kind of discussion would most definitely not go well for him.

The president's secretary placed her phone on its stand. "Mr. Afton, President Collier and Dean Schmitz are ready for you."

She opened the door for him as he stood and walked toward the office. He held his laptop tight to his side feeling confident that its contents would support his position and show the true aggressors. Anyone with even just a reasonably open mind would be able to see that.

Aric found the two officials standing as he entered the office. He nodded and greeted both. "President Collier, Dean Schmitz, good morning."

"Mr. Afton."

"Aric, please take a seat," said the dean.

Aric sat down in the chair they directed him to.

President Collier took the lead. "Mr. Afton, we've had multiple complaints about you over the past two days. These students made some very serious allegations about you, but in fairness, we want to hear your side of the story."

Aric felt a boldness grip him that he'd experienced only a handful of times previously. "May I ask what those allegations are and who made them?"

"Well, you allegedly attacked a student and broke his

arm. You injured a female student's hand and knocked another to the ground. Several complaints were made about your passing out offensive materials. That complaint was also made against others in your group." She paused.

"I see. And those who complained are?"

"We're not at liberty to give you that information."

"So, in a country where legal precedence has been that an accused has the right to know and address his accuser, the college has decided to break that precedence. Is that what I'm hearing?"

Neither official said anything.

Aric continued. "Were you told what said offensive materials were?"

Dean Schmitz nodded. "Yes, material of a religious nature that some students don't agree with."

"We *were* passing out free Bibles and information on various churches in the area, but when did not agreeing with something become equivalent to being offensive? That's a sad commentary on my fellow students. Plus, we never forced anyone to take anything or to stop to talk with us."

The president responded. "Did you have permission to pass out those materials?"

Aric nodded. "In fact, we did. Dean Schmitz can check with his secretary. Our Bible club president got that permission and has the paperwork."

The dean took a deep breath. Aric had called him out.

"I'll have to check with my office."

"What about the other complaints?" asked President Collier.

"Have you seen any video of the event, or have I been called here on hearsay?" Aric felt he knew the answer to that one. "In fact, we positioned our table right in front of a dorm security camera so that there would be video of any problems that might occur with certain members of the student body." He almost started to say "LGBTQ members of the . . ." but caught himself.

"We were told that said camera was out of commission."

Aric shook his head in disbelief. "Well then, somebody either lied to you or doesn't know what's what." He opened his laptop, moved to his collection of videos, and began to play the recording from that specific camera. He held it so both could see. "Here's the video from that camera. I was able to obtain it. I can't speak as to why it was withheld from you."

The two looked at each other, questioning. Neither looked pleased.

As the video progressed, he narrated. "Here you'll see we were simply conversing with students who stopped by of their own accord when five students walked up to our table. Note that none of us had even begun to talk with anyone in the group when this fellow turned over our table. Then this gal picked up and ripped apart one of the Bibles. When I told her she was free to take them all, she and her friend spit on me. They accused me of spreading hate, and when I asked who was acting hatefully, the friend slapped me. That's actually assault, but I've not asked for charges to be brought against her. She then tried to punch me in the face, but I was able to stop her. The first girl then tried to head-butt me, but I stepped aside, and she fell. I never touched her. In retaliation, the guy who turned over the table then tried to roundhouse kick me. He fell and broke his arm after I deflected his kick." He let that and the video sink in. "So, how am I at fault here?"

The two officials again looked to each other for an

answer.

"I have other videos from students if you need to see more." He paused. "I had hoped this would just be another case of harassment by the LGBTQ crowd, and that it would blow over, but clearly it hasn't since I'm sitting here defending myself." He saw President Collier fidget at the mention of LGBTQ.

She sat forward and said, "Would you please step outside for a few minutes while we discuss this?"

Aric nodded, stood, and stepped into the waiting area. He felt good that he had defended himself well and said a silent prayer of thanks. Voices could be heard through the door, and it was apparent that there was disagreement between the two. After several minutes he was asked to go back in.

"Well, Mr. Afton, the video certainly places things in a different light. We were prepared to expel you immediately and record the reasons in your student records. The video record shows us that we would be wrong to do so."

He felt he had been vindicated and prepared to resume life as a student.

"However, your presence on campus has become something of a problem. With only weeks remaining, it would not be right to refuse you the opportunity to finish the semester. And we would be wrong to record this in your records. That said, you may finish the semester, but we will not be accepting your enrollment for the fall. This is your last semester at this college."

Aric felt his jaw drop. "What? I only have one year left to get my degree. I'm the victim in this incident, but *I'm* the one being disenrolled? What about those who assaulted me and damaged our club's property? Perhaps I need to file official complaints for criminal charges against them."

Neither official replied.

The words of Jesus in John 15 resonated in his head,

If the world hates you, know that it has hated me before it hated you.

FORTY-ONE

Adam was back to pacing. The current stipulations for his use of UltraNet still didn't produce enough "dirt" on people to show who the operators were for the WOC. Tracking Bergstedt's communications had confirmed that the WOC was the "wizard" behind the curtain, controlling certain world events. However, those communications had safeguards when it came to identifying those carrying out the orders. Adam had learned to "tiptoe" through the web when dealing with the man's emails and text messages. He did not wish to trigger another alarm and risk exposure.

And while he tracked certain people and information on the web, he could find no information on who was attempting to track him. He knew that Bergstedt, or more importantly, Werner Koch, Bergstedt's boss and head of the WOC, wanted his activity stopped. Adam thought he had convinced them that he was a myth, a man once associated with AlterNet but no longer active. Obviously, they still had their suspicions, and with his defeating their plan to resurrect the surveillance program, they were taking safeguards to protect their current endeavors—the SEER23 pandemic.

As he paced his phone rang. CallerID revealed the caller. "Hey, Lynch. What's up?"

"Hi, Adam. I got your latest report. It was disturbing, to

say the least, but it's in line with the Word."

Adam agreed. He wasn't as well read on the prophecies of Revelation as was Lynch, but his level of understanding increased weekly. He was beginning to agree with Lynch's belief that the prophecy of Revelation 9 with the fifth trumpet's release of hordes of demons, described as locusts, from the abyss to torment men but not kill them, had taken place within the increasing turmoil of the trumpet judgments. From the exponential rise in depression, suicide, and other mental health issues to the sudden rise in trans activists, the push for gender affirmation, and the general increase in Antifa, LGBTQ+, and BLM activity, only such a supernatural occurrence could explain all the craziness.

Adam responded. "Yeah, looks like there's a bunch of internal squabbling within the WHO. Some are balking at various new international health regs that have been proposed. From what I see, they aren't going to be able to pass those IHRs at the meeting next month as hoped and will downplay that failure and state that the meeting is just one to revamp and consolidate those proposals for probable passage in a year."

"Well, that seemed like good news until I read that the WHO is joining the EU by adopting the union's Green Pass digital vaccine passport in order to expand it globally. Have you found out any more about that?"

"Nothing I could dig up easily. The WHO was trying to separate itself from vaccine passports and use the new IHR to do the same thing, but that blew up in their faces with all the squabbling and delay. Now, they're again endorsing the idea and plan to announce the joint effort with the EU in early June, but it's already well underway. They want it in play as this new pandemic spreads panic. But there's more.

They've decided that climate change now counts as a health risk. I also read that the IHR governing body is moving ahead with aggressive plans for complete control over not only health care, but also water, food, travel, shipping, crops, energy, and climate."

"That sounds like the next phase of Revelation's prophecies gearing up for fulfillment. Check out—" Lynch stopped. "Hey, I'm getting way off course here. The reason I called is to ask if you've talked with your brother today."

"Aric? No. What's up?" Adam felt a wave of concern wash through him.

"He stopped by my office to ask for help in transferring to the University of Missouri-Saint Louis' criminology program. Said he's being kicked out of the college here at the end of the semester."

"What?!" Adam had to mentally regroup. His train of thought had been on prophetic events and now he had to change tracks. "Why?"

"He wouldn't say. He was really upset. Said he needed to pray and think about it before he would be ready to discuss it. I hoped maybe he'd called you, and you could tell me what's going on."

Adam had nothing to say. He and Aric had become very close, and it concerned him that Aric hadn't called him about it.

"Wow. My first reaction is to call him, but maybe it's best I let him sort it out and not push him."

"Yeah, I agree that might be best."

"He loves it in Kenosha, and, well, with Jess there, I think it's going to be really hard for him to leave. I wonder what happened."

"Well, I heard he had another run-in with the LGBTQ crowd, and that one of the activists ended up with a broken arm, but I have no details. I think there are videos of the altercation, but I haven't had time to search out any of them."

Adam didn't wait for his friend to finish his statement. At the mention of videos, he was already on the hunt.

FORTY-TWO

Werner had read his prepared statement to the press. Now was the time for questions. He pointed to one of his favorite reporters. In a classic "I'll pat your back, if you'll pat mine" relationship, he often used her to get a step ahead of "problems" when they arose.

"Herr Koch, two questions, please. Are you confident this new vaccine will be safe and effective? And did the demise of PfenRich Pharmaceuticals affect the development of this vaccine?"

He smiled as he replied to her customary softball, and often scripted, questions. "Of course the vaccine is safe and effective. As soon as they were able, BioLogis received emergency authorization from both the European Medicines Agency and the FDA in the U.S. and began joint human trials in Los Angeles, where the outbreak started and the greatest number of cases exist. The results of that trial are in your packets.

"As for the impact of losing PfenRich Pharmaceuticals, that was indeed a great loss, but BioLogis picked up the slack expertly and efficiently. Their scientists and researchers were on top of this new virus as soon as it came to light as having the potential to become the next pandemic. They deserve our applause." With that, he offered a short and symbolic clapping of his hands.

"Next question." He pointed to another reporter well-known to him.

"What role did the World Order Council play in this vaccine's development?"

Werner always enjoyed patting his own back and highlighting the council. "The Council was active in this on several fronts. Of course, after the loss of PfenRich, we played a key role in setting up BioLogis. We worked with the World Bank to organize funding. We used our connections to get them approved by the EMA and FDA. We helped introduce them to the CDC in the US and their European counterpart, the European Centre for Disease Prevention and Control. When the virus broke out, we helped secure funding from the Gates Foundation to initiate the work on this vaccine. Plus, we're working with the WHO and the Rockefeller Foundation to build and strengthen the WHO's Hub for Pandemic and Epidemic Intelligence. This will help drive global collaboration in genomic surveillance, adoption of data tools for pathogen detection, and assessment of climate-aggravated outbreak threats. So, all in all, the Council has been an integral part of this effort to combat the world's next pandemic."

Werner answered half a dozen additional questions from "friendly" reporters while trying to avoid those he knew to be contentious. There was, however, one pert, young, female reporter he didn't recognize, who kept raising her hand.

"One last question." He pointed to the new woman.

"Thank you, Herr Koch. How do you answer reports that the Council is actually responsible for the pandemic by funding another engineered virus and for using the natural disaster in Los Angeles as an excuse to release this upon the world? And when do you and your staff intend to take the vaccine?"

Werner's mind went blank. He looked around. Where was Edvin? He was supposed to screen the questions and reporters. How did this person get into their late afternoon press conference? Several seconds went by as he tried to compose himself and respond.

"Such accusations are preposterous. That's all I have to say on that matter. As for receiving the vaccine, we already have." He paused a moment. "Thank you. That's all we have to say today."

A flurry of questions rose in a cacophony of voices as he left the podium. With his security detail leading the way and protecting his flank, he rushed to the private elevator leading to his office suite. Hurrying off the elevator, he moved toward his office.

"Edvin? Edvin! Are you up here?"

He looked to his concerned secretary for the answer. She shrugged and pointed toward his aide's office door. Werner knocked, although he rarely did. He tried the knob and found the door unlocked. Turning the knob, he tried to open the door. Something blocked his way.

Now concern displaced his anger. He pushed and managed to slide whatever blocked the door aside as he opened the door enough to look in. A body on the floor obstructed his way.

"Edvin!" He turned back toward his secretary. "Call security! We need an ambulance and medical personnel."

He exerted himself further to push Edvin's body aside. Werner was fit for his age but moving Edvin's 90-kilogram body with a heavy door across a carpeted floor was almost too much for him. He managed to move the man far enough to open the door wide enough to slip inside the office. Once inside, he was able to grab his aide's arms and drag him away from the door. He rolled him onto his left side, the recovery position.

Edvin still had a pulse, but his eyes were glassy and his lips blue. He noticed small efforts to breathe, but the young man needed help, help that Werner was hesitant to give.

Edvin's last report to Werner had noted one way that the virus seemed to spread. Upon finding someone struggling to breathe because of the paralysis, many were moving right to CPR and giving mouth-to-mouth respiration. That lifesaving act of kindness became their own introduction to the virus, and they, too, soon developed the paralysis. Word of that transmission route had gotten into the press and had resulted in two things: one, many refused to offer aid and the death toll kept rising, and two, great profits were being made on small resuscitation kits that could protect aid givers from the virus. While Werner took advantage of the second, he never envisioned being confronted by the first.

FORTY-THREE

The news given to him by the college president hit him hard. What had *he* done? Nothing. Those other students attacked them, not the other way around. Were they being told not to return in the fall? Unlikely. Aric found himself sulking in his room. If he had an afternoon class, he would have skipped it, and he hadn't missed a class yet in his college career.

At dinner, he grabbed something fast and easy and took it back to his room to eat. He couldn't face eating with his friends knowing that he'd be with them for only another three weeks. And what about Jess? How was he going to break this news to her?

Yes. Jess. She needed to know. If need be, they could at least sulk together.

He grabbed his cell phone and dialed her number. She answered on the first ring. Before she could even greet him, he asked, "You home?"

"Um, yes. Why—"

"Be there in ten."

He disconnected, grabbed his keys, and headed out to his car. Nine minutes later, he pulled into the Larsons' driveway and walked toward the front door. Jess opened it before he made it to the stoop.

Standing there, with her arms wrapped around her

chest to protect her from the chill wind, she asked, "What's wrong?"

She knew him well. Perhaps it had been the tone of his voice when he called.

He stood in front of her. No hug. No kiss on the cheek. He was almost afraid to touch her.

"I-I'm sorry if I was brusque on the phone. It's been a horrible day. Can I come in? We need to talk."

"Sure. What's wrong? What's happened?" She stepped aside and ushered him into her parents' home. She led him to the couch in the front room, and they sat down.

"What's happened?" she asked again.

Tears welled up in his eyes as he said, "I'm not being allowed to enroll here for next fall. I'm essentially being expelled."

Her eyes widened in shock. "Why? What's going on?" The realization that they might have to spend their senior year apart must have hit her, because tears began to flow down her face, too.

She already knew about the incident at the info table. She had seen the videos. So, Aric explained in detail what happened in President Collier's office.

As he finished, she sat upright, wiped the tears away, and said, "That's just not right. You and the others at the table didn't do anything wrong. You're being persecuted for your faith and attacked for exercising your constitutional rights. And right now, the enemy's attacking and trying to bring you down, to drain you emotionally so you won't fight back." She now looked angry and defiant.

Her attitude surprised him, but her words struck a chord. She was correct, and upon recognizing that, he felt his spirit lift. Instead of sulking all day, he should have been planning his countermove.

"Let me get Dad . . . and Chris." She left the room and a minute later, returned with the two in tow. They sat down opposite Aric and Jess, and she explained what was going on. Aric added a few minor comments for clarification. He also used his phone to show Pastor Larson the video of the table incident.

Jess's father shook his head in disbelief. "That's what happened, and you're the one being asked to leave? Jess is right. You, we, need to fight back."

Jess's brother nodded. "People are getting fed up. Look around. Bud Light sales are in the tank because they got associated with that guy Dylan Mulvaney in their advertising. Parents are growing resentful that their kids are being groomed in their schools and public libraries by pedophiles and homosexuals. Remember the local parent who had his door busted down by the FBI because he dared to question deluded boys being allowed in the girls' locker room? His name's Anson Hardy and he's running for Congress. I hear he's already raised a million dollars for his campaign. Folks are starting to fight back."

Pastor Larson spoke. "I've met with Hardy. He's solid. And I know the Midwest Justice and Freedom Defense Alliance defended him. I'll find out the name of the local attorney he worked with. I bet the college will think twice after being threatened with a civil rights lawsuit."

"And Chris and I can get a few dozen students at school to form a protest. The other side does it all the time, so now it's our turn." Jess smiled.

Chris agreed. "I bet we can get more than a few dozen. I know the guys on the football team that you're friends with will join in. Probably a lot more. And if they shut us down, it's more fodder for a lawsuit."

Jess gave her brother a high five. "If we take too long, we'll run into finals. So, let's shoot for Monday at noon. That gives us three days to get it together."

FORTY-FOUR

Adam stood at the window, staring into the backyard where his children played. Yet, he truly didn't see them. His thoughts were roughly 500 miles away . . . in two different directions.

Upon reflection, there was a third direction as well, and it was nearly ten times further away. His source of information on the WOC, Edvin Bergstedt, had become the victim of their own virus and remained on a ventilator in critical condition. He was not expected to survive.

Rachel entered the room and walked up next to him.

"Penny for your thoughts," she said.

His ears heard her words, but his brain didn't register her comment. He didn't reply.

"Earth to Adam."

She waved her hand in front of his face. That broke his mental meanderings.

"Uh, what? Sorry, my mind was elsewhere."

She put her hand on his shoulder. "I know. You haven't really been with us since finding out about Aric. What's going on in that brain of yours?"

She knew a fair amount about his program, UltraNet, but not everything. In reflection, her knowledge of it was scant. He needed her to understand his work with it without knowing enough to jeopardize her, or the children's, safety.

Learning about his surveillance of Edvin Bergstedt was definitely off the table. He wondered just what he should share.

"Well, it's not just Aric's situation. Do you remember that Good Friday miracle in California?"

She nodded. "How could we forget?"

"You can't tell this to anyone. Promise?"

She zipped her lips with her thumb and finger. "Promise."

"I mean it. That's for our safety. All of us. That poor pastor in Bishop was kidnapped for information on who made the generator, and a man was killed, electrocuted, trying to steal it."

Her eyes widened. "Wow. None of that has been in the news. How did you—" She paused. "Nevermind. Your program, right?"

He nodded. "I've found out who made it. They've got some incredible stuff. Disruptive innovations. The kind that gets inventors killed. I can understand why they're being so secretive."

"So, what's bothering you?"

He smiled. "They need more funding, and I'd like to invest. I can't figure out how to get introduced to them behind the scenes."

She laughed. "Since when have you taken the subtle approach to anything."

"True. Maybe I should just contact them."

"That's more like you. Anyway, I just wanted to let you know that I need to run to the store. The kids are staying here."

"Okay. Got it. I'll keep an eye on them."

She rolled her eyes. "Hopefully better than you just

were."

He feigned being cut to the quick. "Touché."

She gave him a quick kiss on the cheek. "Shouldn't be gone long. Bye."

Adam returned his gaze out the window. The kids hadn't killed each other yet. In a moment, though, his thoughts returned to their mental travels. However, having settled upon contacting the new power company directly and having recognized there was nothing he could do for Bergstedt, those thoughts ran in only a single direction . . . to Kenosha.

While Aric's friends had succeeded in producing protests on his brother's behalf, Adam wasn't sure they would succeed. Lynch had gone to bat for Aric, too, both at the college and by putting in a good word with leaders of the criminology program in St. Louis. That, too, hadn't seemed to change anything. And, at this point, the Midwest Justice and Freedom Defense Alliance hadn't decided whether or not to take on Aric's case.

As a result, Adam had taken to using UltraNet for Aric's benefit. The program hadn't taken long to find something useful. President Collier, it appeared, hadn't been totally truthful with the college trustees. She had padded her resumé, while also leaving out one critical event from her past—an arrest while in college. No doubt she thought that incident to be well hidden, but little could be hidden from UltraNet.

The left had no concern about bringing up alleged incidents from decades earlier to try to smear those they wanted to remove from office. This event, however, was not based upon some individual's questionable memory about something that absolutely no one else allegedly involved in the situation could recall. This was in the public record, albeit obscured.

A year earlier, Adam would have had no issue with using the information to help Aric by passing it along to members of the Board of Trustees. Now, though, he had made a promise to Lynch about how he would utilize UltraNet and its findings. He had promised that all such data would flow through Lynch and Lynch alone. If he passed it along to their friend and he decided against using it, then Adam's hands would be tied. To reveal it to others would make it obvious to Lynch where the incriminating evidence came from. The trust he had earned from Lynch would dissolve.

He could withhold it from Lynch and then use it against the woman. He could do so anonymously, and Lynch would be no wiser, but that would be breaking his promise. He did not want to break that vow. The Bible spoke about the consequences of breaking one's vows.

Despite the inner turmoil it produced, he decided to give the situation one more week.

Heather grew aware of waking up. Or was it waking up *again*? The deep fog that had obscured her mind seemed more like a fine mist now. Hadn't she had this experience before, or had that been a weird dream? As she became more aware of her surroundings, she recognized that she was in a hospital . . . just like in that dream. Yet, that specter was different. With her rising consciousness, she recalled that in her dream something uncomfortable in her throat made her gag, as well as a strange sensation in her chest. This time, those were absent.

She opened her eyes and confirmed being in a hospital

bed. With some effort, she turned her head to the right and saw Dennis sitting there. His chin was on his chest, and his eyes were closed. She noted a clock on the wall. Early afternoon. Right on schedule for his afternoon nap.

She recognized she had a mask over her nose and mouth. Something was helping her to breathe, and she remembered the BiPap machine used on Dennis when he had the virus. The mask felt too tight, yet she couldn't raise her hand to loosen it. Not exactly. She could raise her hand. Just not far enough or with adequate strength.

"Dennis?" His name came out as a soft, hoarse whisper.

The bed control with its call button was near her hand. She had the range to grab it, but it fell from her hand the first time. On her second attempt, she was able to grasp it, but it was only by chance that she pressed the call button. A moment later, a nurse came in.

"Hi there. I see you're waking up." The woman smiled behind the clear visor that protected her face. She wore a yellow paper gown and black latex gloves.

"Water," Heather whispered.

As the woman reached for the water carafe and plastic cup, Dennis stirred and then suddenly jerked awake. He blinked his eyes several times as he looked about.

"Uh, sorry. Fell asleep." He looked at the nurse and reached for the plastic cup and straw, which the woman had already filled halfway. "Angie, I can do that. Thanks."

The nurse took her stethoscope, leaned over Heather, and listened to her chest. "Good and clear." She straightened up. "I'll let the doctor know you're awake."

As she left the room, Dennis helped remove the mask, offered her several sips of water, and replaced the mask over her nose and mouth. She noted tears in his eyes.

After wiping those tears away, he said, "I am so thankful to see you open those beautiful green eyes of yours. I thought you'd never wake up." He took her hand, raised it to his lips, and kissed it.

"What day . . .?" she mumbled. "How long?"

"It's been a week since you last woke up. They've kept you sedated and on the ventilator. Do you remember waking up on it?"

She did, and she didn't. That must have been the dream she seemed to recall. She shook her head. He told her what had happened, how he had found her in the kitchen. She seemed to recall hearing that before. And that was a full week ago? She'd been out of it that long?

"They'll keep you on the BiPap full-time for several more days until you're able to do more for yourself. It's been a rough go. Then we can go back to the, uh, to the house, but they said you're likely to be on the BiPap while sleeping for a few weeks."

At the mention of the house, he looked . . . well, distraught was the word that came to mind. He seemed to not want to go back there.

"Dan?" she whispered.

He shook his head. "Not now."

Now she knew something else had happened. Something was wrong. She shook her head.

"No. Now."

"You're not strong enough."

Those would have been fighting words, were she able to move. "Now," she repeated.

Tears welled up again in his eyes. "Dan is gone. After all he did for us, he's gone." He choked on his words and reached out to hold her hand.

It took a moment for his meaning to register. Dan? Dead? Tears began to flow down her cheeks. How? She couldn't speak and hoped her question registered in her eyes.

"There's a mutation of the virus. That's what you caught. It causes sudden weakness and progresses to paralysis quickly. Few symptoms of illness precede the paralysis, so folks don't even realize they're sick until it's almost too late. Dan was alone in his patrol car when it hit. He lost control of the car and crashed. By the time help arrived, he had stopped breathing. They didn't get to him in time."

FORTY-FIVE

Aric wandered out from the academic building where his Thursday morning class was held feeling a bit overwhelmed—overwhelmed and also humbled by the support he saw being extended toward him. Classes that previous Monday seemed no different, but at lunch that day, over 400 students amassed outside Dean Schmidt's and President Collier's offices. An offshoot of that group also protested in front of the president's on-campus home. The protest dwindled during the afternoon, while classes were in session, but resumed at the end of class and lasted until those two officials had been escorted out of their offices by security.

Chants, like those modeled on student protests of the 1970s, rose in crescendo.

"No! No! He won't go!"

"The students! United! Will never be defeated!"

"What do we want? Justice! When do we want it? Now!"

A dozen or more signs also popped up. Aric's favorite was, "Don't be daft on blaming Afton!" Others included, "Don't blame the victim!" and "We support Aric!" One sign, "Pride goes before destruction," was quickly confiscated by campus security.

On Tuesday, the protest continued at lunch and after classes, but by Wednesday, it seemed clear that President

Collier was standing firm. Also clear was that Dean Schmidt was on Aric's side and had been overruled by the college president. He risked his position by making a public statement about that fact. And yet, by that morning, Thursday, he had announced that he and President Collier had developed fundamental differences, that he could not be effective in his job under her leadership, and that he would be taking early retirement. He had phoned Aric to voice his support for Aric's position.

However, another factor came into play that day. At noon, the CDC held a press conference and again recommended personal protective equipment against the latest virus. Unlike previous experiences with viral mutations which became more contagious but with less severe symptoms, this mutation had defied that expectation by becoming both more contagious and more severe. The media had begun to publicize the current mutation and its deadly consequences. Reports were surfacing that the paralysis could be catastrophically sudden, crippling, and deadly and that attempts to resuscitate its victims could lead to catching the virus. Death rates were rising.

Of greater concern was that the conservative, alternative media was echoing the same message. These reports were not hyperbole. Fear of this new plague was becoming palpable and didn't require propagation by those who had led the COVID propaganda.

There was talk of moving exams up by a week to allow students to go home. Some rumors floated the idea that the college would close *before* exams. Aric had learned not to listen to the campus rumor mill, but no matter what was going to happen, the protest on Wednesday afternoon had dwindled to less than 20.

It was against this backdrop of uncertainty that Aric learned of Officer Dan Dickson's death. The sadness he felt upon hearing that news contributed to his sense of feeling overwhelmed. The statement made publicly by the police department only mentioned Dan's being involved in a crash. However, word on the street said that the accident was minimal, the type one would walk away from with barely a scratch. The speculation was that he had contracted the virus and that the paralysis hit him while on patrol. Aric doubted that the medical examiner would publicly release a cause of death, unless, of course, it fit into the CDC and media's narrative.

For Aric, the loss of his new friend held one ray of sunshine. Dan had made it to church the Sunday before and had accepted Christ as his Lord and Savior that day.

Werner had never felt so hollow. He rarely doubted himself and would never admit to second-guessing his own decisions. Yet, today, as he prepared to say goodbye to his longtime aide and offer condolences to his family, he wondered if he'd been overzealous in pushing out this virus.

Yes, their goal remained to depopulate the world. Yes, the situation in Los Angeles provided the perfect window of opportunity. Yes, they had a vaccine to push out to the world, and money to be made from it. No, it hadn't been fully tested, not that that mattered.

While Werner and the WOC pushed, promoted, and propelled the COVID vaccine to the world stage, they, their families, and their employees were not required to get the shot. Quite the opposite. They knew of the jab's deadly consequences long before its release.

Now, however, the SEERS-23 virus had shifted in a way they had never expected. The vaccine, like that for COVID, would do little to prevent this new contagion, could enhance its spread, and would produce a plethora of systemic health problems far enough into the future that few would link those issues with the vaccine. The plan had been to hype the dangers of the virus, convince millions to get the shot, add billions to their personal bank accounts, and rest comfortably knowing that the virus produced little true harm should they or one of their own catch it.

Now, the virus had mutated in an unexpected way, no true vaccine was available, and Edvin was dead. They were all at risk.

Werner and Liesl made their way to the front of the church. Edvin's parents and sister stood there, doing their best to remain stoic as dozens of family members, friends, and coworkers expressed their sympathy and offered words of comfort. Werner looked about. Anneliese, Edvin's on again-off again girlfriend was not to be seen.

As he approached the parents, he offered a curt bow and extended his hand.

"Herr and Frau Bergstedt, Hannah . . ." He nodded toward Edvin's sister. ". . . my wife and I want you to know you have our deepest sympathies. I-I am feeling lost without Edvin. As you know, he's been with me for a decade. He was intelligent, astute, and hardworking. I will not be able to replace him."

"*Danke*, Herr Koch. He spoke warmly and highly of you and loved working for you." Despite the words being spoken, the man appeared cold, and the words emerged automatically.

As they spoke, Werner heard a commotion behind him.

"Halte sie auf!"

"Lass sie nicht in seine Nähe kommen!"

Stop who? Don't let her get near whom? Werner turned to see Anneliese bearing down on him. His security team was moving to intercept her.

"You killed him! Edvin would still be here if you hadn't released this virus!"

Her words stung. The vengeful look on her face told him she meant him harm. Two of his men secured her by the arms.

"*Ja*, he told me what you've done. He confided in me. I know it was you who authorized this virus! His blood is on your head!"

His men had to drag her from the sanctuary. She fought them every step of the way. He turned back to Edvin's parents.

"Herr Bergstedt, I—"

"Please go now, Herr Koch."

FORTY-SIX

As Pete drove south on Rt. 395 toward LA, he reflected upon the past couple of months. Despite having little or no daily work to perform, he had kept busy with the church and tending to various members' needs, as best he was able to under the conditions. Despite weekly inquiries about project plans and rebuilding, he had heard nothing from the LADWP main office about his damage report. Until the day before when he had been summoned to meet with the leadership on Hope Street today at 1 p.m.

He found it difficult to believe that the dam failure was already two and a half months behind them. The mystery generator had made it easier for all in Bishop, but that, too, had been removed a month and a half ago, and life had become one of tending to the home and church generators, trips north to get fuel and groceries every week, and checking in with LADWP daily through the office in town.

To date, he and his men had not been laid off. He wondered if that was about to change. He wondered about a lot of things. Even with his commitment to his church, he began to feel that God was telling him to move on. Events in California made it harder and harder to stay. With all of the major and minor league baseball stadiums in the LA metro area out of commission, the Dodgers and Padres had rearranged schedules to allow the Dodgers to play "home" games at Petco Park. For their recent Pride Night, they invited a bunch of drag queen "nuns" to be honored before the game. The Sisters of Perpetual Indulgence wreaked the ire of the Catholic Church and denunciations from believers throughout the region. The Dodgers' already minuscule attendance because of the disaster took another major hit.

One thing after another kept adding up to make it difficult to stay. Yet, the most recent act might well be the proverbial straw to break the state's back. The legislature had passed a law that criminalized a parent's right to oppose a child's desire to change gender. If your son wanted to be addressed as a girl and wear girl's clothing, and you opposed that "gender expression," you would be charged with child abuse and the child removed from your custody. The law was so egregious and such a malicious attack on parental rights that even a state senator, a native son of California, now encouraged families to leave the state.

Pete had to agree, but he felt an obligation to his church. Still, within the past week, the church had assisted four young families with moving to Nevada and eight other families indicated a desire to move. His confusion lay with not being sure if God was calling him elsewhere or if he was simply empathizing with those families. Under the current state laws, he didn't want his children to marry and have kids here.

At the end of Rt. 395 he merged onto I-15 heading into the city. He hadn't gone quite ten miles to the Rt. 138 exit when the National Guard directed all traffic off the interstate. As he pulled up to an inspection point, he lowered the window of the LADWP truck he was driving.

"Good morning, sir. May I ask where you're heading and the nature of your business?"

As he flashed his LADWP ID badge, he took note of the young man's rank and name. "Good morning, Specialist Garrett. I'm heading to LADWP headquarters on Hope St. for a meeting. I'm the supervising engineer from Bishop, where the dam failed, taking out our hydroelectric plants and starting this whole mess."

"Name, sir?"

"Pete Manning. I showed you my ID."

"Yes, sir." The soldier scanned several sheets of paper on his clipboard. "Ah, here you are. LADWP advised us to let you through. If you'll pull ahead to the green sign up there, an escort will pull up to lead you there."

"An escort? I know the way like the back of my hand."

The man remained all business in manner. "I'm sure you do, sir, but we can't have you stopping along the way, and, well, the city isn't safe. Too many vehicles are being stopped at gunpoint and being emptied of their gas and anything else of value, while their occupants are having their wallets emptied."

Pete raised his brow in shocked surprise, but then, he shouldn't have been. Rumors about the deterioration in the city had reached Bishop weeks earlier, but the need for armed escort unsettled him. As the soldier waved him on, he pulled ahead and lined up behind another car idling directly behind the green sign. Three more vehicles lined up behind him. Ten minutes later, the military escort joined them and reordered their lineup according to the order of their "delivery" to their destination. Pete continued in the second spot. After that reconfiguration, the line of vehicles moved back onto I-15.

As they headed down the San Bernardino Pass toward that city, Pete could already note a difference. The thick layer of smog that typically lay trapped against the mountains by the offshore winds was gone. Yes, the city and state's push to EV cars had started to make a difference to the city's notorious air pollution, but now, the air was clear, crystal clear.

They continued southwest on I-15, and as they picked up the San Bernardino Freeway, I-10, and headed west toward L.A.'s city center, Pete couldn't say the same thing about what he saw about him as they sped past. Building after building sat in disrepair from vandalism. Shattered glass windows adorned storefront after storefront. Every so often an entire block of buildings remained as nothing but charred shells. Only the boundary streets, acting as fire stops, saved the next block's buildings. He wondered if the area's residential areas had also been hit, but fencing, high berms, greenery, or some other barrier blocked his view.

In West Covina, they detoured from the freeway and escorted the first "delivery" to the Los Angeles County Sheriff's offices on Sunset Avenue. Pete surmised the occupants of the vehicle were department employees.

As they resumed their trip toward Hope St., Pete wondered how many remaining in the city were hope*less*. He had faced that challenge in Bishop among his congregants after the removal of the M-Cube.

On this leg of the trip, however, he was able to check some of the residential areas. While garbage cans and loose trash were strewn about the streets, some homes were still obviously inhabited, and others were boarded up. He noted a police presence and hoped that meant the police were protecting life more than property.

His next shock came as they arrived at the LADWP main offices on Hope St. The parking lot's four-foot-tall cement parapet had been supplemented with a ten-foot-tall chain link fence topped with razor wire. It looked like something from a war zone. Entry to the lot required passing two gates, in between which the vehicle was inspected with mirrors looking for bombs on the undercarriage and open examination of trunks and cargo areas.

Even his LADWP truck underwent inspection. The armed guards were quite polite, with one even being a bit chatty. According to him, the main equipment depot had been looted twice for metals before getting the new security and fencing, while the headquarters building had received numerous bomb threats and one true attempt because of the extended blackout and water issues. He noticed upon driving into the lot that a fair number of trucks were now parked there, along with two large National Guard tankers holding gasoline. The security made more sense after seeing that.

Pete made his way to the main entrance where he again went through a security check. No problem there. He discovered the facility had power and its elevators worked, but few people were presently there working. He found his way to the Financial Services Office where he was expected. A secretary led him to a conference room and offered him bottled water or coffee. That disturbed him a bit. It was as if nothing had happened, but he knew these leaders couldn't be working in a vacuum. The evidence of the catastrophe was all around them.

He accepted the water and appreciated the chill of the drink. As he downed the top half of the bottle's contents, he was surprised that the Chief Financial Officer, April Negwar, entered the room first. He had anticipated meeting with one or two of her underlings, not the chief. Next came Anna

Whitmore, the Assistant Chief Financial Officer, and Marta Ingersoll, the Comptroller. When John Hanover, the "big man" himself and General Manager, entered the room along with the Chief Operating Officer, Myron Lasky, and Pete's immediate supervisor, Mark Dillingham, the Senior Assistant General Manager-Power System Construction, Maintenance, and Operations, he became to feel a bit sweaty in the armpits. Mark, he had met with frequently over the years, but he had never seen all of the main power players in one room together—much less to meet with him.

John started the meeting. "I think everyone here knows everybody else, so we can get right to business. Pete, thank you for making the trek into no man's land. Hope the trip was uneventful."

Pete nodded. "No problems, but I was a bit surprised at needing an escort."

"Sorry, but LADWP vehicles are targets these days. Seems *we're* to blame for all this mess, not climate change."

Pete chose not to reply. His perspective on "climate change" would not be welcomed.

John nodded toward April. "April, why don't you get us started?"

"Thanks, John." She leaned toward Pete. "Pete, when we first got your report and damage estimates, along with rebuilding estimates, we were, well, floored. They were far higher than we'd expected. But as my people dug into the numbers and did some research, we realized we hadn't calculated the extra costs of building within the canyon. Your numbers were amazingly spot on, give or take a percentage or two. Thank you for some excellent work."

Pete nodded.

"That said, we started cranking out the numbers on

projected income from the rebuild. We also had to estimate affected households and businesses. You might not have noticed driving in, but a large percentage of businesses have been destroyed or closed. Current estimates also show that roughly 20% of metro area residents have pulled up stakes and moved, primarily those in apartments and other rentals. Property owners have been less likely to abandon their property."

"But that is expected to change," said Marta. "Property values have already plummeted over 50% here."

"While that's all true, the real kicker comes from our state government," said Myron.

Pete could read the "what else is new" projected between the lines.

"The environmental groups have already put significant pressure on the state to require environmental impact studies before rebuilding anything. Now that the Owens is running wild again, they like that. They're even putting pressure on the state about rebuilding the head gates for the aqueduct system. Without our water supply being restored, a 20% exit rate is a drop in the bucket. No pun intended."

The group discussed the many varied aspects and challenges of rebuilding. Yet, the limitations kept coming back to two main issues: one, whether or not the state would ultimately require environmental impact studies versus granting a waiver for such, and, two, would the demand still be there to justify the costs. They were intimately related. If environmental studies were to be required, that process could take years before rebuilding *might* begin. And the longer the delay, the more people would leave, decreasing the demand. However, even should rebuilding be approved today, the demand could continue to drop.

Pete finally raised his hand to be able to get a word in. "So, what I'm really hearing, but isn't actually being stated, is that the rebuilding isn't likely to begin within the next year and that the employees in Bishop are to be laid off."

Mark nodded. "Afraid so, Pete. And I'm sorry to say, that includes you, too."

Pete took that statement in stride. In reality, he saw it simply as confirmation that God was moving him. Where? He didn't know, but he had faith that God had something better for him.

Mark continued. "We'll keep everyone on through the end of the month, and we're giving two months' severance. During that two weeks, we want to see all the equipment, trucks, etc. moved back to the city's main equipment depot."

Pete nodded while recognizing that under the circumstances, that might take less than a week. There wasn't much on hand in Bishop.

"Sorry, Pete," said Myron. "We hate losing you and the others. If it's any consolation, we've already laid off 25% of the workforce here and 10% across the city in general."

Pete nodded again. What could he say?

At the end of the meeting, he filled the tank of the truck and waited another 20 minutes for an escort out of the city. It was going to be a long trip home.

FORTY-SEVEN

A month had passed since he decided to pass on the info about President Collier to Lynch. At first, Adam thought his friend might move ahead to pass along the news to one of the college's trustees, but that expectation was short-lived.

Instead, Lynch had used his connections at the University of Missouri-St. Louis to secure Aric's acceptance as a transfer student into the criminology program. As one of the country's top, if not *the* top, criminology programs, it was the rare student who would be accepted on transfer.

Adam recalled the conversation.

"Adam," Lynch had said, "to out the president won't change much for Aric here. He'll still face criticism and outright persecution from various groups on campus, and these groups don't care who the college president is. She might look the other way, but who's to say the next president would be different? Christians aren't welcomed on most campuses these days. I know that firsthand, but it would take a lot of money and time to remove me."

"But he'd like to stay. He likes Kenosha and his church there. Jess is there. It's not right that he's being singled out when he was the victim of this attack."

"I agree and understand. I've talked with Jess. I can help her transfer to UMSL, as well, and I'm pretty sure the Southworths would take her in for the school year. She'd only be five minutes from campus there. As for Aric, what's going to look better, a criminology degree from UMSL or from here?"

Adam couldn't argue with anything Lynch had said. Certainly, the UMSL degree would carry him further than a criminology degree from a startup program like that at the college there. In the end, Adam decided not to press the issue, and he wasn't about to go back on his agreement with Lynch.

While the whole issue with President Collier stuck in his craw, he knew he needed to move on. His agenda for the day was to find a new source of information now that Edvin Bergstedt had died.

He wasn't alone in thinking it ironic that the man died from the virus his boss authorized for release. In truth, the mutation had caught the "experts," the U.S. and European federal agencies, and the WOC off-guard. It was much like the guys he read about who used gasoline to start a bonfire. Seemed like a good and logical idea until the blowback from the volatile gas igniting resulted in second-degree burns across the front of your entire body. An ER nurse friend of theirs once told him, they could do a lot in the ER, but they'd never cure stupid.

As Adam broke through some of the defenses in the WOC's local and wide area networks, he thought he might actually have penetrated Werner Koch's personal account. The idea excited him. Who could be a better source than the main man himself?

He set UltraNet to continue his work and headed first to the bathroom and then to the kitchen for a drink. As he descended the steps to the basement where his workstation was set up, he heard the first alarm. Needing to be careful not to spill his drink, he couldn't jump several steps at a time or run down the steps. By the time he hit the basement floor, he heard the second alarm. What flags had he tripped? He had seen no evidence of extra safeguards in the server where his search was centered.

As he gazed upon his monitors, he began to shut down his search. At that moment, however, three words popped up on one screen . . . "I've found you."

FORTY-EIGHT

Heather had required a week to move from BiPap support of her breathing to being able to breathe without assistance and keep her oxygen saturation within a normal range. Oxygen saturation, as described to her by one of the nurses, was the amount of oxygen in her blood, and the ability of her lungs to keep that oxygen level above 90%—preferably above 95%—was the determinant of what kind of breathing support she required. Even after going off the BiPap, she had required supplemental oxygen for a week.

But today would be a bittersweet one. Although she was finally being released home and would require no extra oxygen, "home" was Dan's place, and Dan was no longer there. Dennis had expressed his own reservations about staying there. He couldn't remember the home without Dan being there, whether as kids or later after their parents had passed.

For her, living there without Dan simply made the place feel like an Airbnb or Vrbo rental—living in someone else's home surrounded by someone else's decorating tastes, belongings, and family photos. She longed for her own home, in L.A., with her old friends and the people at the St. Joseph Center. She was surprised at how much she missed the people she worked with and those she once served. Those days were gone.

The house was now Helen's, and she kindly gave them the okay to stay there until their plans solidified. In reality, she was distraught over losing her husband despite having been informally separated. That separation was meant as her way to get his attention focused on her concerns. She had never planned on actually leaving him. That he died while they were on the outs and she never got to say goodbye or that she still loved him, ate at her. She had confided that on a visit to Heather in the hospital.

To celebrate her recovery, Dennis had purchased some salmon fillets, fresh asparagus, and potatoes and grilled them for a late lunch as they sometimes would do in California. Instead of a Napa Valley wine, however, he purchased wine from a local boutique winery, Spirits of Norway Vineyards. Helen had introduced him to their wines while Heather was in the hospital.

As they ate, Dennis brought up the subject of leaving California. "You know, Helen's sweet to let us stay here, but we need to make some big decisions."

Heather nodded as she finished chewing what was in her mouth. "I know. This is really tasty, by the way. What do you have in mind?"

"Well, I know a lot of folks are moving to Texas and Nevada, but —"

"No to Las Vegas. I don't want to move there."

"If you hadn't interrupted you would have learned that I agree with that. Not up for Reno either. As for Texas, their power grid is even more unreliable than what we left, and the summers are hotter. I'm not sure I want to go through something like this again. They're already predicting extended blackouts for this summer."

"What about being closer to Wilson? He and Joy might

be starting a family soon, and I sure would like to be close to grandkids." Their son lived in San Diego where he was stationed with the Marines.

"And be ready to move every two or three years as he gets reassigned? I don't think so. It's one thing to leave a thriving business behind and start over once. It's crazy to expect to do that routinely. If he leaves the service and settles down somewhere, I think I'd enjoy that, too. But not until then."

"So, what do you have in mind?"

I've had a couple of thoughts. With all the folks leaving Illinois and Chicago, this area could support another developer."

Heather shook her head. "No way. Too cold. The only thing that could bring me here would be grandchildren, but I doubt Will would ever settle here. He'll always be a Southern California dude at heart." She paused. "Florida might be nice, but it's getting awfully crowded and is probably full of developers already."

"Well then, how about the Carolinas? Charlotte is growing in North Carolina, and you loved Charleston and Greenville when we visited South Carolina."

Heather considered those places as she ate. "Those could work. Would you be able to work there?"

"Let's plan a trip to check 'em out, and I'll look into that. In the meantime, we need to get our stuff out of the house in BelAir and put the house up on the market."

Heather liked that idea. For the first time in months, she began to feel upbeat about their future. "I'll call my realtor friend back in BelAir and the moving companies to get quotes and availability."

They relaxed and finished their food. She helped him

clean up and then used her phone to look up moving companies. She chose to call them first since she could call her friend after business hours.

"Allied. How can I help you?"

"I'd like an estimate on moving and your availability."

"One moment."

Heather heard the line click and assumed she was being transferred to sales. A moment later, a different voice came on the line.

"This is Richard D. I understand you want an estimate on moving. How many bedrooms and what's the overall size of your home?"

"Three bedrooms and 3,200 square feet." She was surprised that they could offer an estimate based on such details without actually seeing the things to be moved.

"Thank you. And where are you moving from and to?"

Heather realized she should have expected that question. She decided to go with the longest potential trip, based on their earlier discussion.

"BelAir, California, to Charleston, South Carolina."

"Uh, thank, uh, you."

And then it seemed the line went dead. After 30 seconds of dead air, she asked, "Are you still there?"

"Um, yes, ma'am. Um, are you sure you want to do this?"

That was a strange question. "Of course. We need to move."

"Um, yes, ma'am, I understand. Well, okay, looks like it'll run about $35,000 and the earliest we could schedule it would be next May."

Heather was glad she was sitting down. "$35,000? And next May? That's almost a year from now. That's ridiculous."

"I know, right? Here's the deal. No one is moving *to* L.A., so you'll have to absorb the cost of bringing an empty truck in to get your things. And then, of course, there's the cost of moving across the country, 2,500 miles. As for the timing, we have such a backlog of requests to move out of California, not just L.A., that it's become a logistics nightmare making it hard to schedule trucks all across the country."

"I see. Well, I'm going to check around. Thank you."

"Yes, ma'am. Please do, but I think you'll find all of the major companies are in the same situation and the smaller movers will cost more because they don't have the resources for this kind of move. Your Two-Men-and-a-Truck kind of companies rarely do interstate moves, and I've never heard of one moving someone across the country. Anyway, good luck."

After calling the next two companies, Heather thought she might need BiPap again. Their quotes were equally breathtaking, but their reasons echoed those of the first company. Now she understood Richard D's question about whether or not she wanted to do this. It would be cheaper to give everything away and buy all new furniture wherever they ended up. Or better yet, she needed to pray for looters or an arsonist to attack their home and let the insurance company settle. That thought crossed her mind, but, of course, she could never do that.

She dialed her friend.

"Hi, Heather. You guys doing okay?"

"Hi, Annie. We are."

"Well, I heard that Dennis caught that new virus and was in the hospital. Is he out? Where are you?"

"Yes, Dennis caught the original and was laid up for about a week. His brother, Dan, came from Wisconsin to get us, so we're at his house now. He and I caught the new variant. I was in the hospital for over a month. Just got released this morning. Dan . . ." She choked up as she spoke. ". . . died."

"Oh, Heather. I'm so, so sorry. We're still in L.A. With John's position in the sheriff's department, well, we couldn't exactly pack up and leave. At least the department is providing a generator and fuel. We use it judiciously, and several of the wives have teamed up to make joint grocery runs up north. We have to have a National Guard escort in and out of the area. It's surreal."

"Are you going to stay?"

"Well, for now. John feels obligated to, you know, protect and serve. At some point, though, a decision needs to be made. What about you guys?"

"We're leaving, for good. We've been talking about it for a while now."

"You and almost everyone I know. Look, if you're calling about selling your house, I'm happy to list it, but don't expect much. The market here is flooded with sellers. We could ask, maybe, $350,000 for it but it might not even sell at that price."

Heather was shocked. Again. "Three-fifty? But the last appraisal was three and a half million. That's only ten cents on the dollar."

"I know, I know. But the market here has collapsed. How do you sell a house that has no electricity or water, and won't for months, if not years? Plus, there are hundreds of homes just like it on the market. Sorry."

Heather didn't know what to say. Tears filled her eyes. Life as they knew it was gone. They had retirement accounts and a great investment portfolio, but they were expecting to use the sale of their home to purchase a new house. Now they would have to tap into their savings for a home.

"Sadly, arson has become a leading profession here."

Heather blinked the tears from her eyes and shook her head. Did she truly just hear that?

"Yeah, so many places are being burned down that the insurance companies are refusing to pay out if it's ruled arson."

So much for that idea, thought Heather.

FORTY-NINE

For Aric, moving back into his family's home was uncomfortable. In reality, although he was a college student and "expected" to return home during the summer breaks, he had moved out three years ago and hadn't been home except for some holiday visits. Between living in the dorms or at Adam's place on the lake in East Troy in the summers, he hadn't a need to return home. This summer he had lined up a job with a custom vehicle painting company whose owner went to their church and would be staying in a house with four other guys from the church's young adult group.

His transfer to the University of Missouri-St. Louis had negated those plans. His dad had helped him line up some summer employment, and he would be living at home. True, he could stay in the dorms or one of the campus apartments come August, but he decided that removing himself from the campus living environment would let him avoid the campus politics and potential conflicts with the LGBTQ and other activist groups he had been unable to avoid in Kenosha. He wanted to simply focus on his studies and visit Jess in Kenosha whenever possible.

"Aric! Everything okay up there?" his mom yelled from the base of the stairwell.

He left his room and walked to the head of the stairs. "Yeah, everything is fine. Just rearranging my furniture and redecorating a bit. Do you have an extra recliner I could use to read in?"

"Let me check with your dad. We leave in about fifteen minutes to head over to Adam's for dinner."

"Okay."

He looked forward to seeing Adam and his family. He hadn't seen them yet since moving back a couple of weeks earlier. The whole mutant virus thing had everyone on edge. His family—which included the Larsons—had not been affected to date, but few of his friends could lay claim to not knowing someone infected by it.

For Aric, Dan Dickson was one of the unfortunate many, but Aric also knew a couple of classmates who had come down with it and ended up on a ventilator for a while. He had lost faith in the medical community. For COVID, they all rushed to ventilate victims when it was an oxygenation problem similar to malaria and not a simple ventilation problem. Most who ended up on a ventilator died. For SEERS-23, the problem was a ventilation issue, and yet, all of those hundreds of ventilators mothballed after COVID had either disappeared or malfunctioned after being pulled from the warehouses.

If you didn't die by ventilator for one illness, you would die without the ventilator for the other. *It was as if it was planned*, he thought sarcastically.

Yes, Aric missed having his big brother but an hour's drive away in Wisconsin. Not that he'd admit it though. Now, they were less than 20 minutes apart, and he wondered how often they might see each other. Would it be like a born-and-raised local who's never been to the Arch or some other touristy site in St. Louis?

He changed from his workout shorts and sleeveless tee

into presentable shorts and a polo. He was already bounding down the steps as his mom walked out from the kitchen to call him. And as he stepped outside into the St. Louis heat and humidity, he longed for SE Wisconsin's more suitable summer weather.

Adam hadn't cooked outside for a group in years. Their new pellet grill and smoker was prepped and ready for cooking, and their guests were expected any time now. He needed the break. It had been an emotional morning partially fueled by sleep deprivation.

He saw Aric bound around the side of the house, heading for the shade of the pergola over their back patio. Adam understood. Acclimating to the St. Louis weather had taken him several weeks. The *real* summer weather was still weeks away, with its temperatures in the upper 90s and higher, plus humidity matched only in the tropics. Aric would acclimate as well, in time. For now, the outdoor fan on the patio, along with a cold drink, would help alleviate the discomfort.

"Hey, little bro. Drinks are in the coolers." He saw the quirky smile on his younger brother's face at the mention of "little bro." Aric had a good five inches and 30 pounds on Adam, but he loved pulling Aric's chain on occasion. "By the way, I have a surprise for you."

Aric pointed to the coolers. "In one of those?"

"Well, okay, two surprises. Yes, the cooler on the right holds a surprise, too."

Aric opened the lid and pulled out a cold beer, a Wisconsin beer. Aric was legal now, so he had no qualms about drinking a beer. "Spotted Cow?" He bent over the cooler and pulled out another. "Two Women?" Then he retrieved a third, "Totally Naked? How in the world did you get these New Glarus brews? You can only buy them in Wisconsin."

"Special delivery." He laughed. He turned to see another guest round the corner of the house. "Welcome!"

Colonel Southworth and his wife, Mary, joined them. Mary walked over and hugged each young man. She was known for her hugs, among other things, like her cooking.

Rachel emerged from the house and presented her husband with a tray of burgers and brats. She and Mary hugged, and the two walked into the house, but Adam could see them peeking out the window.

"Adam, I hope you don't mind. We have a house guest staying with us for the week. I hope there's enough food for an extra mouth."

Adam grinned. "Sure is." He looked toward Aric, who seemed oblivious to the conversation until the sliding door from the kitchen opened.

"Jess!" Aric nearly dropped the bottle on the patio's stone floor, as he found a table to place it on and ran to greet her. He engulfed her in a hug, followed by a long kiss.

Adam looked toward the window and saw Mary give him a thumbs-up. He laughed and began to place the meat on the grill. While Aric and Jess caught up on events up north, he and the colonel saw to the grill. Soon, dinner was ready and enjoyed by all. With everyone satisfied, Jess joined the women in the kitchen. Adam, Aric, their father, and the colonel volunteered to do the cleanup, but the women insisted they could get it done faster.

"I think they just want to get back inside with the air conditioning," said Alex, their dad.

The colonel smiled. "We didn't marry fools, did we, gentlemen? We should have jumped on it faster." They all laughed.

"And looks like they're teaching Jess, too." Adam poked his brother in the ribs. "Thank you all for coming over. I needed this break. It was a rough morning."

"How so?" asked Aric, his brow furrowed in concern.

Adam paused. Of the three, his father knew the least about his endeavors. He wasn't sure how to proceed. He needed to keep his secrets within a tight circle. It wasn't that he didn't trust his father, but the man often said or confided things to his mom who wasn't known for zipped lips.

"Dad, some of this will be news to you, but I need to stress that I really don't want Mom to know. Period."

Alex nodded. Adam decided to risk it.

"As you know, I made some enemies from my previous employment. The main culprits are dead, but others tried to resurrect their work, and I stopped them. I thought they had given up looking for me, but evidently, some of my recent work with Lynch must have gotten too close to them again. I had my computer looking for information this morning while I went upstairs to the kitchen for a drink. All of sudden all sorts of alarms went off on my system, and I thought I'd triggered something that could lead them here. My computer screen said, 'I've found you' and panic took over. I just about soiled my pants at the thought they could get to my family."

"Did they find you? You seem pretty cheerful now."

"Well, as I dug into what happened, I realized they found one of my alter identities. As a safeguard, I once had my software set up a handful of alternate identities with complete backstops. Whoever is looking for me found one.

As far as they know, I'm a hacker in Iceland by the name of Bergálfur Jónsson."

He wasn't going to divulge that the incident had enabled him to back-trace the intruder. He now had a bot inside the WOC servers that could serve as a backdoor. And while the person who "caught" him had talent, Adam doubted he'd be able to find that bot without great effort.

"A toast to Bergálfur," said Aric, raising his can toward the others. They joined him, but the colonel appeared to do so halfheartedly.

"Something wrong, colonel?" asked Adam.

The older man waggled his head. "No, and yes." He paused. "I mean, don't get me wrong. It's great that you and your family remain safe. Yet, I can't help but lament the fact that society today is even at this point—that people, supposed leaders, feel the need to hide so much of what they do and then protect what they're hiding. And that so much of what they hide is immoral. What they push today has been called perversion for thousands of years, but today they want to make it mainstream and acceptable. Reminds me of the Old Testament kings of Israel and look what happened to them."

"Nothing new under the sun, Solomon said in Ecclesiastes."

Adam nodded in agreement with Aric. "I've been talking with Lynch a fair amount because of the things I'm discovering about the Deep State's plans and its dreams of a so-called utopia. He keeps reminding me that we're seeing John's prophecies in Revelation being fulfilled."

"He's made me a believer," said the colonel. "The wildfires, droughts, pestilence, famine, and more aren't new, but the steadily increasing frequency of them seems to not have any historical precedence. And Revelation foretold of such a time. And then this sudden rise in LGBTQ activism, particularly the trans stuff, certainly seems to have a spiritual, demonic background which the release of legions of demons from the abyss could account for. Plus, the mark of the beast is coming. These vaccine passports and various shopping apps are simply the beginning. None of this is happening in a vacuum, and none of it will happen overnight. Lynch also reminds me that Revelation doesn't reveal a linear timeline and can't be read literally."

Adam thought about that. When had their culture begun to break down? Had it started with the sexual revolution of the 1960s? Before that? In the 1970s when prayer was removed from the schools? Adam was no historian, but certainly, the deterioration of the culture was accelerating. And Revelation spoke to that, too, in John's descriptions of the great prostitute riding the scarlet beast.

What was in store for them? Jesus had foretold that many would fall away from the faith in the end times. That was certainly happening. Would Christ return in their lifetime? Lynch believed so, and his argument for that was persuasive. Adam saw that strengthening their faith was crucial. And along with that, holding tight to God's Word. He was reminded of a quote he'd recently seen from Charles Spurgeon, an English, Calvinistic minister of the 19th century known by many as the "Prince of Preachers:"

> "As for His failing you, never dream of it — hate the thought of it. The God who has been sufficient until now, should be trusted to the end."

FIFTY

Werner shook his head as the most recent applicant for the position as his aide closed the office door behind him. After nearly a dozen interviews, he had come to realize just how special Edvin's combination of talents had been. He realized he needed to stop comparing the current candidates with Edvin. That was unfair to them and exasperating to him.

There was one set of skills, however, that his former aide lacked. While Edvin knew his way around spreadsheets, word processing, and more—all crucial to his job—he had known little to nothing about the inner workings of such software. After the AlterNet2 debacle, Werner realized he needed someone with those specialized skills. Not just a talented IT guy. He wanted the crème de la crème of hackers. Edvin had agreed and had stated he would feel no competition from anyone Werner might select.

It was that fiasco that pushed Werner down a trail he rarely had to follow—one leading to payback. He and Edvin had disagreed on the belief that the mysterious primary programmer on the original AlterNet team was gone. Werner's gut told him that this programmer, code-named "Adam," was responsible for the demise of AlterNet2. However, Werner had no desire to find the man to hire him for yet one more attempt to revive that surveillance program.

No, Werner's goal was to destroy him. Revenge was a dish best served cold.

He had a break in his schedule, so he walked down the hallway toward his newest employee's office. The office itself was spacious. However, the typical furnishings of a modern German business office were nowhere to be seen. The room looked like the computer command center of a military unit or large, urban police force. His new employee had more computer power in her office than the rest of his corporate empire combined.

He knocked on the door and entered the office after her acknowledgment.

"*Guten tag*, Ms. Zhdanov. How is your day going?"

She smiled. "*Sehr gut*, Herr Koch."

Yolina Zhdanov was pretty, despite the punk styling, early 30s, and quite the flirt—not at all what one would expect in a talented hacker. He had recruited her from the Russian firm, Pozitiv Teknolodzhiz, AO—Positive Technologies—which had been sanctioned by the U.S. government for supporting the Russian cyber operations of their Federal Security Service, the FSB. In truth, the company's CEO was on the WOC board, so Werner had her "on loan" for as long as he required her services. He found her flirting, well, complementary, considering he was old enough to be her father. However, her personality had led him to insist on a more formal relationship.

"Someone has been following Edvin Bergstedt's account and cloned his emails and texts. I can't say for sure that this person is the one you're looking for, but he, or she, has the skills to be that person."

"It's a he. Their code names were gender specific, and

this one was Adam. I think he is the one who destroyed our surveillance software project. He's the one I want to find."

"*Ja, herr.* I thought I found him."

He furrowed his brow. "You thought?"

"I used a bot, or some would call it a spider, to crawl back along his route on the web to trace his origin. It landed on a server in Iceland belonging to a Bergálfur Jónsson. With some digging, I found this person to be fictitious, a well-backstopped character but nonexistent."

Werner would not let his emotions take control. He wanted to find this man, and he could be patient. He hadn't achieved his current status by letting his emotions run high.

"One bit of good news, sir. He left behind a fingerprint, so to speak. He uses a unique piece of code in what he leaves behind. I should be able to use it to track him down."

Werner smiled. Yes, his revenge would be sweet . . . and that time was coming.

AFTERWORD

Revelation 8:2-9

2 Then I saw the seven angels who stand before God, and seven trumpets were given to them. 3 And another angel came and stood at the altar with a golden censer, and he was given much incense to offer with the prayers of all the saints on the golden altar before the throne, 4 and the smoke of the incense, with the prayers of the saints, rose before God from the hand of the angel. 5 Then the angel took the censer and filled it with fire from the altar and threw it on the earth, and there were peals of thunder, rumblings, flashes of lightning, and an earthquake. 6 Now the seven angels who had the seven trumpets prepared to blow them. 7 The first angel blew his trumpet, and there followed hail and fire, mixed with blood, and these were thrown upon the earth. And a third of the earth was burned up, and a third of the trees were burned up, and all green grass was burned up. 8 The second angel blew his trumpet, and something like a great mountain, burning with fire, was thrown into the sea, and a third of the sea became blood. 9 A third of the living creatures in the sea died, and a third of the ships were destroyed.

Prior to the seven trumpet judgments, Revelation presents the seven seal judgments which affect a quarter of the earth. While we can't say that a literal quarter of the earth has been affected, nor can we think in terms of a literal third, we can note here an intensification of the judgments. And like the seal judgments, these affect the earth itself, but not mankind, at first. That's still to come.

However, all of these judgments need not be, and in fact, probably aren't cataclysmic in nature. It's not like suddenly a quarter of the trees are burning at the same time and then a third. No, this is likely cumulative, and John is seeing them at different stages.

Could we be seeing these judgments in progress now? Wildfires, extreme drought, floods, famine, and more—all blamed on "climate change"—continue to plague the earth and seem to be worsening. As I write this, over 19 million acres of timber have burned in Canada in the past six months (first half of 2023). To put that in perspective, just under two million acres burned in the U.S. in all of 2022. However, the number of wildfires nationally and globally on an annual basis has varied since 2000. There is no data confirming that these are increasing. I'm still looking for data to see if the idea of cumulative numbers holds water.

Speaking of water, the rainfall, snowpack, and atmospheric rivers that I detail in the story as affecting California were all real and the numbers are accurate. Right now (mid-July 2023) repeat atmospheric rivers across the northeast U.S. have brought fatal flash flooding to those states, and the Wrightsville Dam in Montpelier, Vermont is one foot away from being overtopped.

What about the second trumpet noted above? While I don't use it in this story, an unprecedented El Niño pattern is wreaking havoc upon both the Pacific and Atlantic oceans. We're seeing high temperatures for both land and sea right now. Sustained high temperatures in India, Spain, Iran, and Vietnam are proving fatal. The U.S. Southwest is facing record temperatures, as well, although much of the heat-related media coverage is hyped up. The media made a great deal about the temperature in Death Valley hitting 121°F, but it reached 134°F in 1934.

Still, there are areas in the mid-Pacific that are now 14°F warmer than ever recorded. In January 2022, the Hunga Tonga-Hunga-Ha'apai undersea volcano (*"a great mountain, burning with fire"*) erupted in the Pacific launching 40 trillion gallons of superheated water into the atmosphere. Within a week, this water vapor had circled the Earth. Within three months, it had spread from pole to pole, and the atmospheric water vapor charts went, well, "off the charts." Water vapor is much more effective in heating the atmosphere than carbon dioxide, so various governments' and experts' claims of this all being due to man-made carbon dioxide is also hype. Still, the result is much the same. Australian weather scientists warn that the Pacific and Indian Oceans will be 3°C (37°F) warmer in October than normal.

Water temperatures off Florida and around the Florida Keys are in the mid-90°Fs. Why? Perhaps because several new volcanic vents have been discovered along the mid-Atlantic Ridge, and they're superheating the surrounding water, which is being carried by the Gulf Stream into the North Atlantic.

Climate scientists in the UK report that the North Sea is now 6°F warmer than average for an El Niño pattern, and the Atlantic off the coast of the UK all the way south to the coast of western Africa is seeing temperatures greater than expected by several degrees.

I read that one nuclear scientist estimated that the amount of energy required to heat these vast amounts of water would equal a billion atomic bombs of the size that destroyed Hiroshima in WWII. Put another way, the 36-month running average for the Earth Energy Imbalance is now at a record 1.36 Watts per square meter, which corresponds to an average of 11 Hiroshimas of excess energy <u>per second</u> accumulating in the Earth's climate system over the past three years.

Warmer seas could also mean less wind and rain, creating a vicious cycle that leads to even more heat. These warm temperatures will affect aquatic life negatively. Don't be surprised at reports of major fish kills like the recent one along the Texas coast of the Gulf of Mexico. Could the great mountain burning with fire be the Hunga Tonga volcanic eruption, along with the thermal vents in the Atlantic?

What about the sea turning to blood? Well, millions of dead fish and sea mammals could certainly contribute to such an image. But what about Red Tide, the harmful algal bloom—HAB, as used by scientists—seen annually in recent times along Florida's Gulf Coast, as well as in the Atlantic along the U.S. southeast coast and elsewhere in the world? Some of these HABs literally turn the water red. Recently, thousands of dead fish washed up on Texas' coast from a HAB there. And another HAB along the Pacific coast of the U.S. has killed hundreds of short-nosed dolphins and seals which ate prey contaminated by the toxin produced by the HAB. HABs can occur in both fresh and seawater, and, according to scientists, 90% occur in freshwater streams, rivers, and lakes. Rising water temperatures will almost inevitably lead to more toxic blooms.

Revelation 8:10-13

10 The third angel blew his trumpet, and a great star fell from heaven, blazing like a torch, and it fell on a third of the rivers and on the springs of water. 11 The name of the star is Wormwood. A third of the waters became wormwood, and many people died from the water, because it had been made bitter. 12 The fourth angel blew his trumpet, and a third of the sun was struck, and a third of the moon, and a third of the stars, so that a third of their light might be darkened, and a third of the day might be kept from shining, and likewise a third of the night. 13 Then I looked, and I heard an eagle crying with a loud voice as it flew directly overhead, "Woe, woe, woe to those who dwell on the earth, at the blasts of the other trumpets that the three angels are about to blow!"

There is great speculation about these two judgments. Are they physical (literal) or spiritual (symbolic)? Many believe Wormwood could be a nuclear disaster, as they link the nuclear plant that failed in the Ukraine decades ago to the Russian word, *chernobyl,* which means wormwood. This, however, is based upon a misspelling of the name by a reporter at that time. The town of Chornobyl, where the power plant is located in Ukraine, is named after the *chornobyl* plant, Artemisia vulgaris, or mugwort in English. The wormwood plant, Artemisia absinthium, produces the hallucinogen thujone which was part of ancient absinthe. Because of the "drunkenness" and hallucinations absinthe produces, it was used in the ancient ritual worship of Artemis, the goddess of nature, wild animals, childbirth, care of children, and chastity.

From a symbolic perspective, several scholars link wormwood to idolatry, so a return to idolatry, which comes in many forms, could "poison" the minds and lead to the spiritual death of these people. Perhaps, but how might this link to the rivers and springs? Artemis was closely linked to water and Poseidon, and many of her temples were built near rivers and springs. So, maybe there is some validity to the idea.

Because of the nature of the "star" falling from heaven, two other possibilities come up. One, from a physical perspective, is that it could be a literal meteor. The number of NEOs, or near-Earth objects, has been increasing recently. One passed by the Earth in 2022 at roughly two million miles away, a near miss in galactic terms.

However, the second possibility seems to tie closely to judgment four. If "idol worship" is "poisoning" the minds of many people, could "the third" of the sun, moon, and stars represent a fallen heavenly host? We know that the demons have been locked away in the abyss, Tartarus, but demons are not fallen angels, so they wouldn't "fall" from heaven. Also, the word star is often used to denote an angel in the Bible. The Bible tells us that Satan and his fallen angels are doomed to die like men (Psalm 82:7). Could this represent their final casting down to Earth?

Speaking of demons, the fifth trumpet (Revelation 9:1-11) sees the release of these entities from the abyss. They are released to torment mankind. Well, to torment those who don't have the spiritual mark of Christ protecting them. To see the world suddenly flooded with these beings would likely lead to mass delusions and other mental health problems. The sudden rise of the transgender movement, as well as the rise in LGBTQI+ activism, could certainly have a demonic factor. Yet, we are also seeing great increases in depression, suicide, and mental health issues. These, too, possibly have demonic influences behind them.

The sixth trumpet (Revelation 9:13-19) releases four angels who are sent to kill "a third" of mankind by three plagues: fire, smoke, and sulfur. 'Fire and brimstone" is another way of putting it. TBH, I'm still working to understand just what these "plagues" might be. Today, we associate the word "plague" with infectious disease, but the Greek word here, *plēgē*, is used to denote a public calamity or heavy affliction. This could amount to just about anything, including the modifiedRNA COVID jabs with their resultant heart problems and serious rise in gynecological issues. A recent study has proven that the spike protein of COVID (and the jabs) adversely affects the CD4 cells of our immune system, just like HIV does. The initial wave of HIV seemed to abate only to be followed 8-10 years later with a torrent of immune system problems. Will we see the same in the next decade or less?

Fire, smoke, and sulfur are typically used in the Bible to represent heavenly judgment, such as in the destruction of Sodom and Gomorrah. Recent archaeological digs in the Jordan River valley have uncovered the Biblical Sodom and found pottery and utensils that had been melted. It is speculated that a meteoric airburst produced a fireball intense enough to do that. So, maybe a meteoric Wormwood really is on its way toward Earth.

However, in Rev 9:20-21 we read,

> *20 The rest of mankind, who were not killed by these plagues, did not repent of the works of their hands nor give up worshiping demons and idols of gold and silver and bronze and stone and wood, which cannot see or hear or walk, 21 nor did they repent of their murders or their sorceries or their sexual immorality or their thefts.*

This sure seems to tie back to the previous trumpets in terms of idolatry poisoning the minds and leading to the deaths of many, as well as the demonic delusions that produce the sexual immorality of today.

As I view what's happening in the world today and compare it to the previous seven decades of my life, I see such an exponential rise in immorality that I find it hard to believe that it couldn't be demonic. Yes, there were gays and crossdressers in the past, but then they were "in the closet" and now they're openly in schools and libraries "grooming" our youth. Plus, this radical change seems to have accelerated "suddenly" over the past two or three years. Because of the increase in natural disasters and the rise in sexual immorality, as well as suicide and mental health issues, I personally believe we're witnessing these trumpet judgments in progress.

What do you think? As events unfold, we need to remain aware of what's happening around us. Keep your eyes and ears open, and your mind tuned into God's Word.

On a different note, the technology behind the innovative alternator and M-Cube is real. I've seen the new alternator in action. As for the magnetic induction generation of electricity, much is still under development. If these guys don't mysteriously die, look for significant changes in "green energy" in the near future.

ACKNOWLEDGMENTS

As always, I again want to acknowledge and thank my dear wife, Paula, for her help and encouragement, and for putting up with my spending time writing. With the retirement of my main proofreader, I've started using *Grammarly* for additional error checking. If you find any errors, it missed them. So, please let me know.

And my sincerest compliments to Adrijus Guscia, of Rockingbook Covers, for his incredible covers.

ABOUT THE AUTHOR

Braxton can't lay claim to wanting to be a writer all his life, although his mother and seventh grade English teacher were convinced he had what it would take. A bachelor's degree in Bio-Medical Engineering led to medical school and a residency in Emergency Medicine. He served for a decade in the U.S. Army Medical Corps with tours such as the Chief, Emergency Medical Services at Fort Campbell, KY, and as a research Flight Surgeon at Fort Rucker, AL. Who had time to write?

By the 1990s, as a civilian, his professional and family life had settled down, somewhat, and his mother once again took up her mantra, "Write a book. You're a good writer." In 1997, a Valentine's Day writing contest convinced him that maybe he could write fiction. He spent the next fifteen years learning the craft of writing.

Now, twenty-plus years after that first hesitant start, he has sixteen novels published, as well as non-fiction books and a children's book, and can't find enough time to write. As a Christian, he writes "true-life" Christian fiction (suspense and thrillers) that many call "cutting edge," as he's not afraid to take on such issues as human trafficking, racism, and more. His characters are real-life as well, with all the flaws and blemishes real people have. As such, his books are never likely to gain acceptance by the Christian Bookseller Association. But then, he never intended to tell stories just to the choir.

Books by Braxton DeGarmo:

Still Here Series:

The End Begins – 1
The Shaking – 2
The Beasts – 3
The Trumpets – 4
The Mark - 5

Non-Fiction Study Guides:

Still Here! Surviving the End Times
Still Here! The Apocalypse is Now
Still Here! Countdown Revelation

MedAir Series:

Looks that Deceive – 1
Rescued and Remembered – 2
The Silenced Shooter – 3
Wrongfully Removed – 4
A Zealot's Destiny – 5
Kidnapped Nation - 6
The Khmer Connection - 7
Resurrected Trouble - 8

Seamus O'Connor Thrillers:

The Militant Genome
Ten Seconds 'Til

Other Books:

Indebted

Children's Books:

The Toucan Who Can Can-can